YUEN WRIGHT

wattpad books

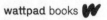

Published in Canada by Wattpad Books, a division of Wattpad Corp.
36 Wellington Street E., Toronto, ON M5E 1C7

*www.wattpad.com*

First Wattpad Books edition: August 2021
ISBN 978-1-98936-557-1 (Trade Paper original)
ISBN 978-1-98936-558-8 (eBook edition)

Library and Archives Canada Cataloguing in Publication information
is available upon request.

Printed and bound in Canada

1 3 5 7 9 10 8 6 4 2

Cover design and illustration by Ashley Santoro
Typesetting by Sarah Salomon

For my sister and my readers. Without you, this wouldn't have been possible.

# CHAPTER 1

## *Wren*

I *can't* find it anywhere, and it's driving me insane.

The thing I wear most has disappeared. During the last week of summer break, I flung all the clothes out of my dresser in a frenzied attempt to find it. Ergo? I now have a room from hell.

In the midst of my search, I catch sight of my reflection in my vanity mirror. A dull ache blooms in my chest as the girl in the mirror stares back at me. For a short-lived second last fall, I thought makeup would be able to erase the dark circles under my eyes. That it would bring back the natural flush to my cheeks.

I'd tried—and failed miserably, might I add—to use said makeup. I ended up looking like I had a bad case of chicken pox. Sighing, I brush the thought aside. There are far more pressing issues right now than how I look. Like the fact that my hoodie is currently very . . . missing.

"Mom!" I yell.

Her response comes back muffled.

"Where's my hoodie?"

I'm met by a hollow silence.

"Hello-o?" I repeat.

There's another empty pause, which my mom fills with a weary sigh. A few seconds later she must figure I'm not going to let the topic go, so she mumbles a defeated, "Check the bottom drawer."

I do, and yep, there it is, nestled among things I never wear. I should've realized my mom hid the hoodie on purpose. She's always trying to find new ways to get me to open up. To people, to new experiences. Whatever that means. All I know is I'd rather stub my baby toe repeatedly than go to school without my hoodie.

"Found it," I call, grabbing my history notes. As I run downstairs in my sneakers, unfiled paper threatens to spill from the pile nestled in my hands. "I'm leaving now."

"Wren," my mother reprimands from the kitchen. "Don't forget breakfast."

I grab an apple from the counter. "Got it."

My mom's a morning person. One cup of decaf and she's good to go. Me? It takes an ungodly amount of strength to pry my eyes open before noon. The state of my hair alone would make Einstein's cut look red-carpet worthy.

A car horn pierces the air. Of course, my charming friend, Mia, has rolled up on my front lawn, crushing our flowers in the process. Poor carnations. They were just starting to bloom. Before she can slam down on her horn again, and we get a neighbor complaint about noise pollution, I call out, "I'm coming!"

As I close the door behind me and make my way to her Mustang, a warm gust of late summer air brushes my bare legs.

Mia Rahman flashes me a bright smile, her incandescent eyes trailing down my frame. "Get in, loser."

Thanks to her Persian mom, Mia's perfected the kohl-lined eye. And thanks to her own acquired taste in fashion, she's never lacking in the clothing department. Today she's wearing a yellow sundress, the hem fluttering over the brown skin of her thighs. If I could paint her, I would.

Chucking my bag into the back of the car, I utter a soft RIP message to the crushed flowers. I slide into the front seat and reach for the seat belt as my friend's bottomless gaze meets my own. "It's almost like you're trying to look like a hippie, Martin."

She isn't wrong. There's this weird paint stain on my jean shorts, but it's not like someone's going to arrest me for being a fashion reject. My hoodie is oversized, but it covers me in a way that makes me feel comfortable. Safe. And most importantly? Invisible.

I love it.

"You planning to change your nun-agenda?" Mia asks. "It's senior year."

She's been trying to drag me out of my shell, and she's tried everything. School clubs, parties, double dates. You name it, Mia's tried it. I mean, sure, I've found guys attractive. On more than one occasion. But they were always either fictional or out of my league.

I shift a wary glance her way. "There's something called priority, you know. Right now, oxygen is at the top of my list—not boys. And after oxygen, it's school. Seriously, M. I need a scholarship if I'm going to college."

"All right, all right. I know the drill." Mia sighs, absently drumming her fingers on the steering wheel in time to a Rihanna song. She glances up as we close in on the school towering over us. "Speak of the devil . . ."

We pull into the parking lot of Eastview High—Massachusetts's dream school. It's a private school, and the building is a fascinating mixture of modern and traditional architecture. I wouldn't be able to attend if it wasn't for the scholarship I've been awarded every year since I was a freshman. As we step out of the car and walk toward the entrance, sunlight washes over us, warming our skin.

"I can't believe you're wearing that freaking hoodie," she laments. "These are the last few days of sunshine we have."

I shrug. My wardrobe has only seen oversized tees, boyfriend jeans, and the occasional jean shorts. Cambridge is notorious for its cold fronts, so you have to treasure the warm days like honey from a pot. Except I don't mind the cold. In fact, I prefer it. And besides, the A/C in chemistry blows. Literally.

I'm halfway through relaying this to Mia when we reach a fork in our path. She passes me a resigned look. "We still don't share any classes, huh?"

I stare down at my schedule then back at her. "Unless you decided to drop theater for physics, then nope."

At the mention of physics, Mia's jovial expression turns sour. "Never mention the *P* word in front of the children again."

I raise a brow as a smile tugs at my lips.

"It's me," she clarifies. "I'm children."

The bell rings then, and as much as I want to prolong her torture, I actually need to make it to class. Mia bids me farewell by throwing a kiss in my direction with her hand. Grinning, I play along, catching the imaginary kiss midair only to chuck it into a nearby trash can. She rolls her eyes, shaking her head with a smile as she disappears in the crowd.

Mia and I—we're polar opposites. Puzzle pieces that don't match yet are somehow glued together. She's the aspiring actress with over a hundred thousand subscribers on her YouTube channel, and I'm the avid watcher of mini-food videos.

The first time we talked was in Spanish class freshman year. We sat next to each other in Spanish and biology, where she ended up copying my work. Not that I minded. One day, a few girls asked Mia to go to a party, ignoring me. I was about to leave, convinced she was going to abandon me, when she outright refused their offer, saying she had plans that day. I still can't believe she did it.

Maybe that was the start of our friendship. Mia could've said yes to those girls that day. She could've stayed far away from the girl who wore a red hoodie a little too often and liked books more than people. She could've. But she didn't.

Faye Archer brushes past me, startling me back to reality. A confident gleam lights up her gaze, and people know better than to get in her way. Faye is a faultless product of the universe. I've never seen her frazzled, or down, or anything but composed. She manages to perfectly balance being on the volleyball team with academics and her social life. She also happens to be my number one competitor for valedictorian.

As she disappears, a sea of painfully slow freshmen close in, and the hallway is bustling yet again. I need to get to math because being late on the first day? It's all sorts of trouble I have no intention of inviting.

I slow my steps as I enter the classroom. Playing with the sleeves of my hoodie, I slide into a seat against the wall. The calculus lesson starts in full swing, and fifteen minutes in, I'm still taking notes when someone snickers behind me. Quicker than a bullet, Mr. Brakeman zones in on his culprit. Zachary Chandler.

5

Born in France, Zach moved to Cambridge in third grade when his dad, a famous basketball player, got traded. With sport in his genes, it's no surprise he's one of the best players on the school's hockey team. And with dark skin, a sharp jawline, and black hair cropped close, he's the subject of many fawning girls at Eastview. Including Mia.

Apparently, his brown eyes are so light they're gold. Personally, I've never gotten close enough to tell. And thanks to Mia hanging out with me all the time, and not the popular crowd where she'd fit right in, he doesn't even know she exists.

"What exactly is it that you find so amusing, Zachary?" Brakeman asks.

"Nothing, sir," Zach mutters.

"Thought so." Brakeman's gaze is stone cold. "Wouldn't be too happy myself if I had the same report cards as you."

There's an audible intake of breath as almost everyone in the room cringes. That was a low blow, and all-round distasteful. Rumor is Mr. Brakeman went through a nasty divorce with his wife so he's now more of a tyrant than usual.

I could've swapped to Miss B—who's miles nicer—but despite his flaws, Brakeman's a pretty decent math teacher. So, if I want to do well on the midterm, I need to stay in this class. Luckily, he doesn't find much to pick on for the rest of the lesson, diving into a lengthy explanation of derivatives instead. Behind me, Zach mutters something once more before picking his pencil back up.

∽

At the end of a long day, the bell rings—a loud, mind-numbing sound students hate and love at the same time. The scent of new

6

books disperses through the air when I drop my bag off at the front of the library before making my way to the fiction section.

A sad confession: I judge books by their endings. It's a habit I can't let go of. I read the book's ending first, and if I like the way it sounds, I'll read the book. Don't get me wrong, I'm not a psychotic fan of happy endings—I believe in a normal kind of forever, not sickeningly happy endings or morosely sad ones.

After combing the shelves, I have so many books they fill my arms and obscure my view. When I stumble to the librarian at the front desk, a frown appears on his face. With a small, bashful smile, I drop the books onto the scanning desk.

"You've taken out over the borrowing limit." The librarian offers me a pointed look. When my smile falters, he sighs. "But I guess I can let it pass."

I'm not sure how to process this random act of kindness, so I just nod, my smile returning. "Thanks."

When the librarian finally finishes scanning, he places my books in a pile in front of me. I try my best to scoop it up, and after a few tries, I finally succeed. My locker isn't too far away, which is a rare instance of good luck.

As I stagger to the exit, an assistant walks out of her office behind the desk. "A. R. isn't a name, young man!" She huffs. "Get back in here and sign this sheet properly, or you can tell Coach to find another place to keep his tapes." She walks back to her desk with a pained sigh, mumbling, "I don't get paid enough for this."

Well, someone's having a rough day.

Behind me, a low "Yes, ma'am," follows the assistant's outburst. I'm curious, but I can't afford to turn, so I push forward. A few grueling steps later, I finally make it out of the library. I'm two seconds away from my locker when I crash into someone, the force sending me reeling backward.

A small, strangled sound grates the back of my throat as my grip on all the books loosens. They fly from my hands and topple to the ground. Praying they aren't damaged, my gaze coasts up, and I can't help it when my eyes widen.

Because standing in front of me is Asher Reed—star athlete and heartthrob of Eastview. Reed's tall, annoyingly so, but maybe it's because I'm all of five feet two. He's wearing a navy-blue varsity jacket, and right now, his eyes are bright as he stares down at me. Sports are big in Massachusetts—after all, we are home to the Bruins, Celtics, and the Patriots. And Asher? As captain of the hockey team, he's . . . well . . . a teenage god.

I'm not particularly fond of Reed. Why, you ask? In sixth grade, Drew McKay emptied his lunch tray over me because I wouldn't write his essay for him. Reed laughed along with all his friends while peas rolled off my head. That year, Drew was suspended for breaking into the school and trying to change his grades. He switched schools after the incident, and Asher took his place as most popular. In summary: Asher Reed is everything wrong with high school, in one frustratingly good-looking body.

As I bend to pick up the collection of books spread across the floor, my knees brush the ground. Reed bends, too, except with ease. When I look up, his eyes connect with mine. They're deep blue, and I wonder what colors of paint I'd have to mix to get that exact shade. We both reach for the same book, and when his hand grazes mine the tiniest fraction, I snap out of it.

His presence is enough to set me on high alert, and I find myself reeling away. When he stands, my hefty pile of books sits perfectly in his grasp. He places them by my locker and steps aside. I only managed to pick up one, and it sits in my hands, almost embarrassed of itself.

"Sorry," I mumble. Folding my arms across my chest, I hold my hoodie as close to me as possible. If I don't, I'm scared my heart will fly straight out of my rib cage.

Reed cocks his head, the corners of his lips lifting. "I didn't quite get that."

I lift my gaze to him in disbelief. We both know he heard just right the first time. Nevertheless, I mutter a quick "I'm sorry." Then, before I can decide against it, "But it's high school. A big, scary place where you're occasionally going to bump into people in the hallways." Then, because my stupid mouth can't stay shut, I add, "Deal with it."

After the last word leaves my lips, I feel an instant and over-whelming need to kick myself. Why couldn't I have just apologized like a normal person? I expect him to drop the conversation. Or dish out some cocky remark. Instead, the curiosity in his gaze only deepens. Folding his arms across his chest, he leans against the locker next to mine.

"Fair enough," he says, and there's a hint of amusement in his voice as he regards me, cocking his head. "Little Red."

My heart jumps under my skin, sending my pulse skyrocketing. Opening my locker, I hurry to shove the books in. My eyes go wide as the books topple out at my face, and I shut my locker with a bang that makes me wince.

Spinning on my heel, I make it one step when I'm tugged back by my hoodie. Is he really . . . ? "Uh, can you let go?"

The air's filled with the sound of his soft laughter. My face drains of any color when it dawns on me. Oh no. Please no. No, no, no. I turn . . . and yep, of course my hoodie is stuck in my locker. Of course it is. I avoid eye contact with him, and it takes a few solid yanks on the material before it finally, finally, comes loose.

Never more eager to get home, I nod once in Reed's general direction then spin on my heel and walk down the hallway.

Male voices resound behind me, and I'm sure his friends have caught up with him. He's never alone for too long. His mere presence commands attention, and people tend to gravitate to him. For a second, I allow myself to wonder what it must feel like to be that revered. That loved and admired.

And as I swerve around the corner, my mind collapses on itself. I place a hand on my forehead, where I could swear a fever's working up. He's the school's golden boy, and I just dropped my books all over him, then chastised him. And then if that wasn't enough, I assumed he wanted to talk to me so bad that he held on to my hoodie.

What the heck was I thinking?

# CHAPTER 2

## Asher

I try to define myself by a few select things.

And I push for clarity in these things. For me, it's always been hockey, maintaining decent grades, and family—making sure my mom and sister are happy. These are undeniably the three biggest facets of my life. And as much as people might think they know me, they don't. And I'm perfectly fine with that, because they don't *need* to know me. The real me, at least. They just need to know enough to like me.

And they do. They love me. I'm acutely aware of this when my teammates send variations of handshakes and side-hugs my way as a form of greeting. I'm captain of the ice hockey team again this year, but that doesn't come as much of a surprise. I was captain last year, stealing the title from the senior starters when I was just a junior.

Coach has been gearing us up for the game on Friday, and

practice is brutal. I'd be lying if I said that I'm not breaking a sweat. Brody Knight, one of my best friends on the team, is already heaving in his gear beside me. I pause to reach for my water bottle, before squeezing water through the cage covering my sweat-drenched face.

Brody and I are both on the same line, and as Eastview's best forwards, we work well together. Zach Chandler is one of the defensemen. He's held the position for years. It used to be a pain in the ass before, when he didn't know how to stop on the ice. Now he's one of the strongest players on the team, and like Brody, he's also one of my best friends.

"Holy shit," Brody groans. "I'm done."

He leans over, still out of breath, but Coach's harsh voice sends us reeling back to our starting points. "*Knight, Reed*, get back in there!"

Swapping wary glances, Brody and I skate back to our positions. Coach barks on about how Harvey's taking his turns too sharp, and how Miller's taking his too lazy. We've run this drill five times already, and it's grueling, but it's Coach's favorite for conditioning. Miller gets an assist and I manage a clean shot, the goal flaring. I shoot him a grin, and he mirrors me as we take our places again.

After a few more rounds, Coach tells us to pick up the stray pucks and dump them near the crease. Finding a puck, I can't resist the temptation and take a fast slap shot right onto the cross-bar, bouncing the puck off it and into the net. The light goes off, emitting a red glow onto the ice. It catches Coach's attention.

"Reed," he yells across the ice. "Do you need a hearing aid, boy? I said *collect* the pucks, not take a shot! What has gotten *into* you kids over the summer?"

Ducking my head with a chagrined smirk, I start gathering them up. I look up at Daniels, who's standing near the blue line where Coach wants the pucks stacked up.

"Yo, Daniels," I say, and his head turns toward me. "Do me a solid?"

He gives me a nod and sets his stick down, ready to receive. Taking one from the pucks scattered around me, I slap it across the ice, watching it skid onto Daniels's stick. He quickly taps it to the right next to the rest.

Popping his head up, he taps his stick on the ice, telling me he's ready for the next one. It becomes a quick pattern, and sharp sounds of stick on puck resonate throughout the arena. When I'm done, I skate to the other side, my stick dragging on the ice.

I close in on Brody and Zach arguing. Zach's talking animatedly and Brody's giving him an "Are you serious?" look. Apparently, they'd both been texting the same girl over the summer.

"You two!" Coach barks. "What are you gossiping about?"

"Nothing," Brody mutters dryly, shooting Chandler a death glare. I stifle a laugh. They'll be over it by tomorrow, but right now, it's fucking hilarious. They deserve it. They're hardly innocent, and I can bet my ass they'd both been texting more than just one girl, anyway.

"Brody doesn't like sharing," Zach murmurs.

"Sharing?" Brody's face flushes, then his voice lowers to a whisper. "You were proposing a threeso—"

"Forget I asked!" Coach says, and his jaw is tight as he shakes his head. "Just get back to practice. *Now.*"

We move toward the rest of the team, lining up behind the others while the two continue to bicker.

Completing the drill alongside Miller, I slide the puck to

him. My stick extends in front of me, waiting to receive it. Miller pushes the puck back to me, but it's way too wide of where I'm standing. My reflexes kick in, and twisting my body, I stretch out, moving toward it.

"Sorry!" Miller shoots from the other side.

I offer a slight nod in acknowledgment. Gliding across the ice, I reach the crease, waiting for Coach's instruction.

"Left," he shouts.

Registering his words, I rotate my skates, spinning to the left, where I face Miller, who's now my opponent. He tries to intercept my shot and I wait for him to come close enough.

Spotting his stick near the puck, I pull back, pushing the puck through the gap between his legs before he can recover. Skating around him, I reclaim the puck then slap it into the net too fast for our goaltender, Hemmings, to stop it.

Finishing the drill, I head back to the start. Miller heads over to apologize to me again.

"Don't worry about it," I say. "Remember to follow through with your shot so that it moves in the direction you want."

Back at the line, Harvey glances at me. "Can we swap for a few minutes?"

I nod curtly, and practice resumes soon after. I have the puck within seconds, and Zach's stick juts in my way, trying to gain possession. Grinning, I draw back, gliding to my left.

"Beat that, Chandler," I yell over my shoulder.

"Fuck off, weed."

He skates at a pretty impressive speed toward me and tries to push me over with his elbow while I try to shove him off me. The rest of the team watches the spectacle, laughing at us. Brody glances over with a small smile, wondering how the hell we're friends. Soon his expression changes, his eyes widen and his mouth opens.

Before he can say anything, Zach and I crash into the wall. Lying on the ice, I pull off my helmet and shake my head, shoving my knee into Zach's stomach. Getting back up, I look at him, and he just sends me a wide grin.

"This is definitely gonna bruise," I murmur, holding my arm and stretching it. "You asshole."

"Payback's a bitch, sunshine." He grins, shrugging. "Go ask the school nurse for some ice. Heard she's hot."

I laugh. "What the hell is wrong with you?"

"More like what's *not* wrong with him," Brody mutters as we skate back to join the others.

Coach strings us along for another ten minutes, but I figure the old man has a soft spot for us, because five minutes later, he calls off practice. Not before delivering a few words of wisdom, though.

"I'm sure you ladies are well aware that we need to kick-start this season with a bang," he says. "Some of you need this for your college applications. Me? I'm just here to make sure the school doesn't drop the funding for this hockey team. Basically"—he narrows his eyes at every single one of us—"I'm ensuring that I keep my job. So, I want you all primed and prepped for Friday, because we *are* going to win."

The school's not going to drop the funding for this team. Looking just at the past few years, we've been the best team in Eastview's hockey history. Last year, we got to the semifinals of the state championships. I'd like to say that it was solely because of me, but that's not entirely true. We really do have some of the most talented players in the high school league, and a lot of our players, including me, have pretty great chances of getting scouted by colleges across the country.

We all intone bored variations of "Yes, Coach," before we're finally dismissed, and I make a beeline for the locker room, wanting nothing more than a shower so I can get home. As I enter, it doesn't smell half as bad as it should with more than two dozen sweat-covered hockey players swarming around. Eastview's got a state of the art facility—we have our own ice rink for Christ's sake—and the locker rooms have a great ventilation system.

Peeling off my gear, I step into the shower, the warm water soothing my muscles as it runs. Afterward, I pull my sneakers out of my duffel, and I'm halfway through pulling on some sweats and a T-shirt when someone shrieks from the shower stall in front of me. *"What the hell!"*

Standing, I walk over. A shadowy figure is visible through the opaque glass door of the stall. Just as another shriek echoes through the room, I raise my hand to knock on the door.

"Is everything all right in there?" I ask as the other guys surround the shower and crowd around me, concern evident on their faces.

The door swings open and a seminaked Harvey runs out, his face red.

"Harv . . ." I say slowly. "You need to calm down. What's wrong?"

"Someone's underwear is in there!" he yells, and I follow his finger to a dark-grey lump on the floor of the stall.

A mortified Harvey stares into the stall in disgust, his hand tightly gripping the towel covering the lower half of his body, as he frantically urges someone to get it out so that he can take a shower. I start laughing hysterically, and the rest of the team joins me as Harvey shoots me a glare.

"Okay," I tell Harvey. "We'll get it out, man. Just relax."

The team shake their heads, refusing to touch it.

"It can't be that bad," I say wearily.

We all flick our gazes to the left, glancing down at the elephant in the room, which in this case happens to be a grey lump on the tiled floor.

Harvey makes a pained sound. "Can someone *please* get it out? I'm freezing my ass off. My nipples are gonna fall off. I'm not going to have any nipples." He pauses. "Don't we need our nipples for, like . . . something?"

Zach is the first to break the silence after Harvey's nipple soliloquy. "There's no way in hell I'm touching that thing. Rock paper scissors. Loser picks up. Deal?"

We all agree. "Deal."

After a series of matches, the last round is between Harvey and me. Miller stands between us as Harvey glances at me. Chandler pulls out his phone and flips it around to record us.

"Rock, paper, scissors," Miller starts. "Shoot."

I whip out a rock, my eyes flicking to the hand in front of me. Harvey's hand does some sort of spasm where he changes his scissors to a paper. He smiles up at me cheekily.

"Go pick it up, Reed."

I roll my eyes. "You cheated."

Harvey's features contort. "Aw, man! Do I seriously have to do it? Damn. I thought I could get away with it."

A sulking Harvey trudges over to the shower, slowly edging toward the lump on the ground. He holds his breath, walking closer and closer. Bending down, he pokes his hand forward to pick it up.

"Shit!" he yelps, running away. "I can't do it."

Harvey looks at the ground and then at a pair of lumo-yellow sneakers on the benches. Before anyone can protest, he runs, picks one up, and hops right back into the shower. He inches forward, jabbing the grey underwear with the shoe.

Daniels yells from the side when he realizes. "You used *my* damn shoe?"

Harvey doesn't pay attention, and chucks the underwear to the other side of the change room. Right where the juniors change. He stands as he looks around at us, proud of his achievement. "That wasn't so bad."

Daniels rushes forward, ready to attack him. "Yeah, because you used my goddamn shoe!"

"Hey! Don't come any closer!" Harvey tries to protect himself using the shoe as a weapon and throwing it at Daniels before running into his shower.

Zach sprints over to me, excitement written all over his face. "I can't believe I got all of this on video!"

I chuckle at him before slipping on my sneakers and packing up my stuff. Brody and Zach look at his phone and eventually land back on the texting-same-girl situation. Brody starts lamenting over the fact that he got two-timed. "Man, I can't believe it."

"It's fine, bro." Zach grins. "We're good?"

"Yeah, man," Brody says, a barely there smile lighting up his gaze. "We're good."

As I wait for them to finish up, my mind drifts to the girl who bumped into me earlier. I was in the library to get some game tape and even got yelled at by some pissed off lady in the process.

After the girl walked into me, I was prepared to help her with the books and leave, but something about the way she made all of two seconds of eye contact with me compelled me to stay a little longer. I'll admit, seeing the flush creep up her neck when I teased her was oddly satisfying. *Little Red*.

I can't believe I'm doing it when I turn to the two idiots I call my best friends—no doubt they'll blow this out of proportion. But it's not like I have anyone else to ask anyway. Between the two of them, at least one should have some inkling about her.

"I need intel," I say as I face them, fully aware of how stalker-ish I sound. "On a girl."

They swap amused glances before they turn back to me.

"What's her name?" Brody asks.

A smile finds its way to my face as I realize I still don't know her name. ". . . I don't know."

"C'mon, weed," Zach says, shaking his head. "You've got to give us more to work with."

The image of her flashes in my mind. It's a damn shame I haven't noticed her around before, because her features are striking—warm skin, high cheekbones, honey eyes—all framed by shoulder-length chocolate-colored hair. I clear my throat, and I'm sure as hell not offering up *that* description to the two. "Short, brunet?"

Zach features contort. "That doesn't really narrow it down."

"Why do you care so much about her anyway?" Brody asks.

"Bumped into her the other day." I shrug it off nonchalantly. "Just curious why I haven't seen her around, is all."

"Oooooh," Zach teases. "Are you in *lurve*? Is our weedy in *lurve*?"

"Fuck off," I say, whipping him with my towel hard enough for it to sting. Chandler just laughs it off as I shove the towel into my duffel before slinging it over my shoulder. I offer the two behind me a two-fingered wave as I exit the locker rooms.

The quicker I can get home, the quicker I can get done with the shit ton of homework I have and finally get some downtime. My sister's been begging me to watch this *Frozen* movie with her, but she always seems to get me at the worst time, so I've been turning her down far too often for my liking. Maybe I can actually do what I promised and watch the damn movie with her.

# CHAPTER 3

## Wren

I'm procrastinating and I know it. I mean, I have an insane amount of homework, including calculus and a history essay, but why not just read for a few hours and push homework to the back of your mind for later, right? Maybe I should procrastinate a little less.

Oh well, I'll work on my procrastination issues another day.

I get halfway through the book before the guilt overrides the pleasure, and I end up researching sources for the history essay, and then completing it. When my hair starts to get in the way, I tie it into a French braid and secure it with a white ribbon at the end. The once-blank page is now filled with my black handwriting. Blowing the imaginary dust off of my polished essay, I tuck it into a folder in my bag to hand in.

I've decided I will simply avoid Asher Reed for the rest of the school year. Oh, scratch that. I'm going to avoid that boy for the rest of my *life*. I'll never be able to live that embarrassing interaction down.

It's been a week but I'm still reeling from our brief encounter. I avoid him at all costs, even when he's just a distant speck in the school hallway. Right now, though, I don't have much time to dwell on it. My babysitting customer's showing up in under an hour, and I couldn't be more thankful for the distraction. I need extra cash, and with school to worry about, this is the best I can do.

I told Mia I needed the money for books, which was only partly true. During the summer, I researched college textbook costs and I almost fell off my chair. Wait, I might've actually fallen off my chair. I decided then and there that if I was going to college, I needed to start planning. Plus, it wouldn't hurt to have a little extra cash to spare.

As if on cue, the doorbell rings. Racing downstairs, I open the door to find my first babysitting customer, Victoria, on the other side. She has kind eyes and a warm smile. Her light hair is pulled back into a low bun at the nape of her neck.

"Hi," she says. "Wren?"

I manage a smile. "That's me."

Lowering my gaze, I find a sweet, dimpled girl wearing a fairy dress hiding behind her mom. The girl's mouth is a puckered rosebud, and concern marks her soft, baby features.

"I love your dress," I say.

She releases her mother's legs hesitantly, looking up at me with hazel eyes that take up half her face. "Really?"

"Yep." I nod. "I can give you some fairy wings to match, if you like."

The girl looks up at her mom, then back at me, before dipping her head once. Then twice. Her movements are animated, and combined with those huge eyes, she might as well be a Pixar character.

"Wren," Victoria says, "this is Everly. Everly, Wren. She's going to look after you until Mommy comes back. Don't trouble her too much, okay?"

"Okay." Everly glances at me then pushes faintly at the back of her mom's legs. "You can go now. I won't trouble her, promise."

Victoria glances at me with a smile. "I'll be back at six."

I nod. "No problem."

The older woman's heels connect with the pavement of our driveway as she strides back to her car, opens her door with a smooth click, and slips in before reversing. Her Mercedes glides over the asphalt like butter, and soon she's nothing but a speck in the suburban distance. Anxious energy radiates off the little girl next to me; her bravado has no doubt worn off.

"So, Everly." I lean down and bundle her in my arms as I walk into the house. "What would you like to do today?"

She tilts her head, scrunching her features as her four-year-old mind forgets the worry, and a bit of that fluttery fairy energy returns. "Can we watch *SpongeBob*?"

She gives me a huge grin I didn't know she could pull and starts an off-key version of the *SpongeBob SquarePants* theme song. I place her down on the couch and switch on our flat screen.

"I like you, Wen," she says, her eyes glued to the screen. "You can call me Ever."

I can't help the smile that tugs at my lips. Or the ache in my chest. A few episodes later, I'm sitting on the couch next to Ever, completing an assignment. She laughs at something happening on the screen, her newly added wings dipping.

"Ever." A thought comes to mind. "Can you sit here for a moment while I go get something quickly?"

She nods as I rise from the couch. Upstairs in my room, I

find a tiny, fragile-looking bracelet, small enough to fit perfectly on Ever's wrist. I found it at the beginning of the summer break while cleaning out my room, and I knew the bracelet would no longer fit me, but I couldn't bring myself to throw it away. Then, that stupid doorbell blares again. It's probably Victoria back to pick her up. Then again, it might not be . . .

"Ever!" I call out. "Don't open the—"

But by the time I'm at the bottom of the flight of narrow stairs, I hear voices.

Too late.

Both sound familiar. One belongs to Ever. The other is deeper. *That* is . . . not Victoria. Unless, you know, she got a voice box implant on the way back. Peeking from the hallway, I can just make out Ever in her dress and fairy wings. She stares up with absolute adoration at a boy.

"All right, Ev," he says. "Cough it up. I know you're only acting like an angel 'cause you've been bribed." He yanks the fairy wings on her back. "And what's with the wings?"

"Don't touch them!" Ever exclaims, swatting his hand away. "I like Wen. She's really nice to me. She gives me popcorn, and fairy wings, and she lets me watch *SpongeBob. And* she's pretty. And I really like popcorn."

I bite back a smile at the ringing endorsement, and decide to come out of hiding. But the smile drains from my face when I realize who the guy is. Eyes widening, I freeze.

It's Asher Reed—and he's staring back at me with equal curiosity. This time, I take in the dark-wash jeans and black long sleeve rolled up his forearms, revealing tanned skin. And I sense the cogs turning in his head while those deep-blue eyes don't hide his surprise. "Little Red?"

I glance uneasily at him. "You're Ever's . . ."

"*Stuuupid* brother!" Ever fills in for me.

"Watch it," Reed says, flicking his sister's forehead, ignoring her vibrant squeal of protest. When his eyes slide to mine, I avert my gaze quickly, fidgeting with the bracelet in my grasp. My plan to ignore him until the end of forever? It's already failed. Horribly.

"Ever." I clear my throat and hold out my hand. In my palm is the tiny pearl bracelet, just big enough to fit on her wrist. "This is for you, if you want. It used to be mine a long time ago."

Ever's eyes are glued to the bracelet. I take it as a good sign, so lean forward to fit the piece over her hand. Trying my best to ignore Reed's hard gaze, I focus on Ever as she immediately fiddles and gawks at her newfound trinket.

Reed sighs like this whole situation is nothing but an inconvenience to him. "Time to go, Ev."

She looks up at him with sleepy eyes and crossed brows. "But I wanna stay."

He shakes his head. "No can do, princess. Besides, you'll probably be back tomorrow."

Ever pouts with a hard-set look on her face that's meant to be intimidating but isn't, not really. Then she crawls into Reed's arms and up across his chest until she's settled on his shoulders. He holds on to her ankles, and when she tugs at his hair like Remy from *Ratatouille*, he doesn't protest.

As he walks to the door, I trail behind, my hands stretching out instinctively to make sure Ever doesn't fall. When Reed's gaze flickers to them, I catch myself, dropping them slightly to fidget with the doorknob instead as I shift my weight from left to right.

Reed tilts his head slightly as his eyes land on me. "Turns out the world is a big, scary place where you're going to bump into people, too, huh?"

It doesn't take a rocket scientist to figure that he's using my own words against me. Frowning, I open my mouth to reply, but my throat is impossibly dry, and nothing comes out.

"And since we both agree that the world is big and scary," he continues, edging closer, "I think we'll also agree that you shouldn't let the four-year-old open the door the next time." He leans down so our gazes are level, his deep-blue eyes so piercing my breath catches in my throat. "Okay?"

I nod slowly, lost for words, but amusement just flares in his gaze. My jaw slackens as I watch him turn and walk away. Ever fumbles in his grasp, yelling a bubbly, "Bye, Wen!"

Managing a smile, I wave back halfheartedly. But deep down? I'm cursing her stupid brother. Reed hasn't changed much from middle school. He's still a jerk. But if I don't want my first job to be a failure, I need to tolerate him. For the time being.

∽

The next day, I take a seat toward the back of the English classroom. Seeing as there's still five minutes until the lesson starts, I ease in my earphones, and the first few chords of "Stressed Out" by Twenty One Pilots hum through my ears. Today, my timetable tells me that I have English lit in the third period. Other days it's in seventh, but either way, I find myself looking forward to it.

Rumbling and laughter slip over the sound of music, and I glance up from my desk as Asher Reed and his two best friends, or what I like to call the Pretty Boy Trio, step into the room.

"Yo, Miss Hutch," Zach murmurs by way of greeting.

She offers him a small smile in return. "Morning, Zachary."

Zach walks past me, flanked by the other third of the Pretty Boy Trio, Brody Knight. Brody's just as frustratingly good looking as his friends. With dark-brown hair and a warm, sun-kissed tan, he has that boy-next-door appeal nailed to a T. They take seats in the back row of the class but Reed stays back, his gaze dropping to me. My throat seizes, and I avert my eyes.

Then, he does the unthinkable. The unheard of. The dreaded.

He walks over.

Edges closer.

And slides into the seat right next to *me*.

Trying my best to ignore the lurch of my stomach, I lift my hand to my face in an extremely lame attempt to seem too busy to acknowledge him. But in actual fact? I'm hyperaware of how close he is to me. His friends are murmuring behind us while I pull on the frayed sleeves of my hoodie.

Reed turns in his seat to face them. "I'm gonna take a break from the back for a while," he says. "I think I need contacts."

Zack flips him the bird but Asher just laughs it off. "Seriously."

"Now I'm stuck with Brody," Zach laments.

Brody scoffs. "More like *I'm* stuck with your dumb ass."

I block out their banter. Once you get a seat it's a nonverbal tradition that you keep it for the rest of the year. Students, especially seniors, don't exactly like it when their routine is interrupted. Does this mean Reed is going to be sitting next to me for the entire year? Great. A dull ache is starting at my temple already.

Not long afterward, people file into the class. Some are clearly confused about why Reed isn't sitting at the back with his friends. Their eyes hop between their beloved hockey captain and me; I want nothing more than to sink into my seat.

Miss Hutchinson assigns us work and sits at her desk. I'm about to start writing when something tugs at my hoodie. Glancing sideways, I find Asher staring at me pensively. He cocks his head. "How do I not know your name yet?"

I stare at him blankly, offering him a noncommittal shrug.

"What is it?" he presses.

My brows pull together. "What's what?"

He sighs. "Your name."

I deadpan as I glance at him. "Beyoncé."

As soon as the word falls from my lips, I regret my very existence. The exact time at which life was breathed into my infant self. This is bad. This is very, very bad. If I could simply dissolve into the air, I would. Yep, I'm pretty darn sure that'll solve most, if not all, of my problems.

It's the longest period of my life.

But the universe is on my side, because after a torturous thirty-something minutes, the bell rings. I scramble from my desk and out of the classroom without a second thought. I don't look back, stopping only when I notice Mia waving me over from the lowest level of the cafeteria.

The shape of the cafeteria is a circle—a unique type of architecture of levels shaped as rings filling the space. The levels rise conically to meet at the highest point of the cafeteria. The more popular you are, the higher you sit. It's a food-chain kind of system that everyone falls into, because as much as people hate to admit it, they crave social hierarchy. Even if it means them not being at the top. We always want someone to place on a pedestal.

Placing my food on the table, I force a smile, but Mia knows something's up.

She reaches over and pokes my shoulder. "What happened?"

"Nothing," I lie. "I'm fine."

"I don't think so." She raises her brows. "Quit avoiding it."

I exhale, figuring Mia's not going to let it go easily, so I meet her dark gaze. "Reed sat next to me in English. And I blurted out something *really* stupid. Really, really, really stupid—"

"Hold up." She pauses, mouth open, fork in hand. "Reed as in *Asher* Reed?"

I make a face. "Well, are there any other Reeds you know who go to this school?"

"That boy is pretty as hell," she says, forking a baby tomato from her pasta into her mouth. "Why'd he sit next to you?"

I huff, ignoring her comment about his face, no matter how accurate it may be. "I'm babysitting his little sister, but I still don't see why he'd—"

Her eyes widen. "You're babysitting Reed's sister? Since when?"

"Yesterday."

"I didn't think you were being serious about the babysitting thing."

I shrug. "Well, yeah, of course I was. I need some extra cash. And I'm also saving up for one hundred books."

"Why would you want one hundred books?"

I'm about to say "Why wouldn't you?" but I hold back, choosing to explain. "I'm making those rainbow bookshelves you always see on Pinterest."

"*Okay . . .*" Mia passes me a disbelieving smile. "And now you've ended up with the devil's sister?"

"She's sweet," I counter. "Not like her brother."

My friend lifts a brow as she takes a bite from her pasta. Sensing tension, she changes the topic. "How're your applications coming along?"

"Okay so far. But there's this thing—" I reach over to poke my fork in her pasta, and she tries swatting me away. "I have to fill out what community service I've done. I've written them down but it doesn't look like it'll be enough."

"You're, like, supersmart," she says. "Why don't you try tutoring? The school's been looking for volunteers."

I'm about to shoot down her idea when I realize that she's onto something. Tutoring might be the only thing I *can* do. I glance back at her as she casually stabs at her pasta bowl.

"Actually," I say, "not a bad idea, M. You—" I pause as Mia's kohl-lined eyes widen at something behind me. I feel a presence, and before I can help it, I'm turning around. Asher Reed is leaning at my side. I stop moving—stop breathing—for a second.

Light fills his eyes, turning them crystalline as amusement glazes over them. "I've been looking for you."

"Oh." I swallow, barely managing to formulate the words in my mind. "Um . . . for what?"

"Wren," he says, and the way his low voice wraps around my name falls down my spine. "That's your name."

My stomach twists but Reed just winks—he actually *winks*—before striding to his group of friends at the highest level of the cafeteria. The buzz of the cafeteria morphs from a dull static to an incessant roaring in my ears. I feel Mia nudge my leg with her own, her eyes wide. "What. Was. That?"

But my mouth is all dried up, and by the time I find my voice, all I can manage is, "I have no idea."

# CHAPTER 4

## Asher

As much I try not to, I care about what people think of me. More specifically, I care about what this girl—the one who bumped into me outside the library and now babysits my sister—thinks. I see the subtle judgment in her eyes every time she musters up enough courage to look at me, and it sends an uneasy feeling down my spine.

I had to do some asking for her name, since she wouldn't give it up herself. First, I'd tried to get it from my mom. But she was on a phone call, so she unceremoniously shooed me out of the home office. I couldn't get much there. So I turned to my next resort: Ever.

"Ev," I'd asked, "what's your babysitter's name?"

"Wen."

I deadpanned. "When?"

She nodded. "Wen."

"When?"

"*Yes, Wen!*"

Suffice to say that conversation didn't go well. Finally, I managed to get it from a guy on the school committee, who knew her from when he was in a group project with her in chemistry.

Wren Martin.

She intrigues me. More than she should. More than I should allow her to, seeing as she has nothing to do with the things that rule my life. The way she looks at me, like she's indifferent to and frankly *bored* by my presence—it gets under my skin. No one's ever reacted to me that way before.

Either way, it's high school, and I have a few months left to mess around with my boys and focus just enough to get into college. I'm planning to get into a hockey college like Grover, and in a few years, hopefully bag a contract as a rookie with the Boston Bruins. When the season kick-starts this year, I'm giving it my all. Sweating it out on the ice is what I enjoy, what I love, and what I'll never half-ass.

Today's the first early morning practice. I get up extra early, go for a short jog, and eat a light breakfast before driving to school. Practice is something I always look forward to. I don't care if it's five in the morning; I think it's pretty cool to start off a day doing something you love.

Coach told us that we wouldn't be going on the ice because apparently our fitness sucked, so the team and I spend the whole morning running laps and lifting weights.

A towel hits me in the face, interrupting my thoughts. I glance up at Zach, who just shrugs. Shaking my head, I chuck it back at him before pulling on a pair of black jeans and a blue hoodie.

"Yo, does anyone have shampoo?" Harvey yells from his

shower, which is now underwear-free. He exits, putting a hand through his hair. "I can't find mine."

Daniels shouts from the other side, "Here, bro," he says, "I got you." Daniels hands his bottle to Harvey, suspiciously eagerly, then moves back to his spot.

"Thanks, man," Harvey says over his shoulder, going back to the shower.

Once he's inside, Daniels grins weirdly and mutters a few words under his breath. He claps his hands, getting back to what he was doing. I raise a brow. Not suspicious at all . . .

"Daniels," Harvey pipes from the stall. "Why doesn't your shampoo foam up?"

"It's just like that," Daniels shrugs, overly innocent.

A few minutes later, a *pink* haired Harvey emerges. I snort. The rest of the team freeze for a moment, then burst into laughter at the sight. As if feeling all our eyes on him, Harvey lifts his head.

"What?" His voice turns panicked. "What is it?"

Miller's the first to sober. "Nothing. Nothing's wrong, man."

Harvey notices something's off and ignores Miller, moving to the mirror. He gasps when he sees his blond hair is gone. Raking a hand through his hair, he turns on his heel, looking at Daniels, who's laughing hysterically.

"If this is your way of getting back at me for using your shoe to move underwear, I'm going to say you failed. I still look good with silver hair." He folds his arms across his chest, thinking he's won the battle. Confusion swirls in his eyes as Daniels laughs even harder than before, tears springing to his eyes.

"Harvey," I say slowly, "your hair's pink."

Realization hits him. Horror marks his face as he flips to face the mirror. "Shit, I forgot I'm color blind."

My laugh blends with the rest of the team's. Zipping up my duffel, I leave as Daniels and Harvey start fighting. I swing my bag over my shoulder and walk to my locker. The school's hallways, which were empty and abandoned this morning, are now full and buzzing with noise. The bell rings as I close my locker door, then walk to my class.

❦

In the cafeteria, I fidget with the cap of my water bottle, thinking about the upcoming game. We're going to be playing Lynwood, one of the best schools in the region. Coach may have let my hand coordination go unnoticed, but my passes are a little off and my reactions are too slow. I make a mental note about perfecting them before Friday's game.

As if on cue, Brody nudges me. "Bro, where you at?"

The guys, Brody and Zach, have had my back since the beginning of time. And if you want to know where they fit in my life, it's somewhere between family and hockey. They're blood. But I can't admit this to Brody because he'll never let me live it down, so I offer him a noncommittal shrug and lazy grin. "Here and there."

"Well, gather 'em up, weed," Zach chimes.

Chandler's taken to calling me "weed" instead of what the team and the rest of the school call me—Reed—because, well, he's a dumbass who likes grating on my nerves. But he's used the nickname so often it's worn its course, so I just shake my head with a ghost smile as he keeps talking. "We're on the ice this season and you need to get your head in the game."

"All right, Troy Bolton," Brody murmurs.

But I nod in earnest. "Got it."

"Can't say shit without this dude mentioning *High School Musical*."
Zach rolls his eyes, and I gotta admit, he's a good-looking guy. We all
are. I guess that explains the girls who flock to our table, but Christ,
ask me to tell you all their names and I'm out flat. Girls are fleeting,
never a permanent fixture in my life, so I never bother to carve out
a new facet for something that won't stick around for long anyway.

"Ha," Brody scoffs. "So you *did* watch it."

Zach shrugs nonchalantly. "I watched it on a date, big deal."

"Sure. *That's* why you know all the songs off by heart."

I fight a grin as I watch them bicker, but I can't help it when
my gaze strays to the lower level of the cafeteria where a certain
red-hoodied girl is seated. I can't see her face because she isn't
facing me, but her dark-haired friend must have said something
funny, because her shoulders are shaking with unrestrained
laughter.

I wonder what it would feel like to make someone like
Wren Martin laugh. With the way she guards her name and
only offers it to Those Who Are Worthy, I bet it would feel like
conquering Everest. I wonder why she's all clammed up, hiding
under that hoodie all the time. But most of all? I'm wondering
why the hell I can't seem to get this girl out of my mind.

~

As Friday rolls around, I find myself charged for the first game
of the season. Yeah, it's a charity game organized by the school
board, but I'm looking forward to it nevertheless. We lost against
Lynwood last year, and it's not going to happen again.

I'm primed for the hockey season. I spent the first half of summer break in the rink, the latter in Miami with my uncle Dean,

swimming a lot and getting the kind of tan that's hard to get in Cambridge. This year, I stand a chance of getting scouted. All the injuries, pain, and early mornings could finally be worth it.

I glance at my teammates, who've been with me through my high school years. We used to wait for this day—the game that would kick off our final year.

"Guys!" I shout, my voice echoing in the rink. "Gather up."

They trudge over in their skates. Normally, we wouldn't be in these before the game, but since it's a home game today, Coach wanted us to come in extra early and do some warm-ups before the opposing team arrives and, I quote, "Steals our rink and pucks from us."

Daniels sends me a lazy smile as he heads back into the changing room. I can bet my ass he'll come back with an excuse for him not making it to the meeting. He finds these things a waste of time.

"Daniels." I smirk as I see his face fall as he reenters the rink. He opens his mouth to say something but I interrupt him. "Coach is on his way. Do I need to tell him that you need to sit this game out because you're not potty trained?"

He ducks his face as it turns red. After the guys round up their equipment and take out the bags of pucks from the storeroom, I start talking.

"So," I say. "First game of the season."

The team hoots and whistles in response.

"These are just preseason games, but it's a good opportunity to see how we all work together with the new skills we have and any game plans you want to try out." They all nod in agreement. "So, let's get on the ice and win this!"

I reach for my stick. One by one, we get onto the ice, gliding over to the right side, where Blake sets up the drill. I divide everyone into groups of three: two offensive and one defensive player.

"Everyone knows the drill. Hemmings, you ready?"

Standing in front of the goal, he lifts his stick, signaling that he is. I nod at Zach so that he can start. He and Harvey pass the puck to each other as Brody crouches low, stick in hand, ready to attack.

One of Brody's best skills is that he can see when the attacker will slip and make a mistake, and that's when he lunges. The only problem with this kind of tactic? It's time consuming. On the ice you rarely have time to mull over things, you just have to trust your gut and go for it.

Standing on the side of the play, I watch as Brody's skates move at a slight angle while he stares intently at the puck and the two controlling it. Then, before Harvey can pass it back to Zach, the puck is in Brody's possession. His blank expression disappears as he looks up at them with a smile on his face.

"Knight, I need you to be faster with your attacks. That goes for you two as well." I look at Chandler and Harvey. "If you can't get past the defense, spread out and use the boards if you need to."

After multiple drills, and trying to perfect our power plays, Coach arrives. "Reed!"

I break away from the group, skating over to the opposite side where Coach is standing. He gives me a passing look. "Did you go over all the drills?"

I nod. "We're finishing off the last play."

He lifts his hand to glance at his watch. "The game's in twenty minutes. Dale should arrive just now. Round 'em up in five minutes."

Muttering a lukewarm response, I head back to the boys, the cool air of the rink whipping past me. As soon as we get off the ice, green shirts fill the front of the arena. They watch us shake the ice off our skates and stride to where Coach is sitting.

"Shit, look at number seven," Brody whispers to me, his cheeks flushed red from the ice. "He's *huge*."

"That's what she said." Zach grins.

I shake my head, huffing a laugh as I loosen my skates. Chandler's a real-life version of Michael from *The Office*, so naturally, he can't go a day without saying "That's what she said," at least once.

Coach shows us diagrams of what the game plan for tonight is, while some of the guys get distracted by the sounds of pucks being hit across the rink, or the fact that Dale has a collective tendency to shout aggressively when they play.

Soon the stands are filling up, and the noise level in the arena increases. We tug on our skates and place our mouth guards in. My eyes flicker to the red timer on the wall that's slowly counting down. My heart rate picks up. I let out a breath. This is it.

I signal the team over. Standing in a circle, I look at Hemmings who starts our chant.

"One, two, three—"

"Eastview!"

The cheers get louder. I crouch, holding my stick while looking at the opposition. The buzzer goes off, and we start.

I kick off the ice, and little remains fly behind me. Almost immediately, Miller slides the puck over to me and I hold it against my stick, carrying it farther up. Driving all the way to the left corner of the rink, I make a turn to cut inward, knowing the defense is in front of me leaving the other side of me open.

38

As I move to the opposite side of the rink, I pop the puck to Harvey, who's stationed behind me, part of the defensemen that follow me. He holds the puck, waiting for the perfect moment.

"Now!" I yell.

I drift toward Harvey, drawing the opposition farther away. Before they can realize their mistake, it's too late. Zach appears on the outer side as Harvey passes the puck to him. The defense tries to move back but Zach makes a shot into the net. The whistle goes off.

Our side of the crowd goes wild as we laugh and come into the center. I slap their backs. "We need a few more like that."

Miller salutes me. "You got it, Cap."

I chuckle and take my position again. This is what hockey is. A game full of twists and turns, where anything's possible. It's something I'd never want to leave. I glance up at the timer. We still have a whole hour left.

෴

At intermission we get off the rink, instantly reaching for our bottles. The game's tied at 2–2.

"Boys, you're playing well out there," Coach says, "but there's still a few things I want you to pay attention to. Knight, you don't have eyes at the back of your head; look up before you make a pass. Right now, all of your passes are going straight into the hands of the other team. Daniels, your grip on your stick needs to get tighter. And Reed, you're sitting off for the next ten minutes."

I nod, but a few minutes on the benches and I feel like ripping all my hair out.

"Harvey, stay on your side!" I shout from the sidelines. "You're pushing Daniels too high up!"

Harvey looks up at me, dazed and confused, and way too slow to react when a player skates past him toward the net. By the time he notices, he's heading back as he tries to attack.

"Reed," Coach huffs. "Get back in there."

I rush by the halfway line, yelling for him to come. Harvey makes his way to me and I tap his stick with mine, as a form of encouragement, before gliding onto the ice.

We're neck and neck. I gaze at the timer. Five minutes. We need to make one goal. One goal to change the outcome of this game. Their right winger has the puck, and he's making his way toward me. I don't waste time. Taking off, I block him from the game, isolating him. Zach's on the right side of me, covering my back.

Curving my stick, I pull it toward me before stepping to the side and sliding the puck over to Chandler. As soon as it leaves my stick, I skate straight up to the goal. Two minutes.

Collecting the puck, Chandler rounds to the right side, sending it down the line to Brody.

Come on. *Come on.*

Brody turns his back to the goal, keeping the puck in front of him.

"Brody!" Coach screams from the side. "Pass it!"

I slide in front of Brody just in time for him to make the pass to me. Pushing the puck with full strength, I take a shot at the left corner of the post. I close my eyes as I hear the buzzer go off. Sweat drips down my face.

I got the shot in.

Several guys jump on top of me, roaring. I fall onto the ice, losing my stick somewhere. Brody and Zach slap me on my shoulder. Grinning widely, I take off my helmet, rake a hand through my hair, and tell them to line up to shake our opponents' hands.

I look around the arena. This is where I want to be. Always.

# CHAPTER 5

## Wren

I launch a pillow from my notebook-strewn bed at an annoying Mia. She dodges it from the other side of my room, nearly falling out of the chair she's stretched across. Her dark hair whips the span of her shoulders as they shake with laughter. "Your aim sucks."

"Shut it," I say. "I don't want to go."

We were halfway through *Clueless* when Mia clicked the space bar on my laptop and announced that she wanted to go to Dunkin' Donuts because, apparently, they're having this huge two-for-one promotion if you eat in, or something like that. And I'm as enthusiastic about the idea as I sound.

"Come on," she persists. "*Please.* You've been studying the entire week. You were studying before I showed up today. You're going to burn yourself out."

"Nope."

"Think about the donuts. The freakin' donuts, Martin! If I don't get coffee in two minutes, I'm gonna blow."

"We have coffee downstairs."

She scoffs. "Go to hell, it's gotta be Dunkin'."

"Yeah . . ." I pretend to think about it. "No."

"*Come on*," she nags. "You love me, right? You won't let me slowly descend into darkness because I can't get my caffeine fix. Right? *Right?*"

I raise a brow. "So this has nothing to do with your fear of missing out on that stupid promotion?"

"Oh come on," she says. "Don't act like you've never been a victim of blatant advertising schemes."

She hurls the notorious pillow back at me. And because I have the reflexes of an injured animal, it collides evenly with my face. I place the pillow behind me and offer Mia a sour look.

"Okay." I sigh. "Fine."

"*Yes,*" she hisses. "Let's go, bitch!"

"*But—*" I stuff some money from my drawer into my phone cover. "We get the donuts and leave. I need to get back and start my history assignment. Plus, I want to squeeze some reading in."

She makes a face. "Isn't the history assignment due, like, next month?"

"There's nothing wrong with being prepared."

Don't be fooled. I have this nasty habit of starting assignments early but somehow still leaving 80 percent of the work for the night before, and Mia's well aware of this.

She rolls her eyes. "I literally hate you."

"Finally," I say, tightening the ribbon at the end of my French braid before I shove on a pair of Converse. "Something we both have in common."

When we arrive at Dunkin', I'm surprised at just how many people are victims of blatant advertising schemes. I recognize a few faces from Eastview, and Zach Chandler's signature yellow sports car can be seen from a mile away. Mia tenses beside me.

"Guess who's here," I tease her.

"Crap."

I start cracking up. "Well . . . this was nice. Let's head back, shall we?"

"We *shall* not." Mia shakes her head. "I came here for my coffee and donuts and you bet your tiny ass I'm gonna get 'em. So . . ." She glances at me. "I haven't exactly dressed up for this scenario,"—I raise a brow at her pretty floral dress—"but here's what we're gonna do. We are going to walk in there, and for Christ's sake, Wren, *do not* look at him."

"What do you mean 'don't look at him'?" I send her an incredulous look. "I'm not gonna look at him."

"Really," she says sarcastically, "because who else does a freakin' *one eighty* to look at someone like they've committed a felony, right after I say 'don't look'?"

I burst into laughter. "I don't do that!"

I do that.

She looks at me with a straight face and then continues. "We're going to walk in there, order, pick up, then grab a table on the other side of the room. As far away from—"

"He Who Must Not Be Named as possible." I nod, grinning. "Right. Sounds like a plan."

We enter, and Mia's doing way too much. Clearly, she hasn't mastered the art of invisibility as well as yours truly, because she literally lifts a hand to her face to block sunlight that just isn't there.

I gotta admit, it's pretty funny seeing Mia as the less confident one for once. But it's a lot less funny when I realize it's all because of a boy. In my humble opinion, boys are hardly ever worth your time. Or energy. Oh well. One peek won't hurt, right? I look up as discreetly as possible.

Sitting in the corner booth is the Pretty Boy Trio: Asher, Brody, and Zach.

I freeze.

This is a code red. In my dictionary, this is the *reddest* freakin' code red in the history of code reds. Because I failed to consider that since Zachary Chandler is here, the rest of the trio would be here too. Including Reed. As if he can hear my thoughts, he lifts his head from the opposite side of the café, and his eyes connect unerringly with mine.

All the air in my lungs is sucked out. It's like he's a lighthouse. Constantly exuding and radiating an effortless, confident energy from his spot in the corner. Dazed, I tear my gaze away from him and fumble to catch up with Mia, who's already in the process of ordering.

After a few minutes, we settle in at the table farthest away from the trio, and Mia starts going on about how she almost broke her phone but I can't focus. Somehow, my gaze shifts behind her.

Reed's face is settled into a frown and Zach has stopped stuffing donuts into his face. Brody just looks amused. Mia turns around to see what I'm staring at, and when she realizes, her eyes widen. "I thought I told you *not* to look!"

"I didn't look!"

I did.

It isn't long before we hear screeching chair sounds, and all three of the boys are seated at our tiny table. What the heck? I glance at Mia, whose eyes have widened considerably. Nevertheless, she manages a smile as her gaze settles on Zach. "Uh, hi."

"Hi." Zach offers her a grin. "Bea, right?"

"Mia, actually."

Zach's smile is blinding white. "Did it hurt when you fell from h—"

"Bro, shut the *hell* up," Brody says, proceeding to smack Zach upside his head. Zach responds by shoving Brody so hard that he nearly falls off his chair and on top of me. Now they're both grumbling and our table's attracting attention. I take in a slow breath.

Asher ignores the two as his eyes land on me. "Wren," he says, like he's testing the waters.

Suddenly, the other two stop fighting to look at me, and Mia joins them. I glare at Reed. I was hoping I'd come out of this situation unnoticed, but it seems like the universe enjoys sprinkling bad luck all over me.

"You two know each other?" Brody asks.

I'm quick to answer. "No."

Reed grins. "Yeah."

I shut my eyes and sigh. When I open them, Zach's brows are furrowed. "How?"

Reed's gaze slides languidly to his friend. "She's babysitting Ev."

"*Ooh.*" Zach winks. "Good with kids, huh?"

Reed and Brody offer Zach blank, unimpressed stares but he just sits back in his chair and kicks back his long legs, his grin intact.

I shrug. "Uh . . . I guess?"

"You go to Eastview?" Brody asks, his gaze settling on me.

I know I said I like being invisible, but damn, I must've gotten really good at it. I've been in at least one of Brody Knight's classes since freshman year. But I can't really blame him, so I just settle with a clipped, "Yeah."

"Oh." Brody draws back a hand to rub the nape of his neck. "Haven't noticed you around."

I sip on my frozen chocolate drink, glancing at Mia, who's enamored by Zach's smile as he talks to her. She's clearly handling this well. Me? I'm feeling what Leo DiCaprio probably felt when he was slowly dying in *Titanic*.

"You don't like coffee?" Brody asks, eyeing the drink in my hand and snapping me out of my thoughts.

"Not really," I mumble. "It has a weird aftertaste."

Immediately, Zach faces me with a mischievous smile. "That's what she said."

Brody rolls his eyes with a grin tearing his lips apart. "You're sick, man."

Zach winks. "You know it."

Brody lets out a chuckle. I risk a glance at Reed, who's sporting a small smile. Up close, his features are striking. Strong bone structure, deep-blue eyes, and the faintest trail of freckles that stretch across the plane of his cheeks and nose, which is slightly sunburned from summer. His gold hair falls over his forehead, brushing his brows, and he has a tan that makes his skin glow. It's no wonder he has half of our school's population swooning.

His gaze flickers to me, and I look away a second too late. Way to go, Wren, you just fueled his ego, which is already the size of a small country.

"Take a picture." He winks. "It'll last longer."

"I would," I offer dryly, "but flash photography scares animals."

Brody chokes on his iced coffee before he starts laughing. Reed's composure cracks for a second, amusement glimmering in his eyes before he covers it up with a look that's predatory. He leans forward so his lips are just inches away from my ear.

"Careful," he whispers. "Animals bite."

His voice sends a shiver down my spine, and it's my turn to choke on my drink. Before moving away, though, Reed sneaks his fingers behind me and tugs the ribbon off the end of my braid. My hair comes apart slowly, loosening down my back. I narrow my eyes at my ribbon, now held captive between his fingers. He smirks, seeing that he's succeeded in his little game. I huff and take a sip from the remaining iced chocolate as I run a hand through my hair in an attempt to neaten it.

"Bro, tell 'em," Zach murmurs, giving Brody a slight shove.

Mia frowns. "Tell us what?"

"We're actually . . ." Brody pauses to give me a trapped look. "Not meant to be here."

I can't fight the grin that finds my lips. "Why not?"

I mean, it's just Dunkin' on a Wednesday afternoon. Nothing taboo about it. If you told me these boys were more dramatic than Mia, I wouldn't have believed you, but life throws you surprises every day.

Brody just sighs. "Ah, you don't get it, do you? We"—he gestures from himself to Zach and Asher—"have a game this Friday. And if Coach found out we made a trip to bum it out on donuts and milk shakes, he'd flay us alive."

I cast a look of disbelief Zach's way but he just shrugs as if to say "And that's the gospel truth." Brody stares at me like I'm supposed to be registering something I'm not.

"*Oh,*" I say, realizing that it's my cue to swear to secrecy. "Well, my lips are sealed."

Brody grins, holding up a fist with only his pinkie finger extended. "Pinkie swear?"

"Um, yes," I murmur, calmly easing his hand down. Afterward, I feel guilty for not just completing the stupid freakin' pinkie swear, but it's not every day that a guy who looks like he fell off of a *Teen Vogue* cover actually talks to me, forget exchanging sacred oaths with me.

"You guys are coming to the game this Friday, right?" Zach asks, his eyes hopping between Mia and me.

Mia shrugs. "I'll go if Wren goes."

Brody glances my way, waiting for my response. I rack my brain for a good enough excuse, but in the end all I can come up with is a sullen, "No one invited me."

Reed holds back a smile. "You don't need an invitation."

There's a small pause where I chance eye contact with him. He meets my gaze right back, daring me to look away first. I don't, even when the blue in his eyes makes me feel like I'm drowning.

I avert my gaze, clearing my throat. "I'll see."

But anyone who uses the two-syllable phrase knows exactly what it means—I'm not going to that game.

# CHAPTER 6

## Asher

By the time game night rolls around, I'm wound as tight as a coil. I stretch a bit to ease the tension in my back, but it does little to help. Lifting my leg to rest it on the bench, I shift my gaze to Zach as I pull on my gear. Dude's struggling to distinguish between his left and right shin guards. A ghost smile makes its way on my face, and Zach doesn't miss it.

"Yo, Reed, get that shit-eating grin off your face," Zach mutters. "You put your skates on the wrong way that one time, I ain't forget."

"What grin?" I smile innocently. "And you had them right the first time."

He groans, pulling his socks off more violently than necessary as he swaps his guards for the third time in the last ten minutes. I snicker to myself. He didn't have them right the first time.

When I chuck my jeans into my duffel bag, a red blur tumbles out of the pocket. Frowning, I reach down to find a red ribbon. It comes back to me in waves. This is Wren's ribbon—the one I stole a few days back at Dunkin'.

Half of me has the strange urge to tie it around my wrist as a sort of lucky charm, but the other half doesn't believe in luck or superstition. Eventually, the latter wins, and I shove the ribbon into my duffel along with my jeans, making a mental note to return it to her later.

Now that some of the anxious energy has rolled off my chest, I start tying the laces to my trainers, which some of us wear to avoid walking around with skates on. The game's against Maris Stella, one of the best high school teams in the state. For the last five years, Eastview seniors haven't won against Maris Stella. That thought alone adds a lot more pressure on my shoulders than there already was.

"I think I'm going to shit myself," Harvey murmurs.

"It'll be fine," I say. "Don't worry about them; stick to the game plan and we'll be good." I stare at them. Determination fills me as they raise their heads, promising to play their best.

"Yeah," Daniels says to Harvey, patting his back. "We'll be fine, Oompa Loompa."

"That's *so* funny." Harvey throws his hands in the air. "*So* freaking funny, man."

I roll my eyes with a lingering smile, ignoring their banter. Today's game is at Lynwood, meaning we don't get the extra warm-up time on the rink that we normally do. Taking my phone out of my duffel, I check that I haven't gotten any new messages from my mom. Coach pops his head into the changing room. "Everyone out in five! Meet me at the benches on the far right."

A few of the guys follow me out and we walk along the hallway leading to the large, transparent doors. The clamor gets louder as we get closer. A rush of cold air strikes me as I trudge to where Coach is standing.

When I reach him, I sit down, placing my helmet and mouth guard next to me. The rest of my team arrive, and they sit and start shit talking our opposition. Coach told me that there would be some important people in the crowd today. *Scouts.*

"Okay, boys!" Coach says. "This is the second game of our season. The first one wasn't the greatest, but we've improved during practice these past few weeks. I know it's hard adjusting to new positions." He pauses to look at Miller, our center, and Harvey, on defense. "But it's no excuse. You all know who's starting: Reed, left winger, Miller, center, and Knight, right winger, Chandler and Harvey at the back. For today, I want to go back to our original setup—Knight, back up Reed." He looks over at Brody, who gives him a firm nod. "The rest of you are on the bench for now. Get ready to go on now, and Chandler, for heaven's sake, keep your damn mouth guard in! Break a leg, boys."

After Coach leaves us, we put on our guards and helmets, then huddle up. We stand in a circle, looking at each other before letting out a loud cheer: "Eastview!"

We line up, then walk onto the ice. I can't help but smile at the smoothness of the surface and the bite of cold air at my face as I glide to take my position. But my smile diminishes as a sense of uneasiness washes over me. I look down at the ice that has a red line streaked across it. I stretch my neck. Rolling it, I try to get rid of that feeling.

But when I lift my head, I catch sight of him. Drew McKay. The boy who almost got me expelled in the eighth grade because he thought that breaking into school, ruining private property, and trying to change legal documents was fun.

I had said no, but Drew broke into the school anyway, and when he was caught? The asshole implicated me. And when I said I didn't have any part of it, he called me a snitch. He eventually left, and I often found myself questioning why I had been friends with McKay in the first place.

He gives me a smirk I'd like to believe has no malicious intent and takes his position right in front of me.

"Long time no see," he says. "*Reed.*"

Yeah, it was definitely malicious.

"McKay," I say, acknowledging him with a tight nod of my head. As much as I feel anxious, I'm not going to let this affect the game. Personal matters stay out of the rink. Staring at the referee, I wait for him to drop the puck so that we can start. He blows the whistle. The puck drops, and my chest caves.

The first forty minutes pass quickly. Zero–zero. We're tied. The team and I are exhausted, and as we chug our water, Coach explains a new game plan. My muscles are aching and my skates are killing me but I need to push through it. I can hardly hear Coach over the blood roaring in my ears.

Something is nagging at me though. Drew. He's being awfully quiet, sticking to the corners of the ice when we play. Something else I've noticed? Drew can't play for shit. I bet his dad waved a wad of cash at the school and Drew got what he wanted, like always. But McKay staying away from me is good, and maybe he's finally let his ancient grudge against me go. I decide to ignore him and just play the game.

The last twenty minutes on the clock starts, and the puck falls. Miller wins it and passes it to me. It glides across the ice, right onto my stick. Skating past a defenseman, I keep the puck on my stick as I move it around the players before passing it into the space in front of Brody, who skates forward to collect it. The crowd gets louder with every pass.

*Come on.* I watch Brody maneuver the puck toward the goa. Stepping forward, I wait to receive it, just like we practiced. *Come on.*

For a split second Brody looks up and makes eye contact with me. It's my cue. I push forward, calves burning, blood roaring in my ears. Now, instead of ignoring the rush in my veins, I channel it. Focus it. I'm close.

Then a giant blur attacks me from the left. Before I have any time to react, it completely wipes me out. A loud pop echoes as immense pain shoots down my leg. The cold, hard ice does very little to comfort me as my pressure points spike, and black dots linger in my vision.

The whistle is blown and slowly the cheer of the crowd dies down. People quickly surround me, peering down at me. I open my eyes; my vision is blurred.

I hear Brody's voice. "Drew? What the *hell*?"

"Brody." From the voice, I can tell it's Zach. "Touch him and you're suspended for the season. Let me beat this *asshole* up instea—"

I choke a laugh despite myself, but there's the metallic taste of blood on my tongue. Then Coach is here, above me and he's shouting for the medics. And everything goes black.

↶

"I'll tell him."

Someone's sniffing, and there's a warm hand in mine. Blinding white walls are the first thing I see. And it feels like there's a boulder on my knee. I turn my head slowly to look at my mom. Red rims her puffy eyes. "Asher, honey? How are you feeling?"

I attempt to sit up but everything aches. It pulls me back, stopping me from doing anything. Panic rises in my chest. What the hell happened? Why does my knee look like that? And why does it feel like I hit my head against a fucking wall?

The doctor standing in the corner notices my confusion and alarmed look. He walks gently toward me, holding something in his hand. His white coat is embroidered with *Dr. Greene*. "Asher, I'm going to need you to calm down. All right? I'm here to explain everything."

Gathering my thoughts, I take a deep breath. Then everything comes back to me, and my roaring headache worsens. The game. Drew. *My knee*.

As realization makes its way to my face, the doctor stops in front of me. Fear makes its way up and closes my throat, making it hard to breathe.

"You sprained your right wrist and injured your knee." He pauses. There's a look on his face as he gives my mother a fleeting glance. There's a moment of silence.

"There's more, isn't there?" I ask slowly, looking at both of them.

My mother holds my hand. What's the big problem? I hurt my knee and my wrist. So what? It's not the first time. It swells up then I have to ice it and bam, done. Knee healed. Wrist healed. Then I'm back on the ice. I'm always back on the ice. What makes this time any different?

"You tore your ACL."

My world falls. Completely off its axis. And sound doesn't exist for a few seconds. I can't hear my mother or Dr. Greene. Some pro hockey players who tore their ACLs have had their careers end before they even started. So what does this mean for *me*?

"Is there any possibility that he can play hockey?" Mom asks, but her voice is just some noise in the distance.

"Well, as of right now," the doctor says, "no. According to Asher's chart dated around October two years ago, I believe he hurt the same knee. His left knee was already giving him slight trouble; you said he used to complain sometimes after games that it was bothering him." He glances at my mother, who nods in response as she tries to understand. "There's slightly more pressure on the recovery of his injury. After surgery and some physical therapy, he may be able to play after five months or so."

That's too late. I can't play this season. I won't be able to go to the state championship. *I can't get scouted.*

Mom grasps my hand tighter. "It'll be fine. You might still be able to play. Don't jump to conclusions, all right? I'm sure everything will be fine."

I'm not so sure.

# CHAPTER 7

## Wren

Reed was injured during the game on Friday. Badly. The entire school is abuzz with the news that he might not be able to get scouted. Which, for someone like him, must be a big deal. The chair next to me in English stays empty for two weeks.

Then, on Tuesday morning, Reed walks into math class late, with shadows under his eyes, his left leg in a brace, and a cast wrapped around his hand. It's not the first time he's arrived at school battered and bruised, but this time is definitely the worst. The class hushes, but he doesn't make eye contact, just stares blankly ahead as he slides into his seat.

It doesn't take a genius to gather he's majorly out of key and more broody than usual. I tell myself it isn't any of my business and continue with my notes.

After class, I make my way to my locker. I'm already exhausted, but maybe it has a little something to do with the fact that I stayed up until four o'clock reading on my phone. Just maybe. Reaching into my locker, I grab the books I need and perch them in the crook of my arm. Trudging to the cafeteria, I make my way over to Mia. I place my books and lunch on the table then sit down.

Both Mia and I are surprised when Zach comes up to us with his usual grin and asks us to join them at the higher level of the cafeteria. Mia and I exchange apprehensive looks, aware that this could be social suicide for both of us.

"Are you sure?" she asks him.

"Yeah." Zach shrugs. "There's plenty of space so that shouldn't be a problem."

I grimace. Sitting at that table will mean sitting with Reed, who I've been consciously trying to avoid because, for some reason, I always manage to be more clumsy than normal around him. But I figure I can't be selfish.

Mia's been extra gooey since the scene with Zach at Dunkin', and I don't want to be the one to crush her dreams. I give her a reassuring nod and get out of my seat with my tray and my books balanced in my hands, then head up the slope to the higher level of the cafeteria, behind Mia and Zach.

"Hey, everyone," Zach says. "This is Mia and Wren. Be nice."

Everyone lifts their heads, which is my cue to duck mine. Mia takes a seat next to Zach, and . . . she fits right in. I realize I've just been standing here staring at the floor for a good few seconds, so I shuffle over and take the nearest empty seat. I'm sitting next to Brody, and he offers me a bright smile. I acknowledge him with a small one in return.

The air is filled with the sound of people engaging in small talk, except for the two people making out, and Asher, who's silent, his jaw set in a hard line. He's still in his mood from earlier, but since his hand *is* kinda broken, I can't judge him for it. I take a slow bite of my sandwich, before Zach yells, "I found it!"

"Reed!" Zach pulls a bright-pink marker from his bag, and runs over to Asher. "Let me sign your cast."

Reed frowns. "No."

"Come *on*. I've always wanted to do this!"

He opens the marker and goes crazy. Reed's lazy attempt to swat him away is futile because Zach's already drawing a disfigured . . . stick man—*nope*, definitely not a stick man. That's a penis. My cheeks warm as I watch a string of inappropriate words appear on the once-clean cast.

Asher holds back a smile. "Chandler, I swear to God, if I end up in detention because of you . . ."

I'm still distracted by Zach's antics when Brody reaches forward and grabs my juice box, popping the opening with the tiny straw.

My mouth drops. "*Hey.*"

Reed lifts his head at my voice. Brody just smirks and takes a huge sip from the juice box while ruffling my hair with his free hand. He cocks a brow and tilts the juice box toward me with one hand. "Want some?"

I pause. The *nerve* of this boy. Is he seriously offering my own juice box back to me?

"No," I say. "You already got your saliva on it." I gag. "I could catch an incurable disease."

He just laughs while I grimace. Suddenly, the sound of a chair scraping across the floor makes everyone snap up their heads. I look up to see Reed leaving the table.

᠅

In seventh period, Reed still sits in his usual place—next to me. Not surprisingly, he pays no attention to me. Facing the front of the classroom, he trains his cobalt eyes on the blank whiteboard and nothing else.

Miss Hutchinson walks in, and the class doesn't halt their mumbling. "Quiet down, everyone!"

The class gradually gets softer and more hushed. Miss Hutchinson's eyes find Reed next to me. "Welcome back, Asher. Glad you're doing better."

Reed just nods curtly, and Miss Hutchinson turns to the rest of the class. "Okay, everyone, we need to get to work. Midterms are approaching fast." She pauses, turns to pick up a large pile of books, then hands them over to someone in the front. "Pass these out, please. We're going to be doing a comparative book study which will count toward your final English mark."

She finishes with a smile, her red lipstick making her teeth stand out more. "The title of the first book is—"

"*Romeo and Juliet*," I whisper to myself as the book lands on my desk and I scan the title. I feel Asher's gaze flicker my way but when I turn to face him, he's back to ignoring me.

"*Romeo and Juliet*," Miss Hutchinson continues, "and although I'm sure some of you have already read it, I'm also aware of the fact that there are many in this class who have not. To those who have, I'm sure you will have no objection to reading it once more."

Miss Hutchinson beams, and for a millisecond she aims it at me, a twinkle in her eye. Running my fingers over the old paperback, I open it to the familiar first page. I groan under my breath.

"Sorry, I didn't quite get that, Wren?" Miss Hutchinson lowers her eyes to me. Benign amusement lines her gaze, and anxiety creeps into my chest. "Please repeat."

"Uh," I repeat a little louder, mostly to drown out the hammering of my heartbeat in my ears. "The plot is entirely flawed."

I hear some hushed murmuring behind me. Miss Hutchinson just smiles. "Would you like to explain why you think so?"

"I just . . ." I exhale. "Um . . . *Romeo and Juliet* is, uh . . . it's a huge romanticization of death. I mean, after seeing that Romeo killed himself for her, Juliet decides to take her life too. From my point of view, it's mere teenage infatuation that drives her to do this after seeing Romeo dead. If she really had been in love with him she would've been content living with only the memory of him."

"She believed a life without love wasn't a life worth living," a deep voice objects.

I turn to find the voice belongs to Reed, and he's finally looking somewhere other than ahead of him. He's looking at me.

"But there were other people who loved her," I say. "She still had to live for her family."

"The same family that banned her from loving someone?"

My chest catches fire. "Yes. Maybe she didn't want to live for her family, but she had to have some reason not to end her life. If she gave herself a chance, she could've been able to fall in love again. Her judgment was clouded. She was too young and too in love to make the right decision."

"If you're saying age is the problem," he says, "then I can't agree with you. You can be the oldest person on earth and still be immature as—"

"She was *thirteen*. And okay, maybe you're right; maybe you can't judge someone by their age. But what about the way they fell in love? It's hard to believe they fell so deeply in love within a matter of days—he fell in love with her after seeing her once. In other words, he fell in love with her appearance, not her character."

Reed shrugs. "Sometimes love doesn't need time."

Frustration runs down my jaw. "You're not being *realistic*—"

I furrow my brows before Miss H. interrupts. "That's enough, you two. Thank you for very graciously supplying the entire class with an informative little debate." She glances between Asher and me, not hiding the amusement in her eyes. "The rest of you can think about the points they made when you have time. For now, you need to complete the questions I've put up on the smartboard after reading act 1, scene 1. They're simple, so don't give me those dying seal impersonations, Zachary."

She raises a brow at Zach, who'd groaned at the mention of work. The class laughs, and the lesson moves on. At the end, I'm packing up my things to leave when Miss Hutchinson stops me.

"Wren," she says.

"Me?" I squeak.

"Yes, dear. And Asher."

I glance sideways at Reed, who stares back blankly. She's definitely going to have a few words about the stupid little Shakespeare argument we had.

"Taking notes in class is imperative to passing this subject," she says. "And as you know, Asher over here has injured his writing hand. And I'm very happy you volunteered to help him out."

What?

"I volunteered?"

Miss Hutchinson looks at me like I've grown another head. "Of course. Asher let me know before class."

I stare at Reed in surprise. He stares back, the corners of his lips lifting. What the *heck*? That's why he left the cafeteria early?

Now that I really think about it, I could care less about Asher Reed and his wrist injury. He signed up for it when he decided to join the hockey team. Sure, I feel bad, but that's about as far as my sympathy extends. I have enough on my plate as is, and I don't need some rude jerk wasting more of my time. Does that make me selfish? Maybe. But I don't care, not really. Besides, why me? Doesn't he have a plethora of people willing to sacrifice their lives for him, or something?

I'm about to say I haven't done anything of the sort, but Miss Hutchinson just smiles before walking out. I turn to Reed in a storm. "Why couldn't you ask someone else?"

He shrugs. "I'd like to see *you* do it for me."

"What?" I make a face. "Why me?"

"You have my attention now, Wren Martin," he says, waving a careless hand. "Do with that what you will."

"What the heck?" I exclaim. "I don't *want* your attention."

Reed's gaze darkens and he leans in a little, offering me a sardonic smile. "Liar."

I shoot him an incredulous look. "What?"

"I call bluff," he says, shrugging. "You don't want anyone to notice you but you wear a red hoodie. You know what a red light means? It means *Stop. Look at me. I'm here.*"

"Or," I say, clamping and unclamping my jaw, "it just means I'm wearing a red hoodie. Life isn't some elaborate literature study."

"C'mon," he says with a steady look. "Miss Hutch won't be happy to hear that you decided to leave the poor handless kid on the side of the road, now, would she?"

"You're not handless!"

But Reed ignores me, veering out of the classroom. Just as he reaches the door, he grins, then gives me a mock salute, which proves just how *not handless* he is. Frustrated, I rub at my temple, suppressing the urge to scream out loud.

# CHAPTER 8

## Asher

I've been feeling like shit since the game. Physically and emotionally. I don't want to complain about it too much, especially in front of Mom, who's already stressing a fair share over this stupid ordeal. I can't drive myself to school until my knee and wrist heal, which means there's more pressure on Mom to get me to school. Basically, life sucks.

But getting that big of a reaction out of Wren Martin, who's been avoiding me like the plague, is the first modicum of amusement I've felt in two weeks. And, all right, maybe I am an asshole for it, but she doesn't *actually* have to do my notes for me if she doesn't want to. She can just tell me to piss off. But she doesn't. Not outright, at least.

I take it as a good sign, and swing my backpack over my shoulder as I walk out of the classroom, chuckling as the image of her shocked face replays in my mind. It wasn't even that deep; I got to

English early and Miss H. asked if I needed help with my notes, and I said, "Nope, I've got it."

You know, like a liar. My right hand is fucked up. Severely. And I can't write with my left, but I was planning to use SparkNotes anyway. Then Miss Hutchinson said, "Is Wren helping you out? She sits next to you, right?"

And I was about to say no, but I pulled back, and nodded, the idea already planted too firmly in my mind. "Oh, yeah," I said, you know, like a liar. "Wren's helping me out."

Miss H. smiled. "She's a sweet girl."

Right. *Sweet.* I sat next to her for an entire period and she didn't say a word to me. Save for the passive-aggressive argument over *Romeo and Juliet*, of course. And then she blew up when Miss H. left. But it was . . . cute. It's the biggest range of emotion I've ever seen the girl display, and to be honest, her anger is more endearing than offensive. Plus, I deserved it.

In math, I begin to realize just how much I've missed in two weeks. At the end of the lesson, I figure I've got a lot of catching up to do. I glance at Wren, and when she gives me a fleeting glance, panic flares in her eyes and she looks away quicker than fire catches. I find myself grinning as she practically throws herself out of the room.

I'm going to figure out why she's been avoiding me sooner or later, but for now, I need to get to practice. I'm sitting out this one, obviously, but I'll stick around to keep the team on track and watch them play from the bench. My next checkup is in a week, and I'm hoping they can tell me what to do to speed up this whole process.

When I lean down to pick up my backpack, pain shoots up my arm. Not exactly a stellar sign. I look down and see that I tried to pick my bag up with my bad wrist. Zach and Brody are by my side, ready to help.

"I'm good," I say, dismissing them curtly.

I don't miss the looks of pity they pass my way, but I can manage just fine. I can't help but feel a lick of animosity toward Drew. He's the reason I'm in this position in the first place. He didn't get out scot-free, though. I'm betting his heroic little act has cost him his place on the team. I'm also betting he's malicious enough to not care.

When we reach the rink, Zach and Brody pull away and head to the changing room. I sink down on the bench, looking at the ice. It looks different from this point of view, one where adrenaline no longer rushes through my body. Closing my eyes, I rest my head in my good hand, elbows on my knees.

"Reed."

I open my eyes and look up to find Coach beckoning me over. "You're still captain," he says. "Go tell those boys to hurry up."

Trudging away, I scoff. *Captain*. What use am I now? I can't play for three months minimum. I reach the door of the changing room and open it slightly. The voices from inside travel.

"I don't think we're going to make it to the state championships this season. We can kiss that shit good-bye."

I look through the little gap in the door to find the team standing in a circle.

"What are you talking about?" Daniels says.

"You weren't there, up close, man. I saw the way Reed was checked. He's going to be out for the season."

"And he's being a little bitch about it. I said hi and dude just ignored me."

"Leave him alone," Brody says, staring at Harvey, who I presume made the previous comment. "He's just going through some stuff."

"That doesn't mean he can treat us like crap," another player pipes up.

My throat clogs up.

"He didn't come to practice for two whole weeks. Everything is falling apart. Daniels can't play his position anymore! He's lost without Reed. Our formations are going to shit. Christ."

"Did Asher ask Drew to slam him into the ice?" Zach says, anger lining his words.

"Maybe if Reed hadn't snitched, this wouldn't have happened at all," Harvey replies.

My mouth drops slightly in disbelief. This is *my* fault?

"Yo, shut the fuck up, Harvey," Zach shouts. "It happened in eighth grade. That asshole should have gotten over it."

"Let's be honest," Brody starts, looking at all of them, and Harvey in particular. "All of you are being too demanding. Reed's not perfect. You think he is, but he isn't. At least appreciate the fact that he kept us together for four years, some of us even longer."

There's a moment of silence. Brody opens his mouth again, looking everyone in the eyes. "And c'mon, man, if he was standing right here, would you be saying this shit to his face?"

I stand at the door, holding on to it until my knuckles turn white. Swallowing, I push it open. "Hurry the hell up."

Some of them duck their heads, but Knight and Chandler walk past them and follow me out.

Taking a seat on the benches, I think about their words. It pisses me off. I didn't want this. I wanted to be enjoying my senior year playing hockey. Fooling around with my friends. *I'm* the one stuck with a sprained wrist and a torn ACL, not them. I actually thought they'd get it, but they don't, not even a little. Nothing's going right.

A tap on my shoulder pulls me out of my thoughts. I look at Coach, who raises an eyebrow at me.

"Sorry," I mutter.

"Any words for the team, Reed?"

I look at them, contemplating my next words. "Your formations are going to shit. Fix them."

They look at me, guilt written on their faces as clear as day. Zach and Brody choke down laughs. Coach gives me a stern look but I can't care less. I want them to know I heard. The team heads off to the rink. And I sit. Staring at them. I don't think I've ever felt more left out in my whole life.

Coach makes his way over to me. "Son, I know you want to get on the ice. I do too. Be patient. You're getting your checkup next week; it'll all work out."

I manage to give him a tight-lipped smile. "I hope it does."

I really hope it does.

He walks off to shout at the team, who clearly aren't doing the right thing on the ice. Coach sits with them, figuring out a new game plan. Rearranging players. They all shift awkwardly as Coach asks them why my spot is empty.

Then I see it. Slowly, the team morphs. They shift. Someone takes my position. Just like that, they replace me. The team starts playing without me, and it feels like I never was there in the first place.

I try not to focus on the ache in my chest as practice nears its end. Everyone starts getting off the ice. Gathering my belongings, I leave without saying anything. And because of my stupid damn knee, I can't even drive home. As I walk to the main building, I pull out my phone to message Brody to tell him I'll be waiting by the locker room.

# CHAPTER 9

## Wren

As I stride down the hallway on the way to the library after school, I notice a lone figure seated on a bench outside the boys' locker room. It's Asher, and he's glancing down at his phone. My heart skips a beat, and I'm about to make a run for it when his head lifts at that precise moment. I'm inwardly cursing myself, but it's too late—he's noticed me, and he's shoving his phone in his pocket. "Martin."

I clear my throat. "I'm making copies of my notes for you."

All right. Even though it was annoying of him to make me do his notes, I'm not heartless. If he asked me directly, I would've said yes. I just don't appreciate him putting me on the spot like that in front of Miss Hutchinson. She probably thinks I'm a lunatic.

When he doesn't offer any reply to my statement, I chew on the inside of my mouth. "Do you want to come to the library with me?"

Reed deadpans. "I'll skip."

*What?* So much for being nice. I give him an unimpressed glare and try to ignore the little sinking feeling inside. I'm really beginning to hate these weird internal feelings. Like, is there an off switch for them? Because I would totally use it. I can't understand the way he makes me feel, and I don't want to.

"I don't read in school," Asher says, trying to justify himself, probably after noticing the look on my face.

A pathetic excuse, really. Clamping down on my jaw, I turn on my heel to leave, but an arm lands on my shoulder from behind. Turning, I register Brody's brown eyes and next to him, Zach.

"Yo, Juliet," Zach says. "Nice work today."

I smile awkwardly. "Thanks."

Brody quips, "What are we doing?"

When his gaze lands on me, I feel compelled to answer. "Oh, uh . . . I was just heading to the library."

Zach looks genuinely confused. "We have a library?"

Brody rolls his eyes. "Yes, dumbass."

"Whatever, *fatass*," Zach says, swinging his car keys around his forefinger. "I'm gonna head home. You coming, Reed?"

Reed's eyes settle on Brody and me. "Actually, I have nothing else to do, so yeah, guess I'm going to the library too."

I stare at him in surprise. Really? What a jerk.

"Okay, then." Zach gives us a mock salute. "See y'all tomorrow."

The three of us make our way to the library. Asher and Brody hardly ever come to the library—I know this because I'm almost always here, dragging Mia along with me occasionally.

Despite what most people say, Eastview's library is pretty great. Something about the way the books are set up, like a maze—one I wouldn't mind getting lost in. I love working on assignments here. It's peaceful. Except for that one time I walked in on one of the guys on the football team making out with a girl in the back row. A shudder runs down my spine at the memory.

I wander around the aisles of books, losing Asher and Brody along the way when something in particular catches my eye. I stare at the painting attached to the wall.

It's vibrant, with an elephant silhouette as the focal point, painted with dark, oil paint. The sunset behind the elephant is brushed on with shades of cerise, auburn, and yellow. I feel a pang of jealousy toward the artist, who could probably paint freely without having to worry about getting nightmares later on.

I love art, and all forms of it. My favorite art medium is, without a doubt, painting. I love the feeling of the paintbrush between my fingers. I love the soft, subtle sound of paint layering canvas. The colors descending into darker shades, then lighter again. I love the feeling of being able to create as much depth on a canvas as I want to. But that was all lost two years ago.

According to my psychologist, painting made my nightmares and visions worse.

Painting requires you to fill a certain picture or image in their head with color, and then translate that image onto paper, with paint. The problem with me is that two years ago, after that night, I'd messed up a certain part of my brain, and ended up with PTSD (post-traumatic stress disorder).

Painting somehow made my recall of the experience more vivid, and dulled my responses to others and the outside world. So I had to stop it. Quit. Completely abstain. Dr. Tselentis told me that there was a possibility that painting was my trigger. Suddenly, the thing that calmed me did the opposite. And so, to prevent the intensity of the side effects of PTSD, I had to refrain from things that triggered it. Common sense, right?

I turn to find Reed staring at me curiously. Snapping out of it, I brush past him. After choosing a pile of books and finishing copying the notes, I look around the library to find the two guys. They're sitting next to each other at a table.

Reed looks like he's playing some sort of game, presumably Candy Crush, his uninjured leg resting on the table itself. Brody's chewing gum, scrolling on his phone. I stomp over, and when they see me glaring at them, Brody stops blowing bubbles and Asher lowers his leg faster than the speed of light.

"You two do know this is a library, right?"

"Yes," they say simultaneously.

"So that means you know what you're supposed to do in a library . . . right?"

They both stare at me blankly.

I burst. "You read, you idiots!"

Brody's eyes are wide. "Holy shit. *That's* what you've been hiding this whole time?"

I frown. "What?"

He tilts his head. "I don't know. I've never seen you all angry and worked up. Guess I don't know you as well as I think I do, huh? We've got to hang out more."

Suddenly, I'm very conscious of the fact that he's right. A little. I'm not antisocial, just a little socially awkward. Until you get to know me and I'm comfortable with talking to you, that is. But that's the thing about most introverts—they're really just extroverts in disguise, and it's when they get comfortable enough that you get a real glimpse of their personality.

Brody must sense that I've coiled back, because he sends

me one of his easygoing grins. "Relax, Wren. Just means you're human. Plus, when you're angry, it's pretty hot."

I choke. Asher grunts, and I'm reminded that he's still sitting right there. His jaw is tight, and he's sending Brody daggers for some reason. When I recover, I mutter, "Can you just go get a book? Please?"

They both stand and slowly walk away, but my face is still warm from Brody's words. Were these boys born with no filter?

Thankfully, by the time they're back, I'm more composed. This time, they each have a book. But one look at the books in their hands and my mouth drops. The books are erotica, published in the freakin' middle ages. Why does our library even have these? They're grinning at each other like idiots as they stride back to their seats. Huffing a breath, I choose to let it go as I take a seat across from them and flip open the cover of my own book.

After a moment of reading, I hear someone flicking quickly through the pages of their book. I glance up. The culprit's Brody. Reed apparently reaches the same conclusion, because he uses *his* book to smack Brody in the back of his head. Brody lets out a profanity and does the same to Reed, using his own book as a weapon.

Reed's about to retaliate when I stop their idiotic little game. "Quit it, both of you!" I hiss. "Why are you acting like four-year-olds?"

"He started it," Reed mutters.

"I did *not*."

"Did too."

"I was just looking for the good parts," Brody murmurs.

I give him a silencing glare, and soon, the two return to their stupid books.

At least, that's what I think. But when I look up at them again, Asher's leaning on his hand and staring at something behind me, and Brody's book doesn't look quite readable at the moment. I stare at them dryly. "Reed, close your mouth. Brody, your book literally isn't even the right way around."

Asher frowns. "*Reed?*"

I raise a brow. "That's your name, is it not?"

"No." He shifts uncomfortably on his seat. "That's what the guys on the team call me. Can't you just use my first name?"

I consider the way his face softens a little, and I almost crack. "No."

Brody laughs, and slowly sobers up at the sight of my straight face. He offers me an uneasy grin. "I actually like this book."

He's making the issue worse. I really don't think he actually registers what he's said until a few minutes after. We all stare at the seductive looking pinup on the cover of Brody's book, and they both burst out laughing.

"You two disgust me." I grimace, but this only fuels the intensity of their laughter until they are both on the verge of tears. I can't help the slow smile spreading across my face because they look . . . cute. Their energy seems to spill out in colors more vibrant than the rainbow. It's endearing. I don't even know why the librarian hasn't stopped these two lunatics yet.

"You read a whole lot, right?" Brody asks. The question comes out of the blue.

"Definitely," I reply anyway, with a smile.

"So, do you prefer happy endings? Over, you know, sad ones?"

"I don't like endings at all," I say immediately. "Hate them more than anything. I wish that books could go on and on forever. The good ones, at least. But they can't, and they don't. So, I guess we never really know what happens to the characters. Other than the fact that they'll all eventually die."

"Unless they're immortal," he notes. I'm impressed.

"Yep, unless that," I agree.

"Hey, Brody," Asher starts. "Zach just texted. Apparently, Tristan's hosting a party this Friday? He asked whether you're going."

"Why can't he just text me?"

Reed laughs. "He's probably too lazy to scroll through his contacts to find your name. Mine's at the top."

"My name starts with a *B*."

Asher snorts. "Your name's saved as Fatass."

"*F* isn't that hard to scroll to!" Brody wails. "And I'm in his Recents." He rolls his eyes and waves a dismissive hand. "Just tell him I'll go." Then his eyes flicker to me. "You coming, Martin?"

They both look at me, waiting for my answer. I place my book down. "No."

"Why?"

"I don't like parties."

Reed is silent for a while. "If you come," he says, slowly, "you don't have to take my notes for—"

"I'll go," I intercept.

"—*one* day."

I drop my jaw, and Brody and Asher high-five, laughing.

"Deal's off," I huff.

Brody lifts a brow. "You already said yes."

I groan, slapping my forehead with my book. It takes an annoyingly long time for their laughter to die down, and when it does, someone calls out that the library's closing. I groan to myself, because thanks to Asher and Brody, I got hardly any reading done.

When we exit the library, I clutch my books to my chest. "I'm never asking either of you to the library again. Never."

# CHAPTER 10

## Asher

Sheets of paper are scattered across the surface of my desk, and I realize I'm officially in over my head. I've missed a lot more homework than I anticipated. And the more time I spend playing catch-up, the less I have to complete the new work that piles up every day. But every time I try to focus, I'm pulled back to the scene in the locker room, which leaves a bitter taste in my mouth.

Continuing my work, I halt when I come across a drawing on the side of Brody's paper. Zooming in, I find an obscure doodle of boobs. Chuckling, I know it's Zach's work of art. I flip my page over and start the next assignment. With my wrist slowing me down, it makes everything harder, but I have a concession to hand in work electronically until my wrist heals.

A few minutes later, a head pops into the room. Mom. I swivel on my chair, looking at her.

"I'm heading out to drop Ev off, then back to work," she says. "Have you had something to eat?"

I'm halfway through murmuring a vague answer and Mom's nodding, leaving my room, when a stupid, ill-informed idea worms into my mind. I'm probably the last person Wren wants to see, but I'm past the point of caring. She's undoubtedly the best person around to help me with the shit ton of work I have to do. I'm fully aware that this could blow up in my face, but it's a chance I'm willing to take.

Before I can think about it, I'm shoving my books and MacBook into my backpack and rushing out of my room. "Mom, wait."

She pauses midstep, glancing up at me with impatience in her gaze. "Yes?"

"Can you drop me off too?"

My mom narrows her eyes a little, and there's this little dent between her brows that always forms when she's thinking. And as much as she tries to be The Cool Mom, she's also naturally curious. "Why?"

"Homework," I say as I slowly descend the staircase.

"With Wren?"

I nod. "Yep"

Her brows cross. "I didn't know you two were friends."

"We are," I say. Okay, maybe that's a bit of a stretch. But the full truth isn't exactly going to help my case, and what my mother doesn't know won't hurt her.

She sighs. "You better not be lying to me. I know you think I don't know what the kids are up to nowadays—"

"Mom," I say, cutting her short. "Have you seen Wren? Does she look like the kind of person I'd do a line of coke with?"

Her hazel eyes are wide. "*Coke?*"

"It's a joke, Mom." I laugh, undocking the keys from the key holder attached to the wall. "Wren's great."

My mom raises a brow.

"And Ev loves her."

I chuck the keys to her unceremoniously. She's forced to catch them, and it cuts our nice little conversation short. My mom shakes her head as she walks out of the house, me trailing not far behind her. When I slide into the backseat next to Ever, she pouts. "Why are you coming?"

"Because I want to," I reply, half-offended.

Ever frowns. "I don't like you."

"Yeah," I say, flicking her forehead. "That's 'cause you *love* me."

At this, Ev shrieks like the little brat that she is, and Mom chastises me from the front. I roll my eyes as I scroll through my phone. A few minutes later, my sister promptly forgets that I'm The Enemy and peeks over at my screen in a way she'd like to believe is discreet. Grinning, I exit my chat with Zach and open my camera. When Ev's face lights up on my screen, she looks up at me sheepishly, caught in the act.

I grin. "You're not sly, Ev-bug."

"What does that *mean*?" she shrieks.

"Enough, both of you," Mom hushes. "We're here. Behave."

A glance out the window shows we've pulled onto Wren's street. With its matcha-green paint job, her house is quaint. Homely. The lawn is neat, even though some of the flowers look . . . squished? Jumping out of the car, I wince when the impact sets off a sharp pain in my knee. As it fades, I walk up to the door with Ever waddling not far behind me while Mom reverses.

A few minutes after, I ring the doorbell, and the door opens, revealing Wren. She's still wearing her red hoodie, her chocolate-brown hair tied back in a braid. There's a teal ribbon at the end. When she notices it's me, her honey eyes widen a fraction, and her mouth opens slightly. She blinks as she stares up at me. Then blinks again.

I clear my throat, fighting the urge to grin. "Aren't you going to let us in?"

She looks around me, searching for my sister. "Where's Ever?"

As soon as she says this, my sister catapults into Wren in a flurry of pink. "Wen!"

Wren gathers her composure quickly; I'll give her that much. She hugs Ev back before setting her down on her couch and switching on the flat screen. Her wary eyes follow me as I walk straight in and drop a pile of books on the table.

"Um . . . no offense or anything," she says, standing in front of me. Her gaze is accusing as she buries her hands in the pockets of her hoodie. "But why are you here?"

"Easy there, panda bear." I bop the tip of her nose with my index finger. Her hands fumble as she tries to swat me away, but I ignore her as I continue. "I need help with my homework." I pause for a second before continuing. "I missed two whole weeks, no? And you volunteered to help me out."

"I did not *volunteer*."

"Semantics."

She shoots me a baffled, slightly repelled look. "Your mom's paying me to babysit one child. Not two."

I pause for a moment. And I'm really testing her patience now, but I can't help it. A grin plays on my lips. "How about I pay you for two, then?"

For a minute, she's silent, and she just stares at me. I glance her way quizzically. "What?"

She tilts her head. "You wear glasses?"

Realizing, I curse under my breath. I'd been in such a rush to catch a ride here I forgot to put in my contacts. Yeah, so my eyesight isn't perfect, so what? That's what optometrists are for. She's trying to fight a smile, but a second later it splits her lips apart.

"Was that a smile?" I ask, edging closer to her. "Pretty."

My words clearly take her by surprise, and just as quickly as it appeared, her smile fades. I can see her fumbling, desperately searching for a fitting reply. She chews on her lower lip. "Didn't you say you needed help with something?"

A crystal-clear attempt to change the subject.

"Yeah," I say. "Homework."

"So, you show up at my house?"

I shrug.

"Okay." Wren takes a labored breath. "Okay." She lifts her honey-eyed gaze to me. "I haven't started, either, so let me just get my stuff."

We spend most of the afternoon trying to complete the homework with the low hum of Nickelodeon on for Ever in the background. Wren sits next to me, and I can tell she's trying her level best not to be disconcerted by my presence. She's a great tutor—genuinely patient, and she doesn't get frustrated when I ask her to go over something twice, explaining everything in earnest.

"So," she explains, "whenever you're talking about perfect circles on Euclidean surfaces, then pi, which represents the ratio of the circumference of the circle to its diameter, is a constant—"

She stops. I'm still focused on her but I can't fight a smile.

"What?" she snaps.

I point to the closed textbook on the table. "How do you know everything without even opening the textbook?"

She stares at the textbook, realizing that my observation is accurate. She looks at me, chewing the inside of her cheek. "I like pi."

"I'm not going to lie," I say. "That's kinda strange. What's with the unnatural love for math symbols?"

"Not all math symbols, just constants like pi."

"Why?"

"I don't know." She shrugs. "Unlike people, pi is forever, it doesn't just die, and it doesn't just end. It's constant, but at the same time there's no pattern to it. It's different. Unpredictable."

I consider my words as my gaze meets hers. "Nothing lasts forever."

The soft brown in her eyes melts into honey as a shard of dying sunlight falls on her face. "I won't take your word for it."

Less than an hour later, I exhale and finish off my last problem. Typing out math is a fucking nightmare. Wren shuts her book then disappears somewhere in the house.

"Hey, Ever," she says, appearing a few minutes later from the kitchen with a tray of iced cupcakes. "I got something for you."

Ev looks up at Wren like she's given her the Krabby Patty secret formula and grabs one. My lips lift as she turns to face me. Without saying a word, she shoves the tray into my face. I take one, a ghost of a smile spreading across my face.

"You done with your other homework?" I ask. My mouth is full of cupcake, and normally I'd think twice about eating this type of shit, but a cheat day is allowed. Besides, my team already thinks I don't care about them.

"Most of it," she says. "I still haven't started studying for midterms."

I look up at her. "Those are in a month."

"Yeah," she says, like it's obvious. "So?"

"So . . . you're studying a month in advance?"

"Asher," she says. My chest tightens at the fact that she used my real name. "One month isn't enough. People start two to three months before. These grades are really important for college applications."

"Fair enough." I nod. "Where are you applying?"

"A few places," she says. Then, she flicks her eyes to me in thought, as if making some mental decision to offer me more. "But I really want to get into Yale. And if I don't get a scholarship, I won't be able to. So yeah—" She sighs. "The midterms are really important to me."

"Why Yale?"

The question takes her by surprise, and her demeanor is jilted for a second. "It's an Ivy League."

"So is Harvard," I say. "And it's close to home."

She chews on the inside of her mouth, alarm flaring in her eyes. I get it. I asked her a question that she doesn't have the answer for herself. Deciding to change the subject, I tear my gaze from her to my sister, who's licking the icing off her cupcake. She holds it with both her hands. "She's clearly in love with you."

Wren lifts a brow. "That's an exaggeration."

"I don't think so, no," I say. "I guess I just want to know why Ev likes you this much, this quick. She's selective."

"I honestly don't know," she admits, nervously. "I'm not . . . sociable."

"You're talking to me."

84

Then, she just stares at me. "What's that supposed to mean?"

An unabashed smile creeps onto my face. "What? I'm attractive and I know it. The world's littered with people who have exceedingly low opinions of themselves, and I'm not going to contribute to the cesspool of self-loathing."

Her stare is dry and deeply incredulous. "How very humble of you."

I huff out a laugh, and as I do, one of the paintings on the wall catches my eye. I'm captured by it for a moment. It's good. Great, even. It's a field of roses. And in the center of it, a single daisy. There's a hint of innocence and authenticity to it, and it doesn't look like something you can get from a store. "Did you paint that?" I ask her.

She nods, and for a second, I'm floored. My eyes widen as I glance her way. "You paint?"

"It's not that good." She shrugs. "Besides, I stopped painting."

"Are you kidding?" Either she's trying to be humble or she genuinely has a distorted view of her art. I turn to face her. "I can't even draw a stick man properly. What does it mean?"

She hesitates for a second, then gives in. "It asks: In a field of roses, who would really choose the daisy?"

For a second, she's staring at me wordlessly, and I'm staring back. My phone buzzes in my backpack, and a quick glance at my watch tells me it's probably Mom back for us. Peeling my gaze away from the painting, I reach behind her for my backpack. When my upper body brushes against hers, she freezes completely. Only when I draw back does she release a breath, her gaze flickering to mine.

I send her an easy grin. "Give yourself a little more credit, birdie."

She makes a face. "Birdie?"

"Yeah." I nod. "A wren is a small bird. So, birdie."

Wren's features are contemplative. "You're smarter than you let on, you know."

"Oh, I've let on." I offer her a pointed look. "You just haven't noticed."

As I make my way to the door, my gaze lingers on the canvas on the wall, then skips to the girl in the hoodie.

"I would," I say to her. It's two words too cryptic, but I don't elaborate. Then, I collect Ever, who's only eaten half of her cupcake, and walk out the front door.

# CHAPTER 11

## Wren

I'm not sure when I fall asleep. But when I wake up, my skin is on fire, and a bloodcurdling scream fills the air. My vision is blurry but I can make out the faint outline of my sister. Her eyes are shut, her body covered. Blood-red splashes of paint—and she's the canvas.

"Emma," I scream loudly. Tears are drying on my cheeks as I try to pull her out of the car, but she sinks farther away from me. I hear voices screaming my name, calling for me to get out of the burning car. *Wren.* But I can't. *Wren.* I can't leave her. Sirens blare in the background, slicing through the ringing in my head. *Wren.*

"Miss," I hear someone call. "I'm gonna need you to relax while we remove you from the car. We're here now, you're safe. I need you to stay awake while we . . ."

"*Wren!*"

Someone is shaking me, but I can't move.

"Wake up!"

The voice gets louder, and my eyes finally open before I'm crushed between a soft chest and the bed. The scent of my mom's flowery perfume fills the air. I'm awake; it's a dream. It's a dream, I repeat to myself, taking deep, irregular breaths. *It's a dream.*

Except it isn't.

Sweat trickles down my forehead, plastering my hair to my face. A warm hand pushes the strands behind my ear.

"You're okay." In the dark, my mom's delicate brow wrinkles. "Breathe, honey."

Mom holds me tightly as my breathing returns to normal. She reaches to my bedside for the all-too-familiar orange prescription vial, popping it open with ease before placing two small pills onto her palm. She hands them to me with a bottle of water from the nightstand. I accept it wordlessly.

She bends down and sits on the floor. "You scared me."

I bury my face in her shoulder, and I can't hold back the tears.

"It's all right, honey." She curves her hand, cradling the crown of my head. "It's all right."

My mom is a nurse, assigned to the ICU and long-term patients at Altemore. In third grade, my English teacher told me to never use the word *nice* in creative writing because it was a boring word, and so it was forbidden. But I can't find a better word to describe my mom. She's nice.

I can't even begin to imagine the kind of shock she went through when she saw her daughters being rolled into the hospital during her shift. Dad died on scene. Emma was in the ICU for weeks while I was in for the first few days. When I woke up, Mom was sleeping on a chair, her hand clasping mine. I was the only person she had left.

After the accident, Mom and I were forced to pick up the pieces, but things were never the same again. We'd lost half of our family in one night. Everything was unbalanced, off key, and just all-round awful. How do you deal with that kind of grief? Where do you put it? Where does it go? How do you fit it all inside your body when there's not much space left for something that big?

When I wasn't eating, Mom would have to make sure I did, and when she wasn't eating, I'd have to do the same for her. It took us months to claw out of the deep chasm the universe had dumped us in.

When reporters asked to cover the story, we chose to omit our names. It was hard enough walking into school without the pity-glances. That little piece of normal was mine to hold on to, and I've only ever given it up to Mia.

My dad and sister are dead. I write it on a paper in my mind, crumple it, then bury it deep inside of me. But the edges are sharp, and every so often I'm reminded that there's this giant festering mess stuck inside me. And it will always be there, no matter what.

∽

I'm missing something. It's either that or I've severely under-estimated how hard I studied for this calculus test. Because sitting here, at my desk in math class with everyone taking the test, I can't explain the flurry of anxiety that creeps up my chest. Like a contagion, it lodges itself in my throat and stays there, and each time I stare up at the clock, it tightens.

When I look up from my test, I spot Faye, her head down as she checks her paper. She's already finished. Taking a deep breath,

I try to calm myself, but it doesn't work. When I try to write my answers down, my unsteady hand distorts my writing.

Looking down at the questions on the paper, I know I know this stuff. But . . . nothing. My mind's gone blank. The pit in my stomach grows. Leaning my head on my hand, I let out a shaky breath. Frustration gnaws at me. A guy sitting at the front of the classroom plays with his pen, clearly indicating he's done. This isn't good. This isn't good at all.

A voice cuts the silence like a knife. "Pens down."

My hand freezes.

"Miss Martin?" I feel the weight of a thousand eyes on me, and my chest constricts. Looking up through blurry eyes, I find Mr. Brakeman looking down at me expectantly.

I hand my paper in, and rush out, fast walking before slipping into an abandoned corridor. My chest is contracting faster than I can control my breathing, and my breaths are sharp and shallow. I lean down, and when it gets too hard to stand, edge slowly to the ground. Pulling out my phone hurriedly, I text an SOS to Mia, then try to focus on my breathing.

"Wren?"

I lift my head to see Mia careening toward me, phone in hand. She reaches me out of breath, leaning down to meet my gaze with worry flooding her face. "What's wrong?"

"Mia," I whisper, tearing up. "I don't . . . I don't feel so good."

"Okay," she says, nodding. "It's okay. You have your meds on you?"

I nod, pointing weakly to my bag as I try to calm my breathing. Mia reaches into one of the compartments and pulls out a bottle of water before dropping two pills in the palm of my hand. Two, because she knows my prescription. She knows me.

My eyes tear up more as I drain the bottle. When I'm done, I wipe my mouth with the back of my hand, covered by the sleeve of my hoodie, and look up at my friend, who's missing class to be here now. "Thanks."

Mia shakes her head, a small smile on her lips. "Don't mention it, stupid."

Something jumps at the benign word, and before I can help it, I look up at her in panic. "Am I really?"

She's confused. "Really what?"

"Stupid?"

Mia furrows her brows. "What? No. No way. I was just kidding, you know that. You're one of the smartest people, if not *the* smartest person I know. Where is all of this coming from?"

Sighing, I don't reply.

Mia's voice softens. "What triggered it this time?"

"Math test," I mumble.

Determination flares in Mia's eyes. Grabbing my wrist, she tugs me toward the school entrance. "Let's go. You need a break."

"Wait. M." She faces me, confused. "We can't just skip."

"Wren," she says. "You just had a legitimate panic attack. Over a math test. And you're smart as *hell*. You studied hard for that test. I know you did. So something's clearly wrong here. Either you take a break, or I'm walking into the counselor's office to demand she gives you the day off."

"What about your classes?"

She shrugs. "Don't worry about it. I'll catch up."

I contemplate it. As much as I hate to admit it, she's right. I've been studying for almost a week for a *test*. I guess I do need a break.

"Fine." I swallow. "I'll come with you."

It's easy to slip out of school, especially if you leave through the back exit. Once we're in Mia's car, we drive for a while, but everything's just a big blur for me. I occasionally feel her gaze on me, but she remains quiet.

I can tell she's worried. After the night of the accident, it took me a few months before I could sit in the front seat of any car. I silently push the thoughts away because thinking about it only makes the knot in my throat grow.

Mia's voice interrupts my thoughts. "You wanna grab something to eat?"

I shrug nonchalantly. "It's fine. I don't think I'm hungry."

She gives me a pointed look, lowering her head slightly. "I can bet you a hundred dollars that you didn't eat breakfast because you were too busy studying."

Turning my head, facing the houses and trees, I grimace, guilt taking over my face.

"Called it." Mia pauses, sending me a passing look. "So, where do you want to go?"

I play with the ribbon at the end of my braid absently. "I don't know. Anything's fine."

As she taps her fingers on the steering wheel, her bracelets jingle. "Well, then, what do you want to eat?"

"I don't know."

Mia's blank face changes to one of frustration. "I swear on Harry freakin' Styles, if you give me another vague-ass answer, I *will* throw you out of this car."

I burst out laughing but sober quickly. I know it's serious when she pulls out the One Direction threats. Eventually, we end up at the McDonald's drive-thru. The monotone lady in the intercom asks what we'd like to have. Mia glances at the board in front of us, then turns, waiting for my order.

I grin. "I don't know."

Her head whips back, irritation flashing in her eyes. A laugh bubbles up my throat, making its way out, and I struggle to get out words. Mia turns her head with a huff, a small smile sneaking onto her face.

"Fine, fine." I lift both my hands in surrender. "I'll stop."

The lady on the intercom speaks again, no doubt annoyed with our antics. Mia turns to me and grins. "Fries?"

I beam. "I'll have the cheeseburger, with a Coke, *and* fries."

She gives me a dubious look but continues nevertheless with, "I'll have the same."

After our food is handed to us, Mia takes out her purse to pay, but I stop her by leaning over and handing the money to the employee myself.

"Why'd you do that?" Mia protests, lifting a fancy-looking credit card from her wallet. I shrug as I take the brown paper bag from her hand.

"I have a job now, remember?" I joke, while she shakes her head in disbelief.

"I can't stand you," she murmurs.

I huff a laugh. "Kneel, then."

The scenery changes and we slow down, stopping at the top of a small hill. I recognize the place as a children's park. This is our place. It might sound stupid, but sitting on a swing talking about nothing with my best friend is sometimes the only thing that helps.

"Let's go." She grabs the bag and steps out of the car, and by the time I catch up with her, she's already sitting on a swing, her legs stretched in front of her. I take the seat next to her, my sneakers grazing the ground.

"You finally arrived." Mia grins as she takes a bite of her burger. "I thought at the rate you were going you'd reach here earliest tomorrow morning."

"Ha, ha," I murmur sarcastically. "So funny. I'm dying of laughter."

I look up at the vibrant yet soothing streaks of color filling the canvas of the sky. There are strokes of cerise and auburn resembling the soft, supple skin of a ripened peach. Light illuminates several clouds in the sky, outlining them in a silvery-gold halo. I'd paint it, except . . .

"Why don't you just tell people?" Mia asks, taking another bite of her burger. "Talking about what happened will help. I know you think you're alone but there are people who've had similar experiences."

"I've been to therapy," I remind her as I toss a fry into my mouth.

She shakes her head. "I know. But that's not what I mean. I mean actually talking about it. Not just to a therapist. Not running away or avoiding it."

"I don't avoid it."

She gives me a pointed look.

A smile tugs at my lips. "Okay, fine, maybe I do."

I sigh. "But everyone acts like they care about people with trauma until they actually meet someone with trauma. It's frustrating and annoying and—ugh—if *I'm* annoyed with myself, how can I expect someone else not to get annoyed too? Like, I'll be doing fine and *bam*. I'm not fine anymore."

"I'm not annoyed," she says, gently. "I'll never be annoyed."

"I know," I say. "But I've known you for the longest time. And I don't think I'll be able to find anyone else to talk to so easily."

It's true. I trust Mia. She never looks at me with pity. Pity is the worst. It's the lamest excuse for love. People tend to mix up the two. It's like pity's red and love's blue, and when you mix the two up, you end up with a disastrous-looking purple.

"Don't make me feel so important," Mia says. "You'll give me a complex. And all right, if you don't want to talk about it with anyone, maybe, I don't know . . . try to find some peace about it yourself?"

I smile a little. "Thank you," I say. And I mean it. "I'll try."

"I'm always here for you, you know."

My chest warms as I sway faintly on the swing, and I believe her. "I know."

# CHAPTER 12

## Asher

Sitting on an uncomfortable chair in a waiting room isn't exactly how I thought my Friday afternoon would go. The hands of the clock move slowly. Torturously slowly.

Scrolling mindlessly through my phone, I find a series of messages on the team's group chat in response to my good luck message. Zach and Brody send me private messages telling me that everything will be fine. If I wasn't injured, I'd be on the ice today playing Clifton. A sigh escapes my lips as I lean back in my chair.

Mom, who's sitting next to me, notices.

"Asher," she says, reaching over to cover my hand with hers. "Everything's going to be okay."

I'm getting real tired of hearing that phrase, and I open my mouth to reply, but the sound of a door opening distracts me. It's Dr. Greene, the physician in charge of my care.

"Good afternoon," he says, offering me a polite, clinical smile.

I offer a curt greeting back, while Mom talks to him a bit more as he leads us into his exam room. The doctor gathers the papers that probably detail my case. "It's been a few weeks since your injury. This is your first checkup. Am I right?"

Nodding, I answer him.

He notices my somber mood. "Well, okay then. Asher, how's your knee feeling? And your wrist?"

I wince slightly as he examines my knee. "Much better than last week."

"That's great," he says. "If you don't mind, I need you to follow me to the other room where I can examine you properly."

Hesitantly, I stand, making sure I land on my right leg first before following. About an hour later, I head back to the main room where my mom sits. Dr. Greene comes through the doors a few minutes later with multiple sheets in his hand. He starts talking before my mother can ask him. "The cast on your wrist can come off within the next few days. Just make sure that you apply the ointment and regularly ice the area." He offers a passing look to my mother. "About your ACL . . ." The doctor pauses.

I get an overwhelming urge to hurl. He pulls out X-rays and MRIs of my knee.

"As we know, we looked at your X-rays previously and found no fractures. But with your MRIs, we've noticed that your ACL isn't *completely* torn. This is the first one, and when we compare it to the most recent one, we can see that there's been a slight improvement along this side.

"The fibers have been disrupted, as you can see by these wavy lines. Your tibia has been pushed up in relation to the femur," he says, "so I'm afraid you still need to have surgery."

My mother looks at me, hope brimming in her light eyes. I know she's worried about me. She's hoping that I can keep playing. This year is the most important year for me, hockey-wise. It's the year that decides whether I can get accepted into Grover's sports program. I *need* to play this season. Clasping my hands tightly and tucking them behind my neck, I look at the ceiling, feeling two sets of eyes on me.

"Asher?"

"I'm fine." I shift my gaze to Dr. Greene. "When can I go for surgery?"

He nods, flipping through books and looking through the calendar on his screen. "I suggest a few more weeks. During this period, try to attend some physical therapy. Obviously, don't push yourself too much. This is just so that we can strengthen your knee." He pauses. "So you have two options: you can either reconstruct your ligament with another from somewhere else in the body or you can choose to repair."

"Which one is better?" my mother asks.

"Well, I would suggest repairing it. Asher's ligaments can be stitched back in place. So instead of completely reconstructing his ACL, this would be a much safer, less painful, quicker operation. I also think that we could add an internal brace. Considering the fact that Asher wants to get back to hockey as fast as he can, this structure could aid the rehabilitation period and provide better support for his knee. I understand if you want to take your time and then make a decision. Please tell me what you'd like to do at least two weeks before. I'll send more information to you, Ms. Reed."

Muttering a small okay, I sink farther back in my chair. Blocking out my mother's conversation with Dr. Greene, I play with my fingers. About a million thoughts flow through my head, all making me more upset by the second.

There's a lump in my throat as I feel the walls around me closing in. I close my eyes; darkness surrounds me, imagining crowds going wild on the benches, my team, Coach shouting orders from the sidelines, the cold air hitting my face as I skate across the ice, and the overflowing happiness that surges through me when the puck careens into the net. And then, tapering toward the end is the satisfied look on my father's face. *You'll never amount to anything.*

A hand on my shoulder pulls me out of my thoughts. I look up to see my mother giving me a small smile. "Let's head back?"

After an uncomfortable ride, we finally reach the house. Before I can even step out of the car, Mom is by my side, offering her help. Shaking my head, I refuse. It's meant to be the other way around, goddammit. I'm supposed to be the one helping *her*. I stroll toward the staircase, ready to go to my room. My mother stops me, nodding at the kitchen.

Walking into the kitchen, I pull a bar stool out and sit on it. Mom moves to the other side of the white countertop. She places her brown bag on top. Leaning forward with her hands against the counter, she asks, "Are you okay?"

I stay silent for a while before muttering my go-to answer. "I'm fine."

A frown crosses her face. She can tell I'm lying. "You don't have to pretend to be okay for me, Asher. It's fine, love. I know hockey is important to you. You've held on to a stick since you were three." She lets out a chuckle as I stay silent. "You were such a little riot."

"I don't think any of that matters now, Mom."

"It's not over. You may think it is, but it isn't." She ruffles my hair as I try to move away from her hand. "After your knee is healed, you can play again. This injury isn't going to stop you."

"What if I can't play anymore?"

"Then no matter what happens, what you choose to do, your sister and I will be by your side, cheering you on. Sometimes things happen for a reason. Maybe with all your time, you can try other things. Who knows? Maybe you'll find something that you're more passionate about."

"Hockey's it," I say, shaking my head. "It's always been it."

"I know, honey. And I'll do everything and anything to get you back. I promise."

Nodding at her, I slip away. As I trudge to my room, every step gets heavier. Opening the door, I'm only reminded of how much hockey has ingrained itself into my life. My room's littered with hockey gear, and signed jerseys hang above my bed. Framed certificates litter one wall, and on the right, there's a glass cabinet housing all my trophies and medals.

I lie on my bed and pull the covers over me, and as I face an empty wall, I feel tears of frustration well in the corners of my eyes.

I wonder what Dad would say if he saw me now. He'd probably shake his head or clench his jaw, and say that real men don't cry. And maybe he'd give me a shiner to rough me up a little. It builds character, he'd say. And I'd have to cover it up the next day in school. Say I tripped and fell. And people would believe it.

I wake to a knock at my door, which is followed by a creaking sound.

"Asher." It's Mom. "Dinner's ready."

I don't turn to face her. "I'm not hungry."

She sighs, closing the door as she leaves. I'm left in silence once again. Reaching for my phone, I scroll to Brody's and Zach's messages asking what's happening and why I'm not answering their calls and texts. Sighing, I chuck the phone somewhere on my bed. The darkness around me doesn't comfort me. I turn onto my back, glancing up at the ceiling where small bits of light are reflected from my window.

The door creaks open again; this time a small figure is standing in the opening. Ever tries to walk toward me quietly but makes a little squeaking sound when she trips over something lying on my bedroom floor. Lifting myself slightly, I flick the lights on. I glance down to see her holding a plate of food.

"Here," she says, shoving it at me.

"I'm not hungry, Ev."

"Mommy says you gotta eat or you'll get sick." She looks at me with a stubborn expression, pushing the food toward me again.

"Fine." I give in with a small smile. "Give it to me."

Taking the plate from her, I sit upright on my bed. As I fork the food into my mouth, my appetite returns, and I start scarfing the stuff down. I pause when I see Ever struggling to climb onto the bed. Placing my food down next to me, I pick her up easily and drop her on the other side of me. She bounces slightly, and is able to keep quiet for a total of two seconds.

"Ash?" She tilts her head as she looks up at me. "Why are you sad?"

"I'm fine," I say, my mouth full. "Don't worry about it."

"I don't think you are."

"I am. Now shush."

Ever listens for once, pouting absently. As she swings her legs to and fro, I twirl my fork, wiping the plate clean. When she sees that I'm done, she puffs air into her cheeks.

Did she wait for me to finish? I train my eyes on her. "What?"

She pulls out a small piece of candy wrapped in purple. It's probably melted from the way she's been clutching it this whole time. "This is for you. Mommy said it was."

I crack a small smile, knowing exactly what she wants. Holding my hand out, I wait for the chocolate to be dropped into my palm. Ever just holds on to it, looking up at me as a guilty look takes over her face. "If you're not sad, can I have it?"

I grin. "What if I am?"

She falters, her grin dropping slightly, but she smiles brightly again. "Then you can have it."

I'm surprised when she hands the chocolate to me and hops off my bed before walking to the door.

"Ev," I call. "Come 'ere."

She runs back over to me and takes the chocolate before hugging me. "Thank you."

Smiling at her, I ruffle her hair. And then I think about the first time Dad hit me, and I take another look at my sister. I realize there are way worse things than not being able to play hockey. And there's some solace in that.

## CHAPTER 13

### Wren

The cold, chilling air creeping through the crevice around my window, temporarily freezing me, is enough to announce the start of winter. Frost flowers appear in vectors in a thin layer, blossoming around the entire glass's surface. Snow dusts the pavement outside, covering everything in a crisp, white shade.

After slipping on my boots, I run downstairs, ready to ask my mother for a cup of hot chocolate to warm my insides. It's a miracle I haven't injured myself on this very staircase yet, considering the frightening number of times I've rushed down it.

I smile when I see that my mother has already prepared a cup of cocoa for me, and I sit opposite her, slurping my scalding hot drink unattractively.

"How're you doing, honey?" she asks, stirring her coffee, the strong aroma pervading the house.

I blow air into my cup then take another sip before pulling the sleeves of my hoodie higher. "Okay."

She smiles, and I notice creases at the corners of her eyes that weren't there before. My mom is objectively stunning, with high cheekbones and the most beautifully shaped eyes. But I'd be lying if I said the accident hadn't taken a toll on her.

Just as I finish off the last bit of my cocoa, Mia's honking bursts the bubble of silence. I let out a soft chuckle, grab my bag, and utter a quick good-bye to my mother. She pulls me into a hug and lets me go, the warmth from her arms appearing and disappearing in an instant.

Walking through the thin layer of snow, I flip the hood of my hoodie over my head as the snowflakes tickle my skin. Even the red material my hoodie's made from can't hide the small smile I have stuck on my face. Snow, like rain, brings back the good memories. The ones I want to remember. The ones that bring a smile to my face and add warmth to my soul.

I get into Mia's car, watching as the windshield wipers swipe from left to right. I've always hated the way the windshield wipers don't stretch to the far corners of the window, instead always forming a semicircle.

"It's colder than my heart outside," Mia says, sniffling while bringing a tissue to her light-red nose.

"Mia," I say, "if it was that cold, we'd all freeze to death."

She rolls her eyes and tucks her tissue away. "That was so funny, I forgot to laugh."

I grin, glancing outside as the car gets into motion. The trees are dusted with a soft white, like icing sugar covering chocolate cake. Winter's just too beautiful for words.

"I hate winter!" Mia groans, pulling out her tissue again and proceeding to obnoxiously blow her nose when we reach a red traffic light.

When we get to school, after pausing briefly so Mia can blow her nose again, we rush into the entrance so we're not pelted by the heavy snowfall. The crowd at the front of the school is insane, packed with sophomore students going on some sort of school trip.

Mia gets lost somewhere in the crowd, and I'm about to call her name when I bump into a warm back covered by a dark leather jacket. Reed turns to face me, an annoyed look plastered across his face. There's a troubled look in his eyes that I've never seen before, not even when he walked into school all bruised just after his injury.

When he recognizes me, his frown slowly turns upside down. "Hey, birdie."

"Hey," I reply, continuing to walk as the crowd at the main entrance thins out. He stays by my side, and we silently walk to the math classroom.

I'm nervous. We're getting our math tests back today, and my hands go cold. Mr. Brakeman insists on summarizing how good or bad our results are in a twenty-minute-long speech. Did I answer all the questions? Then I freeze for a second. Did I even write my name on my sheet?

Finally, he hands the papers out. Within a few minutes, my test lands on my desk, a B- in the top right corner of the page. My heart sinks. The gnawing feeling tucked in my stomach grows, creeping up my throat.

I frantically flip through the pages, searching for where I went wrong. It looks like a murder scene. Blood-red marks are everywhere, contrasting against the pale white. I glance at the front of the room where Faye looks happy. I take deep breaths, trying to calm myself. This is going to bring my grade down.

It's fine. I'll just push harder on the next test.

Behind me, there's the fluttering of paper as a test is flung, and there's an audible groan. I know I should be minding my own business and worry only about my grade, but I turn to see what's going on. Zach stares at his page with confusion. A blood-red F is inked inside a circle on the page on his desk.

Zach glances up at me. The frustration in his eyes disappears and concern swirls in them. "You all right?"

"Yeah," I mumble glumly. My eyes burn a hole in the paper sitting on my desk, taunting me.

"Well, if it's of any help, keep your eyes on Brakeman." His eyes flicker to Mr. Brakeman's desk, as if he's waiting for something to happen. "It might cheer you up."

I turn to face the front, furrowing my brows in confusion. Mr. Brakeman picks up his coffee mug to take a sip out of it, but it's glued down. Zach, you evil genius. I get a glimpse of a satisfied Zach when I turn to give him a quick glance.

"Keep watching," he whispers. I shrink into my seat, wondering how I became his accomplice. Nevertheless, I watch as literal steam pours out of our math teacher's ears.

"Who has *dared* to do this . . . this dreadful deed?" Mr. Brakeman's voice seethes with anger. His bird-like eyes roam around the class before settling on Zach. His eyes narrow in on his target.

"You!" He points an accusing finger at Zach behind me, gaining no reaction whatsoever from Zach. I would feel bad, but Mr. Brakeman really does try hard to make everyone's lives a misery, and now he's gotten a taste of his own medicine.

"Hey, man." Zach shrugs. "No body, no crime."

"I will report you to the principal for this, young man! Who do you think you are?" Mr. Brakeman reaches for the telephone in a rage, but unfortunately for him, the handset doesn't budge. It seems to be glued firmly.

He tries frantically to lift other objects from his desk, but everything, *absolutely* everything, is superglued down. His phone, his stationary, his computer, and his textbooks. Mr. Brakeman looks like he's about to explode.

I'm pretty sure you can hear the laughter from a mile away. The bell rings, and the entire class grab their tests and dash out in a blur, and I find myself among a crowd of people, including Reed, who always manages to escape classes first. When he notices me, he offers me a lazy smile. I'm not sure what to do with it. Zach's antics make me forget about my grade for the rest of the day.

In English, Miss Hutchinson walks in, greeting the class with a polite smile. "Today, class, I'm going to challenge you to channel your inner dramatic selves!"

Various people groan, probably since they haven't signed up for drama.

"As we all know, the book for this semester is *Romeo and Juliet*. A huge part of Shakespeare's writing consisted not only of stimulating composition but also performance. As you all may have guessed by now, you will all be paired up and expected to perform a scene from *Romeo and Juliet*. I'll give you ten minutes to prepare, and then you'll come up here and perform!"

She smiles like she hasn't just assigned me the hardest task of my life. I can't even act in front of a mirror. How the heck am I supposed to do it in front of an entire class?

"Remember, everyone, this counts toward your term mark, so

I would like to see some effort being put into it. Right, that's all for now. Get started!"

A few seconds into reading, someone pokes me in the arm with a pen. I narrow my eyes at Reed.

"Hey," he says. "You're my partner."

"What?" I frown. "You can't just announce it. You have to ask *civilly*. What if I'm going with someone else?"

The corners of Reed's lips tilt upward. "Really? Who's that?"

I narrow my eyes, looking around the classroom. Milo, a lean guy from the computer club, sits behind me. When I face him, he looks up at me in surprise, his curly hair framing his eyes. I don't know why I'm doing this—probably just to prove a point.

"Hi," I say. Milo stares at me, confusion lurking in his dark eyes. "Can you be my partner?"

I'd talked to Milo once or twice, in the library. He stares at me in contemplation, and he's about to agree, when he stops, his eyes darting over to look past me. I gaze at Reed, who's watching poor Milo intensely.

"Uh . . . I think you already have someone who wants to be your partner," Milo stutters, terrified at the mere prospect of being paired with me. Great. He avoids eye contact and continues scribbling something on his page. I glare at Reed, who just smirks back at me.

"So?" he asks, oh so innocently. "You gonna be my partner or what?"

I glance at the plastic clock on the wall, getting restless. "Fine!" I hiss. "But we only have a few minutes—"

Reed just shrugs. "Leave it to me, birdie."

I scoff in response, clicking my pen as I wait for him to choose a scene. He pages through the paperback for a while, and shuts the book, assuring me that we have a scene. I just open my mouth to suggest I approve the scene before we perform it, but Miss Hutchinson interrupts. "Okay, everyone. Time's up! Time to perform."

I fidget with my hoodie, unsure whether I really need a whole lot of people criticizing my acting skills. Reed looks at me as if to say "Relax, it's going to be fine." But it does little to appease my fraying nerves.

"As usual, it's volunteers first. Any brave souls who would like to volunteer before I begin choosing myself?"

Zach, sitting at the back of the class, shoots his hand up. Asher laughs. Brody elbows Zach, hard, but it's too late since Zach's already shuffling to the front of the classroom. Brody grumbles under his breath and follows him.

Brody starts the prose, and it isn't long before I realize they're doing the famous balcony scene. Zach responds in a high-pitched voice in an attempt to be Juliet.

In summary, it's hilarious. For every line that Zach delivers with airy "love," Brody responds with deep contempt. When the two complete their scene, they receive a vigorous round of applause.

"Good effort, you two," Miss Hutchinson says. The slight concern on her face is laughable. "Who wants to go next?"

There's an awkward silence. And how absolutely coincidental is it that I have to be making a split second of eye contact at that very moment?

"Wren, come up here with your partner." Miss Hutchinson smiles. Great. My hands grow clammy as I walk up to the front, but I clutch my book for reassurance. Asher stands and follows me to the front, walking nonchalantly. I open up to the page he's marked. My heart skips a beat. I stare blankly at Asher, which earns me a smug expression.

Suddenly, he takes my hand, starting the verse with ease. "If I profane with my unworthiest hand . . . to smooth that rough touch with a tender kiss."

I jump slightly from the contact, but Reed's smooth, deep voice is strangely comforting. I take a quick glance at my book before looking into his clear blue eyes, my words slow and my voice precarious. "Good pilgrim, you do wrong your hand too much . . ."

His lips tilt upward slightly, and I realize I haven't messed up my lines. He holds on to my palm tighter, the warmth of his hand reassuring. Enigmatic.

"Have not saints lips, and holy palmers too?" He faces the class with a dramatic air, his tone and voice so well combined you'd mistake him for a drama student. A few girls at the front can't take their eyes off him, and I'm having problems myself. How the heck is he doing this so well?

I deliver my next line, facing him and trying to forget about the audience. "Ay, pilgrim, lips that they must use in prayer."

"O, then, dear saint, let lips do what hands do . . . "

I blink. He wants me to kiss him. Well, in the scene at least. I stare at the words on the page, gulping. Finally, I open my mouth. "Saints do not move, though grant for prayers' sake."

I move slightly away from Reed, but he just edges closer. "Then move not, while my prayer's effect I take."

The words in the book stare back at me: *He kisses her* it reads, but my mind modifies the words, so I see them in three different places instead of just one.

"Thus from my lips, by thine, my sin is purged." Asher ends the verse with easy superiority. His hand finds mine again, drowning my small fingers. I follow his lead and we both bow.

Miss Hutchinson nods at the two of us, with a smile. "Well done."

Relief pours through my veins. I glance at Asher only to find he'd been staring at me the entire time, a lopsided smile creeping onto his striking face. He doesn't bother looking away either.

～

Returning home, I can't help but replay Mia's words in my mind. *Try to find some peace about it yourself.* As much as I don't want to admit it, she's right. I can't keep avoiding what happened, sweeping it under the carpet like age-old dust. I need to at least try. I owe them that much.

"Mom?" I call.

I find her on the couch with a mug of coffee resting in her hands.

"Hey, honey." A slight smile appears on her face. Her eyes linger on the red of my hoodie. "I've never quite understood that hoodie."

"I don't have an obsession." I frown. "Never mind my hoodie." I dismiss her words curtly as I land on the couch next to her. "I wanted to ask you about something."

"Go on."

"There was this box. It had all of our photograph albums and a bunch of other stuff."

She nods as I explain, and I can imagine her recalling the event in her mind.

"I don't know why, but I was on the verge of burning it all," I continue. "You said I'd regret it. You said you'd keep it until one day I'd come and ask you for it. I . . . I think I'm ready."

She looks at me, and I can't quite place the emotion on her face. "Are you sure?"

"I'm sure."

It takes a lot for me to wait. I can just refuse and turn away, leave it for another day. But there's something inside me, a voice, screaming at me to finally get past it—to knock down the already crumbling wall around my heart.

And for some reason, all I can think about, all I can see in my mind, is Asher, his eyes a shade darker, drawing me in, telling me again and again and again that nothing lasts forever.

∽

It's midnight when I finally decide to open the box. All evening I've been staring at it as if it'll jump up and bite me.

I swing open the worn-out, brown leather top. My breathing is heavy now, but I try to control it. I spot a thick black album, and my hands tremble as I pull it out. Strangely, it draws me to it, my fingers bending around the heavy cover. After a moment's hesitation, I open the book.

The first picture is one of my parents, my mother smiling up at my dad. Her skin is the same tone as mine, her hair the same shade and texture, but a little shorter. It's tied back in a loose ponytail, with coffee-colored strands framing the front of her face. My dad was a little more serious than her, but they balanced each other out. I look like my mother, but I got my personality from my dad.

Tears prick at my eyes and I force them back, because they're making my vision hazy. The next few pictures are similar to the first, all with my parents as the sole subject. Then there's a change in the timeline. The pictures morph into ones that include me, first as an infant, then a toddler, and then a preschooler missing a few teeth.

I look different. Happier.

My eyes latch onto a certain picture of me with my arms wrapped tightly around my mom, our faces close together. I was about five at the time—you can tell by the hideous pigtails on my shoulders. We're both smiling, and I can see the immediate resemblance. It makes me wonder why I'd ever deny just how much I look like her.

Dad isn't in a lot of the pictures now, he's the one behind the camera. Then the Emma photos start, and there's an impossibly stubborn knot in my throat. I find one with her in my arms, me with this goofy smile on my face as I hold her in my lap. I can still remember that day. Mom was so scared that I'd drop her. There are little tufts of hair on Emma's head, and I'd taken to styling them with my makeover set.

But now she's gone.

It's this photo that gets me crying, and I'm crying so hard that my face is just a wet mess. I let it all out, slow and steady. Breathe in and out. After a while, I dry my cheeks with the sleeves of my hoodie and close the album.

## CHAPTER 14

# Asher

When you spend most of your life defining yourself by a select few pillars, and one of those pillars crumbles, your entire world suffers a shake. I feel something similar—an unbalanced, off-kilter, in-the-clouds kind of feeling.

It's Friday. Another day when Eastview will play a hockey game. Without me. The team's been acting stranger. Yesterday when I walked into the arena, they all kept deathly quiet, like they were talking about me before I entered. Or maybe I'm just becoming more paranoid. Who knows?

I walk into the cafeteria, making my way to the upper level where I usually sit. Passing a table, I catch sight of a familiar red hoodie. Hair tied in a braid, a white ribbon at the end today. Wren. She's writing on a piece of paper as she talks to her friend, Mia. I think that's her name. Zach's mentioned her once or twice.

Eventually, I peel my gaze away, finding myself at my table

only to discover that my regular place is filled. They look at me. Guilt covers their faces. The dude in my chair stands to give it back to me but I shake my head, telling him to stay put, and take a seat in the corner instead. Lifting my fork, I swirl the spaghetti on my tray. It doesn't look very appealing anymore.

"Asher."

I lift my head to find Brody looking at me. He starts again, "What happened at the checkup? Everything okay?"

Everyone's staring at me now, expecting an answer, and my grip on my fork tightens. Zach must notice something's wrong, because he steers the conversation away from me.

"So . . . the party's at Daniels's, right?" he says.

I look at him, giving him a tight-lipped smile. He simply nods. Lunch continues without anyone asking me any more questions, and the conversation eventually steers to today's game.

Not in the mood to sit and hear about it, I mutter a quick excuse about taking a leak, pack my stuff, and leave. No one notices me go except Knight and Chandler. I scoff. The rest of my "friends" don't care. They're too invested in the player who took my place on the team. Sitting in my seat. *Harvey.* I don't hate him. Honest. It's not his fault that he's been placed there, in my position. There's an unsettling feeling in the pit of my stomach. Sighing, I walk to my next class.

At the end of the day, I hear my phone ping. Looking at it, I see a message on the group between Zach, Brody, and me.

ZACH: *Am I picking up A later?*

A few seconds later, Brody replies.

BRODY: *I am*

Chandler sends an eggplant emoji. I furrow my brows. Right after, a thumbs-up comes through, followed by him saying he tapped the wrong one.

ME: *There's no way that can be so close to that emoji. Unless . . .*

BRODY: *Unless what?*

ME: *He has that under his most recent*

BRODY: *HAHAHA. Who are you sending this shit to, Chandler?*

ZACH: *Shut it. And Brody, quit acting like you haven't done the same*

BRODY: *Never. I'm a child of goat*

BRODY: *goat\**

BRODY: *GOD. GODDAMN*

Zach attaches a meme of Kermit holding a knife. I can picture him grinning at me; a light chuckle escapes.

After a silent drive with my mom, I lie back on my bed, glancing up at the empty spaces on my walls. Once, they held things that gave me happiness. Now those same things anger me. Frustrate me. So I threw them in the spare room. I didn't want the reminders. I try hard to forget about it, but every attempt is a failure . . . and that's what I am. A failure. The word leaves a bitter taste in my mouth.

I don't want to bother my mom with my problems more than I already have. She has to leave work early to come pick me up, check on me, drive me to appointments, and worry about college and hockey.

She does a great job, fulfilling two important roles in my life. She plays the part of my mother *and* my father, who, might I add, left us a few years ago. I don't recall much, but I do remember my mother crying when she thought I wasn't watching. I used to try to take as much of the pressure off her as I could, but eventually she found out what was going on.

When the bruises became too hard to hide, she was livid. I'd never seen her so angry before. Nothing was really the same after that, and sometimes I wonder what life would be like if I just kept pretending. If I kept taking the brunt of it to protect her and Ev. If we could still be a family. And then I shut down that thought process as fast as I started it, because it's royally fucked up.

It's the same thing with that ass, Drew. What if I hadn't said anything? None of this would've happened. I shake my head; I don't want to think about either of these topics any more than I already have.

My eyes drift to the clock on the wall, widening. I take a quick shower and get dressed. Taking out a black jacket, white T-shirt, and a pair of black jeans, I change into them. I pull my brace on and tighten it around my knee. I look at myself in the mirror, eyes zooming in on my knee. *Pathetic.* It's what Dad would see. And it's all I see now too.

I'm trying. I'm really fucking trying, but it isn't working, so I decide on a plan B instead: going to Daniels's party and getting shit-faced.

All right, it's admittedly not the best plan, but I don't know how else to deal with everything. Ignoring doesn't help, forgetting doesn't help, and talking about it? Oh yeah, it doesn't help. Shocker. My ringtone echoes throughout my room. Brody's name flashes on the screen. Swiping left, I answer the call.

"Get your ass down here. I've been waiting for the past ten minutes because you don't look at your messages."

"One sec," I say, grinning as I pick up the house keys and shove them into my jacket pocket. When I finally get into Brody's car, he gives me an annoyed look.

"What?" I ask, adjusting the seat.

He starts the car, then pulls out of the driveway. "I don't want to pick you up ever again."

"Why don't you come in like a normal person?"

He gives me a grim look and shakes his head. "Madam Flo hates me, man."

I snort. "She doesn't hate you."

He gives me an incredulous look. I want to ask about the game, but I don't think I want to hear the answer. If it was a good game, I'll feel like crap because I wasn't there, and if it was a bad game, I'll feel like crap because I wasn't there.

I swallow the lump in my throat, and, gathering the courage, I pop the question. "How was the game?"

"It was good," he says, and just as predicted, I feel like crap. "We won. Barely, though. It was bad play on their side. We just got lucky."

Nodding absently, I turn to the window, staring at the passing houses. A moment of silence is disturbed by Brody's sigh. He clears his throat, and I turn to face him.

"You okay?"

"I'm fine."

Knight looks at me, head tilted. "How about you don't lie this time?"

"How about this time you stay the hell out of my business?" I murmur dryly.

He deadpans, and I'm 100 percent sure he's about to offer some cocky response, but at the last minute, he changes his mind, turning his head so that he faces the road, jaw tight, hands gripping the steering wheel.

I let out a breath, clasping my hands tightly. "I'm sorry, man. I didn't mean it. There's just a lot going on. I don't know what the fuck I'm doing most of the time."

He stays silent.

"I guess I deserve that," I mutter.

I always seem to screw up. I've already lost so much within a matter of a few weeks: my team, my position, my other "friends," my seat at lunch, my reputation, and my shot at getting into Grover U. I don't want to lose one of the last things I have. I can't afford to.

"You know," Brody says, his gaze focused on the road ahead of him. "Zach and I are worried about you. You don't answer our messages or calls. You don't tell us anything. You hardly talk to us at school. We're trying. We really are. We want to give you your space, support you, and help you if you need it. You were there for us when we needed it. Just . . . let us be there for you. That's all we're asking for. We understand that this isn't easy for you. For Christ's sake, you were the one who encouraged me to play hockey and pushed me to do better. The only reason I'm on the team right now is because of you. It doesn't feel right that you're not there and I am."

"I'm sorry," I say again.

"It's fine, man. Just talk to us. Zach and I . . . we're not gonna judge you. Besides." He grins as he focuses on the road. "We're used to your ass and it's kinda lonely without you."

I manage a smile, nodding as the sky turns to a velvet blue, streetlights illuminating the road in front of us. Eventually, we arrive at the matcha-colored house, one I'd visited a handful of times over the last few weeks. The place where I didn't expect to find her. Wren.

Getting out of the car, I turn around to close the door. Before leaving, though, I hold on to it. "We're good, right?"

"We're good," he says, giving me a small grin.

# CHAPTER 15

## Wren

I'm halfway through studying when Mia bursts into my room with Chinese takeout. The aroma that wafts around my room is so enticing that I can't help but set down my pen and reach for a foil dish, practically inhaling the fried rice.

After we scarf everything down, we're stuffed, so we decide to play a game of *Just Dance*, because according to Mia, "Dancing reduces bloating." I just shrug, because I didn't know Chinese food made you bloated, or that you were supposed to actively try to get rid of said issue.

"Quit making that face, Martin," my friend scoffs. "Not everyone can be blessed with a fast metabolism."

Laughing, I follow after her as we veer downstairs and she sets up the game. We start, and she gets really into it, like *really* into it. The ponytail she's tied her black hair into whips wildly as she dives into each dance move. The whole time I'm just lazily completing the moves, she's stretching her limbs and punching her controller in the air with a vigor that parallels even the world's greatest dancers.

What's hilarious is *Perfect!* keeps flashing on my side of the screen, while she just gets a whole bunch of *Good*s. And when I win, Mia, being the natural sore loser that she is, demands a rematch.

Two hours later, we're still playing.

"Mia," I say, hunched on my knees and out of breath after I win yet another game. "Just give up already."

"*Never.*"

Sighing, I agree to one last game. This time, she switches things up and tries out my stellar method of doing the bare minimum. When it doesn't work, and I win again, I collapse on the floor, laughing to the point of tears.

"No *fair.*" Mia clenches her jaw, not finding the situation half as funny as I do. "Rematch."

"No." I sober up. My muscles are jelly, and they quiver at the mention of another game. "For the love of God, no rematch."

The front door creaks open, and my mom enters, a warm smile appearing on her face as she notices us. "Hi, girls."

"Mom?" I sit upright on the carpet in front of our TV as I look over at her. "You're back so early?"

She pauses, dusting off bits of snow from her coat before hanging it up. "It's six thirty, honey."

Huh. Guess time goes fast when you're forced to play twenty-three rounds of *Just Dance*. Mia's grey eyes go wide. "*Six thirty?* We're gonna be late!"

"For what?" my mom and I ask simultaneously.

"Uh, the party?" she says, like it's obvious. I grimace, wondering how she found out so fast. In fact, if she hadn't brought it up, it would've left my mind entirely. She recognizes my look of confusion and rushes to answer it. "Zach told me," she adds. "You did say you were going, didn't you? Because the only reason I said I'd go was because of you. And they'll be here to pick you up soon."

I shrug. "Maybe."

"Wren." There's concern on my mother's face. "You didn't tell me you were going to a party?"

"Mom . . ."

"No," she says, "this is good. This is *great*. You're finally getting out of your comfort zone. Just be careful, all right? You need to remember to—"

"Mom," I say. "I'm not sure if I'm even going."

"What?" Next to me, Mia lifts a brow. "Why not?"

"Yes," my mom says. "Why not?"

I give her a look. "Aren't you supposed to not want me to go to parties?"

She places a hand on the kitchen island, leaning against it. Our house is an open plan, so I can still see her clearly from the carpet below the TV where Mia and I are currently sprawled. "I know you're responsible," she says. "A bit *too* responsible, if you ask me. Listen, honey. You don't need to second guess yourself all the time. You're allowed to have some fun now and then. Life's short."

The air turns delicate. I know we both found different ways to cope after the accident. Every day, I sink further into my shell, close more and more doors and let fewer people in. The way I see it, the less you have, the less you have to lose. Mom tries to look at everything positively—to cherish everything she has instead of dwelling on the things she lost.

It's part of why she pushes me to live life to the fullest. She thinks I'm punishing myself, but maybe this is just the person I am. The person I've always been. Except this time, she didn't have to do much pushing. This time, it's on me. *I* was the one who agreed to the deal with Asher and Brody. And I guess I'll have to see it through. I chew on the inside of my cheek as I think about it. What's the worst that could happen, right? It's just one party.

"Fine." I sigh. "I'll go."

Mia squeals, and Mom and I exchange small smiles.

Back upstairs, I collapse on my bed, eyeing the book on my desk, waiting patiently to be read. Mia's hovering figure soon blocks my view as she opens my closet with a bit too much enthusiasm. She starts sifting through countless jeans, some ripped, some skinny, and a whole bunch of unicolor T-shirts.

She groans when she finds that I don't have anything close to party attire, and I laugh to myself. Maybe I can get out of this after all. I say, "Told you I have nothing to wear."

But she just grins back at me. "A girl always has that one section of her dresser she never uses, Wren. I'm going to find that section, and when I do, you'll be amazed at what you have stored away."

I snicker. "Well, have at it, Sherlock."

She doesn't reply. Instead, she continues pilfering through my clothes. I bury my face in a stray pillow, knowing full well that her little mission is going to fail. Surprisingly, after a few minutes I hear a ruffling sound and a proud "A-ha!"

Peeking up from my bed, I crane my neck to see what she's discovered. She holds up what looks like a black top. It's one shoulder, and I can't even remember getting it. "Where'd you find that?"

"Told you I'd find something," she says. "It was in the last drawer, right at the back. It's cute, no?"

"Sure." I shrug. "At least only one of my arms will freeze."

"*C'mon*," Mia yells, placing the top on my bed in a hurried frenzy. "Get dressed! I still have to do your hair and makeup!"

In the bathroom, I pick up the shirt tentatively and pull it over my head. I take a look in the mirror and it's . . . strange. The neckline is asymmetrical, and only my right arm is covered to the wrist in black material. It fits snugly on my body. Mia makes a contented sound, when I step out, and sits me down in front of my dresser.

Pulling out a brimming makeup bag, she immediately begins spritzing, dabbing, and brushing at my face. Halfway through the lengthy process, she shoves a brush into my hands, ordering, "Brush your mane, will you?"

Sighing, I send the brush through my hair. It isn't even my fault. My strands tend to knot way too easily, and there came a point in my life when I just gave up. After I'm done, and my roots are all but begging for mercy, Mia decides to straighten my hair. A half hour later, she twists me in my chair so that I'm facing my vanity for the Big Reveal.

"So?" she asks. "Do you like it?"

Coffee-colored strands frame my face, and the eyeliner makes my eyes look like rich honey rather than dark brown. The faint blush accentuates my cheekbones. "It's nice." I send her a small smile through the mirror. "Thanks, M."

"Don't mention it." She picks up her bag and gathers the makeup tools strewn across my dresser table. "Now quick." She throws me a pair of black boots. "Wear these. They're not that high, so don't you dare complain. I gotta go get ready. I'll meet you there."

"Bye!" I yell, but she's already halfway down the stairs. I slip on the boots, and true to her words, they aren't too high. Hesitantly, I trudge downstairs. My mom, who's sitting on the couch watching something on TV, turns when she hears me.

"I like the top." A soft smile appears on her face. "Told you you'd use it someday. Are you sure you'll be all right?"

"Yeah," I say. "Don't worry."

"It's my job to worry," she says, and as if to emphasize her point, her forehead wrinkles. "Call me if you need me to pick you up early, okay? I'll stay up late."

"I will."

The doorbell rings, and she stands, gesturing for me to open the door. When I do, Asher greets me with his signature smirk. He's wearing a black long-sleeved shirt over his usual jeans. His golden-brown strands fall faultlessly over his eyes, and his smile falters as his gaze slides over my figure. He blinks. Swallows. And then, as if being clicked back to life, he clears his throat. "You look . . . prettier than normal, birdie."

When he smiles, his left dimple shows more prominently. My fake blush compensates for the soda-pop feeling that fizzes in my chest at his words. "Thanks," I say. "You don't look too bad yourself."

I shuffle over to awkwardly poke his cheek—the exact spot where his dimple is carved. He frowns, but I don't miss the way his lips twitch into a small curve. My mom comes up behind me, and I clear my throat.

"Uh, Mom, Ree—Asher." I gesture to him, making a split second of eye contact. "Asher, my mom."

Reed dips his head and offers his hand. She's practically beaming. I slip away to use the bathroom quickly, and when I get back, I find them in conversation. Reed's eyes find me, and a glimmer of amusement slips into his gaze. I walk up to my mom's side, and his attention returns to her. "Are we good to go, ma'am?"

"All good. Have fun, you two." She passes me a not-so-discreet look that makes me squirm. It's not like I can blame her. It's the first time a boy—one who wasn't the pizza delivery guy, at least—showed up for me.

When the door closes behind us, it's just the two of us. I find it hard to comprehend how Eastview's revered hockey captain is standing right here, in front of me, on my porch.

Even with the height advantage the boots give me, Reed is still far taller than me. He's staring down at me now, the blue in his eyes dim in the early winter light, and he looks like he wants to say something. Finally, he opens his mouth, and—

"*Reed!*" I turn, recognizing Brody in the driver's seat of his red pickup truck. "Hurry your ass up, man."

Shaking his head with a smile, Reed motions for me to walk ahead of him. As I slip into the back of the truck, Brody winks at me playfully in the rearview mirror, and I give him a small smile.

It's the first time I'm in a car with someone who's not Mia or my mom, and I can't help the nerves that creep in. I scan the interior of the truck as I settle my clammy palms on my knees.

Asher climbs in the back with me and Brody frowns. "I thought you hated sitt—"

Reed rolls his eyes. "Hit the gas, Knight."

Brody mutters something under his breath, but I don't pay attention, glancing out the window instead. Reed's gaze wavers to me as I watch the cars whiz past in rapid succession, forming an illusion of steely colors. "Your mom told me she's prepared to get you a car."

I turn to face him. "Yeah."

"She also told me that you don't want one." He turns to flash me a fleeting look. "Why?"

The question catches me off guard, and I pause, stunned for a moment. "It's hard to explain," I say, truthfully. "Complicated."

"I don't mind complicated."

I sigh, fidgeting with the silver charm bracelet around my wrist. "I can't drive."

He stares at me, disbelief clear in his features. "What do you mean?"

"That's exactly what I mean."

"You haven't been to lessons?"

"I have."

"And?"

I turn to give him a tight-lipped smile. "I failed thirteen driving tests."

Suddenly, I jerk forward in my seat as the truck comes to a sudden halt. My heart flies out of my chest. We come to a standstill just as the traffic light turns from yellow to red, and I feel my throat close as my vision blurs slightly.

I glare at Brody. "What the heck?"

"Sorry," Brody murmurs sheepishly. "It's just . . . *thirteen*?"

"Yes."

They both have no response to this. So we sit in silence for a brief moment, and my pulse slowly returns to normal. Light snow covers the ground as Brody's truck rolls up beside a pristinely cut lawn, and I exhale a quick breath of relief, glad that the ride ended quickly.

Asher steps out on his side, then holds the door open for me, stretching out his hand. I just stare at it suspiciously. He rolls his eyes and retracts his hand just as fast as he'd offered it.

127

I step out on my own, looking up at the way the dark night sky meets the ivory paint of the building to calm my nerves. The snowfall is light, and it's like a painting. The architecture of the house is breathtaking—arches warping into intricately carved windows and meeting saddle-brown roof tiles. I find it hard to peel my eyes away.

"Whose place is this?" I ask.

"Tristan Daniels," Brody replies.

Light illuminates the pathway to the house, and as we near the entrance, the sound of upbeat music loudens. That's when the uneasy feeling worms its way back into the pit of my stomach.

As we enter, Brody disappears somewhere into the crowd. Even though it's lightly snowing, people are scattered outside, on swings and benches. Most of them are talking, laughing, or engaging in copious amounts of PDA. I grimace, and Reed glances my way. "I think Daniels went a little crazy with the invitations."

Swallowing, I enter the party at his side. Swarms of people saturate an open, extravagant first level of the mansion. Lights flash to the beat of some Drake song blasting from the music system in the far corner. I stare at a girl who walks past me with a red Solo cup in her hands.

"You thirsty?" Reed asks, noticing.

I nod. "A little."

"No alcohol?" he asks, raising his voice over the commotion.

I shake my head, and he winks before disappearing. The floor is littered with red cups, and the number of people in this house is surprising, even though the space is big.

Reed returns with bottled water for me. I grab the bottle from him, unscrew the lid, and gulp down half of it. He frowns as he watches me. "Try to savor that, will you? There were only ten bottles of water at the bar. I had to fight with the bar guy for that one. Idiot was treating it like a prized possession."

"Thanks for fighting bravely to serve me with this pitcher of water," I say, then, for good measure, I add, "valiant knight."

This earns me a blank, unimpressed look from Reed. Someone from the hockey team calls his name, and he strides over, slowed by his knee brace. Someone bumps into me, and I lose my balance a little. I quickly collect myself, standing upright.

"I'm so sorry. I didn't see where I—Wren."

"Hey, Brody." I smile.

"You know, I never got the chance to tell you that you look beautiful."

"Thanks." The words fall out of my mouth clumsily. "You too."

"Thanks." He laughs. "Wanna dance?"

I stare at the middle of the platform. The neon lights collide with skin. People are actually enjoying this party? Go figure. Throwing caution aside, I take Brody's inviting hand. "Sure."

We sway awkwardly during the start of a song I don't recognize, and my palms grow clammy. There's a slow burn in my calves, and sure, I'm not doing much, but the *Just Dance* marathon was only a few hours ago, and it was the first time in months I actually did some sort of exercise.

Brody's gaze flickers to something behind me, and I follow it to see a blur of red hair that must belong to Faye Archer getting lost in the crowd. When I look back at him, I see him softly gazing in the same direction. Brody's eyes widen, realizing I'm watching him. I just smile, feigning nonchalance.

After five more minutes of gliding along with Brody, I hear someone scream my name. I turn, never more grateful to see Mia running toward me. She does it at a concerning pace, though, and I have to tell her to slow down or we'll end up on the floor. It's amazing how fast she can run in heels. She reaches me without killing me in the process, surprisingly.

"How do I look?" she asks.

Mia's dark hair falls across her shoulders. It complements her square-neck long-sleeved top, the violet color deep and rich against her brown skin. She blinks, waiting for an answer.

A smile tugs at my lips. "Do you want the truth?"

She almost kicks me with her killer (literally) heels. "Shut up. I look drop-dead gorgeous."

"Modest much?" I laugh. She rolls her eyes.

Zach, a beer bottle in his hand, pulls away from the hockey huddle, his gaze settling on Mia.

He sends her a blinding white smile, and I can almost feel her melt next to me. Zach looks at me as if trying to figure out who I am. Then something clicks, and he recognizes me. "*Juliet?*"

"Hey, Zach." I wave slowly at him.

He recovers quickly, and throws his arm around Mia, pulling her toward him. I can practically see the hearts in her eyes as she looks up at him. Then she snaps her gaze back to me. "Do you have your meds?"

Realization washes over me like ice-cold water. Because I don't. My heart rate spikes and fear wraps me in a tiny bubble, refusing to let me out. Mia's hand settles on my arm, bringing me back to the present. "You do, right?"

I mumble incoherent words as my mind spins.

When the music gets louder, Mia crosses her brows, raising her voice. "I can't hear you!"

"I—"

"You guys up for a game of beer pong?" Zach yells.

Mia turns when Zach pulls on her hand, ready to lead her to the table set up in the far corner. The noise gets too loud, and the room feels like it's closing in on me. Shaking my head, I wipe my hands on my jeans.

"I'm gonna go to the bathroom," I say, moving away from them. "I'll be back."

Looking around trying to spot the bathroom, I find Reed instead. I'm about to walk over to ask him where the bathroom is, when I realize he's kissing some girl. For a split second, we make eye contact. I freeze, my cheeks warming, and I rush in the opposite direction.

My heart races as people loom over me. I have no idea where I am. The smell of cigarette smoke grows so strong it makes me want to heave. The room starts spinning. I push past the horde at the entrance of the house as everything rushes past me in sharp lashes, harsh paint strokes of undefined color.

"Wren." I hear a rushed voice behind me. "Wait!"

Swiveling slightly, I find Mia striding after me. She tries to push past everyone but gets caught in the crowd. My hands tremble at my side while I make my way to the front door. I still can't breathe as I run out to the front garden. And tucked between everything is a dull, itchy frustration at the sight of Reed kissing that girl.

Why do I even care? He can do what he wants. I try to control my breathing. *Breathe, Wren.* In and out. *In and out.* My throat starts closing up, and black dots spot my vision.

I need to sit down. I bend over, trying to control my breathing, but eventually, I sink to the ground. The snow crunches around me, but it soothes my skin in a way that's calming. I lean back, looking up. But I can't breathe. I can't hear anything except for the roaring blood in my ears.

"*Wren,*" I hear a voice yell.

The last thing I see is a pair of worried eyes above me.

They're deep blue.

# CHAPTER 16

## Asher

Standing in the corner of the crowded room, a beer in hand, I catch sight of Wren through the moving bodies. She's smiling up at Brody as they dance. Clenching my jaw, I look away as I take a swig from the ice-cold bottle in my grasp.

I thought coming to this party would boost my mood. Walking through Daniels's kitchen, I realize I couldn't have been more wrong. I chuck the bottle in the trash before picking up another from the countertop. Leaning against the table, I glance at everyone else. They look so at ease. Carefree. Something I don't think I'll be for a while.

"Reed?"

Turning around, I find the person who's the sole cause of the shitstorm that hit my life. *Drew McKay.* Gritting my teeth, I brush past him. I don't want to see his stupid fucking face. He's rude, impulsive, and an all-round asshole who'll stop at nothing to annoy the crap out of me. Drew walks in front of me, blocking the way out of the kitchen. A smirk rests on his face.

"How's the knee?"

I keep a blank face while my grip on the bottle in my hand tightens. He wants a fight, but he's not going to get it. Besides, a fight with him isn't going to make my situation any better. My knee is already screwed, and as much as I want to, punching him might make my wrist worse than it already is.

Drew smiles. "You're still going to Grover?"

I say nothing, crossing my arms as I try to hold myself back from smashing his face in.

"Got a stick up your ass, Reed?" he asks sardonically, opening his arms for a hug. "I'm just trying to be friends. For old times' sake."

I scoff. "I'll pass."

He laughs, bringing his arms back to his body. "Still funny, I'll give you that. At least you still have one redeeming quality."

"I'm getting bored with this," I snap. "What the fuck do you want from me, Drew?"

He walks closer to me, light catching in his dark hair. "I'm just repaying the favor, man. You got me expelled, you know that? You took my place in the group. You took all my friends. And if that wasn't enough, you had to use my sister too."

I glance at him in disbelief. "What? Drew, *you* were the one who broke in. And Gemma was a mistake."

The Gemma situation was a mess, and one of the reasons I don't get involved with girls before making it abundantly clear that I don't want anything more than a hookup. I've never had the time for a relationship, and I should've known that I was going to break Gemma's heart.

"You took what belonged to me. And I had to dish out karma." Drew's voice drips with venom. "Since your daddy wasn't around to do it for me."

He hits a chord. Rage rises up and fogs my vision, and it takes every ounce of strength I have not to punch the shit out of him. But if I did, I'd just become the monster my dad was. So, in the end, I watch as Drew walks away, and let out a ragged breath.

It doesn't make sense. I was with Gemma less than two years ago. How could anyone hold on to a grudge for that long? Beats me. Swinging the bottle up, I down the contents.

As I reach for another beer I wonder: Are people born bad? Or do they wake up one day, tired and reckless, and decide to become the villain? And if it was the latter, how long will it take before I become the one thing I swore I never would?

Catching sight of the rest of the team huddled around the beer pong table, I stride over to them. I know I need to make things right with them about my shitty attitude when I came back from the hospital, but sometimes my pride gets in the way. And it's definitely taken a hit knowing that they won a game without me.

Before I can, though, I bump into a raven-haired girl. Her hair's all over the place and the straps of her dress are falling off her shoulders slightly. She looks back at me, and when she sees me, the frown on her face turns into a drunken smile.

"Hi," she says, wrapping her arms around my neck.

I pull back, giving her a strange look. "Uh, hi?"

Leaning back a little, she says, "You play hockey for Eastview, right?"

Grabbing the stray coat lying on the table next to me, I throw it over her. "You know where your friends are?"

I watch her mumble under her breath.

"Hey," I say, sighing. "Your friends?"

"Oh, um, over there," she says, pointing to three girls standing in the corner of the room.

I hold either side of her shoulders and gently push her off me. "Maybe you should go join them."

"No." She tightens her hands around my neck, standing on her tiptoes and bringing her lips closer to mine. "I want to stay here. With you."

I'm about to create distance between us when over her shoulder, a familiar face catches my eye.

Wren.

She's standing near the door, searching for something. Someone. Her eyes meet mine for less than a second before anxiety and panic flood her gaze, and then she rushes out. My hands drop to my side, and the girl almost topples over. I don't have time for this.

"Go to your friends," I tell her, before rushing after Wren.

As I walk to the door, there's rushed footsteps behind me. I turn to find a worried Mia. She follows as I push past bodies to the exit before catching sight of Wren's figure by the pavement near the street lamp. She staggers, swaying a little. Quickening my steps, I'm right behind her when she falls.

"Wren," Mia says, panic lacing her voice as she comes up behind me.

"What's wrong with her?" I ask, holding on to Wren's limp body.

"Panic attack," Mia mutters.

Wren's eyes flutter shut, and a rush of fear runs down my spine. Does she have a concussion?

"Let me carry her," I say quickly. "Get Zach. Or Brody."

Mia nods and rushes back into the house. Letting out a shaky breath, I carry Wren to the house. It puts some strain on my knee, but I suck it up. Walking through the front yard, I spot Brody rushing toward me.

"Asher, are you—" Brody's voice halts. His gaze drops to the passed-out Wren in my arms.

"The hell?" His voice is laced with confusion. "What happened?"

"No time to explain. Give me your keys."

Unsatisfied with my brisk reply, he says, "Let me carry her. You're going to hurt your knee."

The image of Brody and Wren dancing together flashes in my mind, and my agitation flares. Like hell I'm going to let him carry her. Ignoring him, I push forward until I reach his truck. Brody sighs behind me, but unlocks it anyway. Opening the door, I lay Wren inside gently.

"How much did you drink?" I ask him, running my hand through my hair.

"Hardly anything."

I nod, sliding into the backseat before placing Wren's head on my shoulder and holding her in place. Brody's already up front, and as he pushes his key into the ignition, I explain that we need to wait for Mia. It's not long before the front passenger-side door opens and Mia jumps in, glancing back at Wren next to me.

Knight drives away from the house, picking up speed through the neighborhood. Pain shoots from my knee. I'm not supposed to be putting any strain on it. Dr. Greene told me it might hinder the healing process, but I don't care. I need to know that she's okay. I look down at Wren's face. She's sweating. Why the fuck is she sweating?

Finally, we reach Altemore, and Brody parks at a random point at the hospital entrance. I rush Wren to the emergency room. Mia talks to the lady at the desk while I wait with Wren still leaning against my side.

I pull out my phone and call Zach, who at first declines my call. That idiot.

I phone him again. He answers, "'Sup, weed."

"Zach. . ." I trail off.

There's some noise on the other side and then it becomes silent. "*What?*" And despite the fact that he's probably pretty drunk, concern is evident in his voice. "Are you okay?"

"I'm fine. Something happened to Wren. Get an Uber and get over here,"

"Oh shit, dude. Okay. Okay, I'll be there," he says before cutting the call.

Sending a hand through my hair, I exhale. I can't help but feel slightly guilty for the state Wren is in. She didn't want to go, and I forced her to. How was I supposed to know she gets panic attacks?

I can't erase the memory of the look on her face before she rushed outside. It's like she was screaming for help, and I was right *there*, but I didn't do anything. My throat tightens. I can't seem to do anything right.

## CHAPTER 17

# *Wren*

"I think she's dead."

"For the love of all that's human, Zach, she's not dead!"

"Before I'm forced to jump off this building, can you both shut the hell up?"

"Guys, guys! She's waking up!"

My head pounds, and I try to touch it—a futile attempt, since my wrist is attached to a drip system. My blinking teams up with a monotonous, throbbing headache.

"Hey," I murmur, attempting to sit up.

Brody's at my side, snaking an arm around me to help me up. He doesn't say much, while Mia narrows her eyes at me, bursting. "'Hey?' *Hey?* What were you thinking, running off like that?"

Fury coats her words, and yet I somehow sense the undercurrent of fragility there. Zach and Brody signal for her to stop but she ignores them, edging closer to me. "You can't get away from me that easily."

She sniffles. "I mean, I know I can be annoying at times, but I'm not that bad, am I? Okay, maybe that *one* time when I threw a Nutella jar across the room and it hit you—"

She breaks into a sob as she melts into my arms, and my voice is muffled by her shirt when I say, "Mia, I'm okay, all right?"

"You threw a jar of Nutella at her?" Zach asks. Brody looks like he's having a mental debate about whether it's appropriate to laugh in a hospital or not.

Mia turns to give Zach a glare. "It was a *mistake*."

I release a soft chuckle, despite myself. They all leave when my mom visits the room a little while later, checking on my vitals. She's used to it. This isn't the first time my panic attacks have landed me in the hospital. And this one most certainly isn't the worst.

"Maybe the party wasn't such a good idea after all," I mumble.

"It's okay, baby." She flattens my hair with a soothing hand. "I know you're trying."

With that, she leaves the room, and I can't feel more alone. All I have now is the sweet scent of mint gum. I stare at the empty couch, and that's when I notice the ruffled blanket spread across the seat, looking out of place. I don't know how I could be so sure, but—

He was here.

Asher was here.

～

Reed doesn't come to school for a whole week after the party. But when I open my locker, unpacking books from my sling bag, I find a sticky note placed neatly on top of the pile of books inside my locker. Unfolding it reveals blue ink that turns my stomach inside out.

*I'm sorry.*

I know exactly who it's from, but how did he get the note into my locker in the first place? The cafeteria buzzes with the sounds of students as I sit down in my normal seat. Mia and I figured a long time ago that the "popular territory" just wasn't for us.

I fork a piece of meatball from a bowl of spaghetti into my mouth, savoring the taste. When Mia plops into the seat next to me, I give her a chirpy greeting, which earns me a puzzled stare.

She sets her lips into a hard line. "Spill."

"What?" I ask, twirling my fork in the linguine.

"Don't play stupid." She tilts her head and narrows her eyes. "This entire week you've been moping around and stuffing your face with Skittles."

When I don't reply, she motions as if to usher me to start talking. Did I mention that I have a slight addiction to Skittles?

"I—"

"Oh!" She gives my shoulder a light, understanding pat. "Why didn't I figure it out sooner? It's your period, isn't it?" If she spoke just a fraction louder, even the people living in Australia would've heard her. As it is, a few members of the computer club turn to stare at us.

"What? No!" I splutter, stabbing my tongue with the fork in the process. "That's not it. I was going to say that Asher left a note in my locker. Apologizing. I don't know why or . . . how, though."

She crinkles her nose. "He did?"

"Yeah." I nod. "And I wanted to ask you, did you give anyone the combination to my locker?"

She shrugs and gives me a pained, sneaky smile. "I *may* or may not have given it to someone."

I gasp. "You gave it to him, didn't you? You gave Reed my locker combination!"

"He asked me!" she cries. "He told me whatever he was going to do would make you feel better. I couldn't lie on the spot. I just gave it to him and hoped for the best."

I can't be completely mad at her. She's not wrong. I do feel lighter since I found that note in my locker this morning. Mia offers me a pleading expression. "Are you mad at me?"

"Nope." I point my fork at her accusingly. "Just remind me to never tell you confidential information ever again."

❧

The soles of my boots meet the linoleum floors with a regular rhythm as I rush through the hallway, only coming to a halt when I recognize Brody's dark hair and denim jacket.

"Brody."

He turns, eyes widening when he notices me. He breaks away from Zach and walks over to me, his expression concerned. "Wren. What's up?"

"Do you know what's going on with Asher?" I ask, holding a stack of notes I made for Reed and a small sticky note with *I'm sorry* scribbled on it. "I have his notes."

Brody stares at me blankly. "I have no idea. It's been radio silence from him this entire week."

"Can you take me to his place?"

He pauses for a second as if mulling over the idea, then just shakes his head like he decides it's not a good one, and turns to walk away. I follow him, hoping I don't come off as too annoying. "So it's a no?"

He stops and turns to face me, and I bump into him. He looks down at me, his eyes narrowed, and the blank look on his face is replaced with something soft. "All right." He sighs. "Fine. I'll take you."

The journey to Asher's house is quiet. I watch the scenery to distract myself from the fact that I'm in the passenger seat of Brody's pickup. It's nothing to do with the way he drives, because his driving is pretty smooth, but I still get nervous on car rides, especially when I'm not with Mia or my mom. When we finally come to a stop, I let out a loose breath.

"This is it," Brody says.

I open the door and look over at Brody. "You're not coming?"

"Nope." He shakes his head. "Good luck, though. He's a stubborn one."

The snow has really begun to build up. So much so that I've started wearing boots while waiting for Mia in the mornings, to stop the snow from seeping through my sneakers. There was an impenetrable layer gathering outside the house this morning.

I stand before the mansion, suddenly feeling very small. A mere glimpse of the scene creates countless questions in my mind. Taking a step toward the closed gates, I fumble with the ungodly amount of paper in my hands while trying to press a single finger on the intercom button. It buzzes, and I wait awkwardly outside the building.

"How can I help you?" a female voice finally speaks.

"Hi," I speak into the device. "It's Ree—Asher's, uh . . . friend, Wren."

"Hold on."

The gate slides open, which I take as my cue to walk in. The large wooden door of the house opens, and an elderly woman's surprised face stares back at me. Her dark-grey hair reaches her neck and half of her front is covered by a crisp white apron.

"What brings you here?" she asks politely.

"Hi, uh . . ."

"Madame Florence."

"Madame Florence. Do you know where Asher is, by any chance? I came to drop off some school notes for him."

Surprise is evident in her features, and she narrows her eyes, as if trying to dig deep into my soul. Her questioning stare soon turns into a heartwarming smile.

"Ah." She sighs. "Finally, a decent girl comes around. Patience, *non*? My Asher has chosen well."

I smile, not quite understanding, but going with the flow anyway.

"Hm. He has not been himself lately. Do you want to talk to him?"

I nod.

"Downstairs." She gestures. "The basement."

Whizzing down a spiral staircase, I let my hand graze the banister. It's darker than the main level of the house, and as I wade farther into the area, I hear the sound of people screaming and cheering.

The dark room is illuminated by the light emitted from the large screen. A figure sits quietly on the couch. Reed. His jaw is set in a hard, defined line. I notice the dark bags that have formed under his eyes. He wears them like art. Breaking out of my stupor, I walk in. He ignores me, but I know he's aware of my presence.

"Uh . . . maybe I should go," I mutter to myself, turning.

He continues aimlessly staring at the players on the ice. "Stay."

I halt in my tracks. "Reed—"

"Asher," he corrects, edging over on the couch, seemingly

making space for me. He reaches to the floor for a water bottle, and takes a sip. Taking a small breath, I walk over and sit next to him. Our legs stretch in front of us. I'm halfway through realizing how annoyingly long his legs are compared to mine when he breaks the silence.

He sighs and runs a hand through his hair. "I shouldn't have forced you to go to the party. If it wasn't for me, you wouldn't have had a panic attack, and you wouldn't have ended up in a hospital."

"I chose to go. It was my decision. Don't blame yourself." I pause, glancing at his profile. "But let's focus on the more important part. Asher Reed is apologizing? And to me?" I mock, poking his cheek, which turns light pink at my words. "Who are you and what have you done to the real Asher?"

He rolls his eyes, prying my fingers away from his face, the corner of his lips tugging upward. "Get over yourself, Martin. Why are you here, anyway?"

The air freezes. "I have your notes."

His eyes grow brighter. "You have my notes, or you're using my notes as an excuse?"

I stay silent for a while, looking at him from the corner of my eye. His gaze clouds, and I sigh, offering up the full truth. "And I just wanted to know if you're okay."

Slowly, the corners of his mouth lift. "I'm good."

I swallow. "Good."

He leans forward, impossibly close. "Are you?"

I blink. "What?"

"Okay." His breath fans my face. "Are you okay?"

"Yeah." I release a breath when he finally draws away.

His eyes are fixed on my face now, but he's silent, searching my face. "Good."

I want to look away from his scrutinizing gaze, but I can't. The TV casts a blue-ish glow on his face, and clearing my throat, I shift my attention to the screen. "Hockey?"

He grins. "No, birdie, tennis."

I give him a flat glare. It's not like I know much about sports, either way. We stay silent for a while, just watching the game. It's an NHL one, and the rapid way the players move is mesmerizing, even I have to admit this. I peel my gaze from the screen to glance at him. "Do you miss playing?"

Amusement fills his eyes. "Of course I do."

"In a weird way," I say, "I kinda get it."

His eyes narrow, like he doesn't fully believe me.

I sigh. "Remember that painting you asked me about at my place?"

He nods curtly.

"I used to really like art," I say. "But I can't do it anymore."

Reed's brows knit together. "Wh—"

"Don't ask why."

His mouth slowly closes, and I sigh again. "It's complicated."

"I don't—"

"Mind complicated," I complete for him. "I know. It's just . . . I don't really like talking about it. I can't tell you why I don't paint anymore, but at the very least I can convince you that you're not alone. I know the feeling. You know, when the thing you love most is taken away from you. It's like life cheated on you. It's—"

"Unfair," he says.

I nod. "Unfair."

"Like half of you has disappeared," he says, and it's so accurate that there's an ache in my chest.

Turning to face him, I say, "You're going to play again, though, right?"

146

He tries a small smile that doesn't quite reach his eyes. "I won't give up on something that makes me that happy that easily."

I think back to my own situation. "But what if you're sure it could hurt you again?"

"I don't care." He shakes his head. "If there's a possibility that I can still do it? I'd make sure to do everything to make that possibility a reality."

I can't help the small smile that tugs at my lips. "You really do love hockey, huh?"

He shrugs, a dull complacency entering his gaze as he looks down at me, his hair ruffled and scattered across his forehead in a mess. "What about you?"

I frown. "What about me?"

"Are you going to paint again?"

The question sets off a deep-seated fear inside me, and it spreads through my chest as it catches fire. It's a while before the feeling fades, a while before I'm able to look up at him and think straight. "I don't know."

He must sense that something's off because he shifts a little, changing the topic. "Do you want to go somewhere?"

I lift a brow. "Where?"

He rolls his eyes. "It's a surprise."

I'm silent for a while, mulling over the idea. "I can't get back home too late."

"We won't be long."

"Okay," I say, and I can't help but wonder if I'll regret this later. "Fine."

The cold air brushes my face as Asher pulls me outside and toward a dirt path covered with snow. I breathe heavily as my boots crunch under me. I stop after a few minutes. Placing my hands on my knees, I duck my head, looking at the snow below me.

"You okay there, birdie?" Glancing up at Reed, I see a slight smirk on his face. He clearly isn't as exhausted as I am. I slowly stand, offering him a glare, and continue walking. "I would drive but,"—he points to his knee—"doctor's orders."

Eventually, we're walking down a thin gravel path in a dimly lit forest. The scenery changes, and there are more and more trees. His gaze lands on me and I hold it for a second before looking away.

"What is this place?" I mumble.

"You'll like it." He smiles a genuine smile. "I promise."

"C'mon." He tilts his head, light in his eyes. I grimace, with no choice but to follow him, since I have no idea where we are or how to get home. We walk for about another mile, and I'm pretty glad I wore boots.

The path gets even narrower and grittier, and before I know it, I trip. Almost immediately, Asher turns and is at my side. Sliding a strong arm around my back, he helps me up in silence. "You okay?"

"Um . . . yeah," I lie. He ignores me, holding up my left arm—the one I fell on. Embedded in my palm are dozens of little stones, and the skin is grazed. When he runs his fingers over my palm, I flinch. His eyes flick up to meet mine, but they hold little emotion.

"Stay still," he orders. I watch as he lightly removes the stones from my skin. Then, he edges a little closer to me, close enough that I can feel his breath—which smells distinctly of mint gum—on my face, and tucks a strand of hair behind my ear.

In the process, his fingers brush the side of my face, and tingles flow through my cheeks. My stomach floods with butterflies.

The pain in my palm subsides a little, my skin numbing at his touch. I feel my face warming up.

"Thanks"

"It's all right," he muses, and takes my uninjured hand in his. Probably a precaution since I'm so accident-prone. I try slipping my hand out of his hold, because I know that I'll start getting clammy, but his hold is firm. I give up.

Every step we take with my hand in his hollows out my chest another inch. I can't seem to get used to his touch. The sound of gushing water steals my attention. When I turn, the view takes my breath away.

We're standing before a semifrozen pool, the water at the bottom fading to a dark, velvety color, a stark contrast to the snow around the pool. A little above is a cable line connecting to a tree house.

"This is amazing."

"Told you you'd like it." Reed smirks, pulling me toward the tree-house ladder. "Climb up."

When we get to the top of the tree house, the view looks even better. Asher leads me inside. The walls are made of bamboo sticks, and the house is decorated with collectables and figurines, scattered with piles of comics and large Marvel posters.

The slight sparkle in his eyes is clear. "So, what do you think?"

I glance his way. "How is this possible?"

"The guys and I found this place a while back. It's abandoned. The people who built it own a house a block over. They moved out, and the new owners don't really care much about this place, so it's kind of no-man's-land now."

My eyes are wide. "Does your mom know about it?"

He shakes his head, and his left dimple appears. "Nope. The

only people who know about this place are Zach, Brody, and me. And now you."

I nod slowly, training my gaze on the zip line. "Can I have a try on that?"

"Of course." He gives me a look. "If you promise not to dislocate or permanently injure any body parts."

I brush him off anxiously, standing. "Yeah, yeah, whatever."

"C'mon."

I stand on the platform, and he tells me to put one leg into a harness, and then the other so it rests on my waist. He has to tighten it a lot because, and I quote: "Zach has a fat ass."

I pray the harness is tight enough because if it isn't then I'm getting soaked. Paranoia starts to creep in. "I'm not going to die, am I?"

Reed chuckles to himself as he fiddles with my harness. He's so close I can feel his smooth intake of breath. "No, birdie, you're not going to die. The line is secure. Just hold on tight. When you're at the end, wait for me. I'll be there to help you out of the harness. All right?"

"All right. Okay."

I try to calm myself. Sensing my nervous energy, Asher pulls something out of his pocket. My eyes widen as I realize. It's my red ribbon, the one he'd pulled out of my hair the day Mia dragged me to Dunkin'.

"That's mine," I murmur, more to myself than anything.

"Yeah." He nods. "It is."

I swallow gently as I glance up at him, and I know he knows the words I want to say but can't. *You kept it all this time?*

Silently, he edges closer to me, gently looping the ribbon around my hair, and fixes my hair into a ponytail. I stay quiet, too, although his fingers working behind me sends an unfamiliar shiver down my spine.

"There," he says finally, standing back to glance over me. And I think for a second, just a second, there's a flush to his cheeks. But maybe it's just me, because he reaches over me a moment later with a grin. "Hold on tight, birdie."

Then, there's nothing beneath my feet.

The scream is stuck in my throat. The wind rushes past my face, and the air is crisp around me. As I glide across the line, I try not to look down. But inevitably, I end up peering down to see the tops of the lush green trees, the wild, flowing water beneath me.

I'm flying.

I'm really, seriously flying, and I feel . . . alive.

There's a smile tugging on my lips before I even know it.

Soon, the zip slows and my knuckles burn. Water droplets scatter on my cheeks, but I can't wipe them away. Finally, my boots graze the ground. I look around, still stuck to the line by the hooked harness, floating around like a monkey in space.

"Asher!" I call out. "Hello? Are you there?"

Silence.

"*Hello?*"

The silence becomes deafening, and I frantically rotate on the harness, looking for any sign of the blue-eyed monster. Or any sign of life, yeah, that'd be great too.

The harness feels too tight as I hear leaves crunching in the distance. I pick furiously at the stupid thing to free myself, but the devil tied it well. I hear the crackling of leaves under shoes getting louder, and I begin to panic.

"Oh God no." I huff under my breath. "I'm too young to die. I haven't even met Beyoncé yet."

Suddenly, the hairs on the back of my neck rise. Someone's right behind me.

"Boo," he whispers—and that's when I scream. Loudly. Well, yeah, until Asher blocks half of my face off with his hand, muffling my scream.

"*Sshh*. Don't scream." He snickers as he finally lifts his hand from my face. "It's just me."

I scowl, but he's too busy trying to contain his laughter and not being subtle about it. "I can't help it," I mutter. "Your face is kind of horrifying."

"Horrifyingly sexy, baby." He grins and unclips me from the harness. My dangling feet finally touch the ground. "Yours was priceless. All terrified."

I so badly want to tear off that *stupid* smirk.

"You're a sadist," I spit, walking as far away from him as possible.

"And you're cute."

"Whatever," I huff, crossing my arms, like it'll magically take away my embarrassment. I start to walk away.

"Hey, birdie."

"What?" I call out to him behind me.

"You're going the wrong way."

I turn, sighing with exaggerated flair. "I knew that."

"Uh-huh." He smirks, pointing his thumb in the opposite direction. "Beyoncé's this way."

# CHAPTER 18

## Asher

We're walking back from the park, where Ev insisted she had to go. Except I couldn't take her alone because Mom made me swear not to do anything without Wren's help, then went on to list about a hundred ways things could go wrong because my knee's still healing.

Currently satisfied, Ev's skipping along the snow-covered sidewalk. Wren's tightly wrapped up in a beige coat with her red hoodie—a piece of clothing she always seems to have on her—underneath.

"Happy now?" I turn back to narrow my eyes at my sister. She nods, her fluffy white earmuffs shaking along with her. Chuckling at her, I shake my head as we walk back to Wren's place.

The cold air bites at my skin, and it's like a greeting from an old friend. This is what it felt like entering the arena. Next to me, Wren's boots meet the snow-covered pavement with a crunch as she tucks her hands into the pockets of her jacket.

I pull out my phone and click on Candy Crush. It's practically crack. I even convinced Zach to get it so that we can compete. Yes, I'm aware of how fucking lame it is. Do I care? Not really, nope.

A loud tune fills the air when the app opens. A small smile sneaks onto Wren's face. Pretending to ignore it, I tap on level 133. It's one I can't seem to get past. Furrowing my brows, I glance at the brightly colored candy scattered on my screen.

Something tugs on my jacket. It's Ever, and she's holding on to my sleeve. She gives my phone a glance before knocking it out of my hand, picking it up, and running off with it.

"Hey!"

"*Run!*" Wren yells, and then she spins, her coffee-brown braid whipping midair as she starts running with my sister. Her black boots plow through the thick layers of snow. Ev is practically submerged and gets stuck. She turns around, too slow because I'm already on to her. She starts squealing.

"Quit it, you little *brat*."

Wren just snorts, trying not to laugh when Ev doesn't stop pushing through the layers of snow. "Don't let go, Ever!"

"Wren," I growl.

Wren grins evilly as she looks back at Ever, ignoring my slew of protests. Thanks to therapy, my knee's stronger, and catching up to Ever is about as easy as you'd think it would be.

I yank her up and she shrieks in my arms as I set her down on more secure ground. Collecting my phone from her tiny hands, I find my screen still open on Candy Crush, and a *Level Failed* message rushes up along with upbeat music. Wren bursts out laughing. I grunt at the sound of literal failure being emitted from my phone, and I turn, finding Wren flailing around a few yards away from us. My knee slows me down as I run, but I'm still able to catch up with her. Her honey eyes widen when she sees how close I am. Yelping, she tries to run faster.

It's too late. I'm already wrapping my arm around her waist, whipping her around to face me, stopping her from moving any farther. Her soft breath fans my cheek, and I can almost hear her pulse careening.

"Nice try," I muse.

She looks up at me with those soft honey eyes, her cheeks flushed. Then she smiles sheepishly, raises her hands, and surrenders. She rolls her eyes and sticks her tongue out, while Ever pouts in disappointment. My gaze flickers to Wren's mouth for a millisecond before I tear it away to focus on my sister.

Ever's gloved hand slips into Wren's, and she motions for Wren to bend to her height. Once Wren does, she whispers, "We'll get him next time."

I can't help but smile when Wren nods back, trying to match my sister's grave expression. "The war will be continued."

We reach Wren's house after a few minutes of walking. I trek inside and watch as Wren sets Ever down, and my sister grabs her hand and drags her to the TV.

"What? You wanna watch?" Wren asks. Ev nods, and Wren chuckles in response.

"Sure," Wren agrees, attacked by a sudden light bulb moment. "Hey! We can watch a movie. And build a pillow fort!"

"Yeah!" Ev screams, jumping up and down. "Ash can help with the pillow carrying. He's really strong. Even though his knee is all broken and stuff."

I roll my eyes.

Wren notices, and turns to Ever. "Oh, it's fine. He doesn't have to help. Pillows are light anyway."

"Fine," I grumble.

"Fine what?" she asks.

"Fine, I'll carry your stupid pillows for you."

"I'll have you know my pillows are top quality." Wren's gaze is swimming with fake admonishment. "There will be no shaming of pillows whatsoever."

"Yeah, don't be mean, Ash," Ev adds.

Wren winks at me, which earns her a scowl.

Five minutes later, I'm tumbling down the stairway holding a huge stack of blankets, duvets, and about six pillows. Wren tries not to laugh when Ev jumps on me and all the pillows nearly fall off the pile in my hands.

Dumping all the stuff on the floor, I give them an unimpressed glare. "You said *a few* pillows."

Wren scoffs. "And *you* said you were strong."

The result isn't half bad. The pillows and cushions cover the bottom of the fort in various colors, and the sheets hang over the fort, draping over the blankets. She even adds fairy lights to the opening.

The microwave pings, the sound resonating through the house. Wren walks off to get the popcorn, and comes back with bowls filled to the brim. She leaves them on the coffee table.

"Pretty good, eh?" She nudges me in the arm while holding Ever's hand.

Ev drops her hand and runs inside, quite amused by the fort. I watch the lights bounce on Wren's face. Her eyes sparkle as she looks straight ahead, a small smile playing on her lips. Feeling my gaze on her, she turns, facing me.

I clear my throat. "My mom wanted me to ask you if you'd like to come over with your mom for Christmas Eve."

Wren's eyes widen as she ponders the invitation for a moment. Then she nods and crawls into the fort. "I'll check with my mom." Letting out a breath, I send a hand through my hair. That isn't so bad. I make a poor attempt to follow, but I'm too tall to fit. Crouching my frame awkwardly, I squash into the fort next to Wren.

"We could watch *Frozen*," Wren suggests, digging through a box of DVDs.

Ever nods in excitement, resembling a tiny bobblehead.

"No way." I shake my head and thrust the popcorn bowl back into her hands. "What else is in here?" I ask, digging in the box myself. Shortly after, I let out an exasperated groan. "There's only Disney movies in here. What is wrong with you?"

"Excuse you." Wren makes a face. "It's not my fault you're a party pooper. C'mon, Reed, you can't tell me you haven't watched a single Disney movie."

I frown. "Of course, I have." I fish out *The Lion King*. "Let's watch this."

Wren glances at my sister. "What do you say, Ever? *Frozen* or *The Lion King*?"

Ev's gaze flicks between Wren and me, and a confused look washes over her features.

"Mine's about princesses," Wren adds, in an attempt to sway her decision.

I frown. "C'mon Ev, we've watched *Frozen* a hundred times. Mine's about a lion that kills another lion, and then the son of the lion is sad and—" I stop, realizing I've lost the war. "Just pick already." I groan, frustrated.

My sister walks over to Wren and picks a movie out of her hands. Wren basks in her victory, smiling proudly at me.

"Little traitor," I mutter.

While I set up the movie, Ev and Wren whisper in the corner.

"Hey, Ever?"

It takes a while for her to respond to Wren because she's fighting with something on her little checked cardigan, one of the buttons, and I'm reminded that four-year-olds don't have the best attention spans. She looks up at Wren expectantly.

"How's Mason?" Wren asks.

I grumble.

"*Shh.*"

Ever rolls her eyes. "He's so stupid!"

"Really?"

"Yeah. Every time I try to say hi, he runs away from me. So, he's stupid. Boys are stupid."

"I'm sitting right here," I mutter. But when I get no response from the brats, I huff a disgruntled noise, relegating myself to the popcorn bowl. There's no point arguing. I'm clearly outnumbered.

## CHAPTER 19

### Wren

Asher collapses way too close to me for my liking. He proceeds to inch closer to me until he's right next to me, the side of his body brushing every second or so against mine. Not to mention the fact that heat seems to surge through me every time, bubbling in my veins and reaching my fingertips. It's not like I can blame him entirely. The fort is clearly too small for all three of us.

I can feel warmth radiate off him, and I turn to face him, but he doesn't take the hint. I inch away from him until eventually, I'm almost on top of poor Ever, who's waiting for the movie to start.

"I'm getting squashed!" Ever shrieks.

Reed rolls his eyes. "I'll go sit on the couch."

He worms his way out. Without him, the fort is suddenly much, much bigger, and I'm reminded that he took up so much space because he's a six-foot-one two-hundred-pound hockey player. My skin cools as I spread out, not squishing Ever anymore.

It's about the hundredth time I've watched *Frozen*, but it's the most eventful. Asher and Ever are so alike in mannerisms. First, they both chew their popcorn the same way—obnoxiously loud. Second, they keep their eyes fixed on the screen, so immersed in the movie they don't notice me studying them. Finally, they both make comments at the most inappropriate times. For example:

"What are those two hairy things stuck to his face?" Ever.

"Who starts singing in the middle of nowhere? Get on with it, woman." Asher.

"Is that a carrot?" Ever.

"Forget Kristoff, go for Olaf, the dude's more reliable." Asher.

The movie soon ends, and we change to Netflix. After a while, when I don't hear Asher or sense any movement from him, I lean over to see him passed out on the couch. He fell asleep? I chuckle quietly.

"Ever," I whisper, distracting her gaze from the TV.

"Yeah?" She speaks out loud, ignoring the fact that I whisper to leave the blue-eyed monster asleep.

I point to the sleeping beauty on the couch, and when she notices, the mischievous smile on her face mirrors mine. As I edge off the couch and grab Ever in my arms, an ingenious idea sparks in my mind.

"What are we gonna do?" Ever asks, her eyes wide and intrigued. She knows we'd be stupid not to take advantage of this golden opportunity.

Once we're at a safe distance, I speak. "I have an idea."

After we ransack my mother's room, we remerge with a bunch of makeup and a slightly clued-up Ever. We're going to give Asher a makeover.

"So, we're going to make Ash look ugly?" she asks, her inflection rising.

I shrug. "Yep, pretty much."

It makes me wonder why Ever finds so much joy in harassing her older brother, but I think she loves the reaction she gets out of him. It *is* pretty freakin' hilarious getting Asher all riled up. We make our way back, Ever tiptoeing. He's still there, looking very innocent while he sleeps.

I kneel in front of him, leveling myself with his face. Ever doesn't have to; she just stands next to me, waiting for my signal to start. The outline of his lips is clear, and his longer-than-average eyelashes splay over his cheeks, making him look like a sculpture.

I can't believe I'm doing this. Inviting murder. Destroying the peace.

"I'm having second thoughts about this," I murmur, but Ever's already emptying the contents of the makeup bag on the carpeted floor.

Too late. I fish out the little bottle of liquid that is definitely *not* Reed's skin tone.

"What's that?" Ever asks.

"It's foundation. I think we put this stuff all over his face."

She doesn't doubt my answer for a second. "Okay!"

We slather the cold, soft liquid all over his face, and he doesn't wake up or even flutter his eyes. His cheeks are warm and his skin unnaturally soft. When we're done, I resist the urge to laugh, because he looks like he smashed a cake in his face.

"Ever," I whisper, my eyes widening, "you're supposed to be putting the lipstick on his *lips*. Not everywhere else!"

She lifts her head and stares at the squiggles of red lipstick she's drawn, not only on his lips but *all* over his chin. It's also somehow ended up on his cheeks. At this point, I'm really wondering how he isn't awake yet. He's making this way too easy. We've caked tons of makeup on his face, and my mom is so not going to appreciate us raiding her makeup supply.

Afterward, I do the eyeliner with the little wing on the end and I try not to poke him, or the whole plan will be ruined. We put some sparkly blue stuff on his eyelids.

"To bring out the color in his eyes." I cackle.

At this, Ever bursts into a round of loud giggles. I try to shush her, but it's too late.

She's awakened the monster. Stirred the beast. His hands begin to move a little, and we jump from the sudden motion. He makes this weird grunting sound and turns over a little. He reaches his hand to his face as his eyes open, ever so slowly.

"Wren?" he calls, his voice husky and raw as it should be after a sleep so deep. "Ever?"

We both scramble for the couch.

"Act natural!"

Confusion swims in Ever's hazel eyes. "What's nacho ral?"

"Oh," I mutter, realizing she doesn't understand a lot of things. "Well."

"Can somebody please tell me why I smell like strawberries?"

We snap our heads his way, and he's upright on the couch now. He rubs his eyes, and when he brings his hand down and looks at it, a bewildered look crosses his face. The sparkly, icky makeup comes off on his palm.

"What the hell?"

"Don't curse!" Ever giggles, and I can't help but join in on the laughter. His face looks like a painting gone terribly wrong. There's glitter and lipstick where they definitely shouldn't be.

When it finally dawns on him, he growls. "What have you two *done* to me?"

"We gave you a makeover," Ever explains, while I stay silent, my hand on my lips as I realize how big of a mistake this really was.

"Why would you do that?" His eyes land on me. There's something unerringly creepy in the way he speaks. It's too calm, too serene.

"We figured you liked your face a whole lot, so we wanted to give you a—" I start.

"Give me a what?"

"A . . . um . . ." I struggle for words. "An upgrade! Yep, that's it. An upgrade. A facial upgrade."

He gives me a flat glare, then takes out his phone to see the state of his face. I get ready to run. When he sees it, he lets out a strangled scream—one he'd like to believe is manly. He gives us a deathly glare, a last warning, before he charges at us. Ever and I shriek and sprint in opposite directions; she's faster than me, but at least we create a diversion of some sort.

"You look like Ursula!" Ever yells, and I think I cry a little from laughter.

"Shut it, you little *brat*!" Asher yells back, lunging for her.

She shrieks again, and runs in my direction, and I start running too. We're both trying our best to laugh and run, but the combination isn't exactly effective.

All I can see is blurry figures rushing everywhere, and Ever appearing and disappearing at irregular moments. Everyone's screams and laughter mix together to create a weird soundtrack, one that bubbles over and sounds more like a farm than anything else.

Except if Asher really wants to catch us, he would've done it a long time ago. He's stalling, and I smile a little at the thought.

Eventually, I hear Ever's high-pitched screech, and I know he's finally got her. They reappear with Ever slung over Asher's shoulder, wriggling like crazy to get out of his hold. It isn't going to work—I know for a fact his hold is iron-like.

He drops her on the couch, muttering a monosyllabic, "Stay."

Surprisingly, she listens, but not without staring up at him with a little rebellious laugh. Then his eyes land on me.

"And *you.*" He pauses, grabbing my arm and dragging me to the bathroom. "You're helping me get this off my face."

∽

"My mom really needs to stop paying you for this," Reed says, referring to the babysitting. I mean, he does have a point.

I hand him another wet wipe. "Yeah, I know, right?"

"What the hell is this stuff?" he groans, rubbing the black stuff off his eyelids.

"That would be eyeliner." I offer him a pained smile. "Liquid."

"Might as well be permanent fucking marker," he huffs.

I snort, but try to contain my laughter when he offers me a glare.

"They make it waterproof so you can cry and still look pretty afterward," I say. "Let me try."

I take the wet wipe from his fingers and squirt makeup remover on it. Bringing the wipe to his cheek, I rub it a little before our proximity starts to mess with my brain.

After a while of me dabbing at his face, he places his hand on mine, stopping me. His skin, as usual, is warm. He leans in closer, aiming to close the gap between us. My breath hitches, and I blink. Suddenly, he freezes, pulling away with an evil smirk.

"Do I really look like Ursula?" he asks.

"Yeah," I affirm with a small smile. "I can totally see the resemblance."

～

The next day, I look out my window to find my mother digging with a shovel at the snow covering the driveway. Opening the front door, I regret not wearing something more than just slippers. The snow crunches under my feet, and I feel the cold through my pajamas as I walk over to where she's working.

"Mother," I drawl. She glances up from what she was quite invested in and smiles.

"Yes?"

"What are you doing?" I ask, narrowing my eyes.

"Maybe I should've gotten you those glasses, honey. Can't you see? I'm shoveling snow."

"I can see that." I start to shiver. "Why are you shoveling snow at eight in the morning?"

"It's blocking the driveway and I have to take the car out. Aren't we going to your friend's place today?"

Victoria invited us to their house for Christmas Eve, and when I asked Mom, I was half hoping she'd say no. She agreed, though, and now I'm spending Christmas Eve with the Reeds, apparently.

I run back into the house to grab warmer clothes. A few minutes later, I convince my mother to go back into the house so I can take up the job instead. I zip my jacket up a little tighter, the cold biting at my skin.

Exhaling, I watch as the breath forms a dragon-like shape from my mouth, dissipating in the barren air. My upper arms hurt already. I clearly need to exercise more. To be honest, I'm never the type who gets excited when their gym teacher shouts, "Thirty laps around the field!"

I'm the type who groans, complains the whole time, and struggles to complete the first lap—heavy breathing slowly consuming my body so that it looks like I'm having convulsions. Heaving, I shovel the last chunk of snow from the pavement and tuck it into the straight line, patting it in.

A few hours later, I'm still nervous about this whole dinner thing. I mean, I've seen Victoria before and I've talked to her, but now I somehow feel it's different in the sense that I actually know her daughter, and son, a little more. Maybe now she has certain expectations of me, or maybe I'm just overthinking the whole situation like I always do.

Nevertheless, I think this whole nerve-racking situation compels me to dress a little less like I'm a hippie. I wear black jeans paired with black combat boots. Over my dark grey jersey, there's a beige double-breasted coat and a plaid scarf. It's not model worthy, but it's good enough.

Mia would be proud. Heck, Mia would want to come over and dress me up if she could, but truth is, she can't. Her parents are forcing her to spend Christmas Eve with her extended family over in Vermont. She was literally wailing about her whole ordeal to me over the phone last night, while I laughed.

The electronic gates slide open after my mother buzzes the intercom. We walk up to the entrance of the mansion, and its mahogany doors part to reveal Madame Florence. She's wearing a crisp white dress this time, accompanied by an equally white apron, but her charcoal-colored hair is almost identical to the last time I saw her.

"Ah, I was right. You are a special one!" Madame Florence gushes. She motions for us to enter the large space. "Come, come!"

Lit up, it's like I'm seeing the house for the first time. Everything's spacious, the color scheme neutral with taupe walls. There are also smooth sheets of glass used as partitions, and I can see the snow outside from where I'm standing.

The clicking of heels resounds, and I turn to find Victoria making her way down the stairs with a maroon-lipped smile. She looks graceful, her golden-brown hair settling over a black sweater.

"Oh, you're both here!" Victoria says with a perfect smile, meeting us at the bottom of the elaborate staircase. She hugs me and moves on to my mother. They immediately start up a conversation, and I stand there awkwardly while they exchange pleasantries.

I barely notice when Ever pads down the staircase and tugs at my sleeve. I smile, happy for the rescue. My mother has just met Victoria and they're talking like long lost friends.

Picking Ever up, I balance her on my hip. "Hey, there, my little ray of sunshine."

Her golden hair is fixed into a high ponytail, which bobs when she speaks. I notice her adorable lilac lace tutu, and my pearl bracelet fixed to her tiny wrist. "Tomorrow's Christmas!"

"Aw, isn't she just the cutest thing?" my mother coos, noticing Ever in my arms.

"That's what they all say," Victoria says. "She's actually a little devil."

"Are you making her carry you, Ev?"

I turn, with Ever still in my arms to face an amused Asher. He tucks his hands in the pockets of his dark jeans and leans on the balustrade of the staircase.

"No, she's not," I say. Ever sticks her tiny tongue out at her brother. "And I can, she's really light."

He walks over to where we are standing. "You came."

"Of course I did," I say. "I promised to."

He stares at me with a lazy smile playing along his lips, then leans in and plucks his sister from my grip. I follow him to their living room, where a bare Christmas tree stands, leaving my mom and Victoria still in conversation behind us.

I turn to Asher. "Why is your tree still not decorated?"

He just shrugs. "Decorating it late then keeping it up until the end of January is a tradition in this household."

"Hey, Wen," Ever says. "Do you wanna do it now?"

"Um." I ponder my answer, then decide to give in to that adorable look on Ever's face that screams Say yes, pretty please with a cherry on top. "Sure."

Ever edges over to pass me a few ornaments. I decide to start at the top, and climb up the ladder. But, *of course*, I miss my footing. Suddenly, the ladder isn't beneath my feet anymore and I'm falling from a height of seven feet. I let out a strangled shriek, grasping at the air.

I'm falling all right, straight into the arms of Asher Reed. What's worse is that he's grinning down at me, making me feel all mushy inside. I separate myself from him. Luckily, no one sees what just happened. Or so I think.

"Were you guys making googly eyes at each other?"

Ever.

My cheeks heat, and I think I might just die from embarrassment.

Asher winks. He *winks*. What an idiot. "If that's what you call it."

I glare at him. "Don't listen to your brother, Ever." I lift her, hugging her in my arms. "He's a bad influence."

"You"—I turn my attention to Asher, narrowing my eyes—"are extremely inconvenient."

He cocks a brow. "Yes, because saving someone before they injure themselves is considered *extremely inconvenient*."

"You didn't have to catch me, you know," I say. "I doubt anything serious would've happened if I just fell."

"Come now, Martin." Reed winks. "We both know we can't have you falling for me."

I ignore the lurch of my heart, rolling my eyes as I join Ever, who's picking out more metallic Christmas ball ornaments and little stars. She hangs them at the bottom of the tree. Asher does, too, but not after making some random inappropriate joke about the balls.

One second, he's hooking a red ball to the tree, the next, he's close to me—really close. Close enough for me to spot the faint trail of freckles across the plane of his cheeks. He sneaks his hand into my hair and unties my braid. "There."

I swallow and take a step away, and I know he knows why, because he chuckles. He clearly finds pleasure in watching me transform into a bundle of nerves. And he has a weird fetish with untying my hair. I start draping the lights around the tree, uncoiling the tangled line as I go.

His eyes trail the front of my body. "Nice sweater."

"Thanks." I eye his navy-blue sweater and the crisp shirt collar folded over neatly. "Yours too."

He groans and sends a hand through his hair. "Don't lie,

169

birdie. My mother forced me into this. Said it looked, and I quote, 'decent.'"

I laugh, finding it cute that he listens to his mother. It's true—the sweater seems too pristine and well, yeah, *innocent* for someone like him. Don't get me wrong, though, it still looks good on him.

"I'm not lying," I muse. "It looks nice."

He looks back at me with an equally amused expression. "It looks nice, or *I* look nice?"

I lift a brow. "Are you really fishing for compliments?"

He scoffs. "I don't need someone to tell me I look good. I know I look good. But"—he stares at me for a moment, a mischievous twinkle in his eye—"it'd still be great if I could hear it coming from you."

I punch him in the shoulder. "In your demented, repulsive little dreams, Reed."

"Whoa, somebody has a big vocabulary." He winks. "Sexy."

"Wen," Ever cries. "I can't reach the top!"

I shrug. "Me too."

"Ha." Asher mocks. "Sucks to be you."

"Ash, stop being mean." Ever frowns. "And help me put this star on the top."

I stick my tongue out at Asher, who grins as he faces his sister. "Your wish is my command, princess."

A small smile appears on my face, evolving into a full blown grin as Ever literally *climbs* her brother until she's standing on her own little feet on his shoulders. Asher supports her with his arms.

"Be careful!" I laugh, watching as the pair wobble over to the tree. Ever places the golden star on the top, and the tree finally looks complete. I give them a faux round of applause, and Asher ruffles his sister's hair before setting her down again. Ever frowns, flattening her hair with her little hands, and the three of us pause to stare up at our masterpiece.

Brilliant colors and hues of red, gold, jade, and cerulean drape the previously barren tree. The fairy lights twinkle in the dim light and the metallic balls shine as they rotate. Right at the top of the tree, the star sits alone, sparkling in self-contained splendor.

"Quite good, eh?"

"Great, so now that we're all here, we can go eat!" Victoria finally appears, with my mother at her side. As we all file into the dining room, Victoria stops me, her hazel eyes warm. "I didn't get a chance to thank you."

I blink. "Thank me?"

"For taking care of my babies."

It takes me a while to realize that she's talking about Asher and Ever. After I do, though, I blink a few more times and my mouth goes dry.

"If anything," I say, catching my breath, "it was the other way around."

"Such a sweet girl." She smiles. "Those two must be driving you crazy."

I smile. "A little."

We walk into the room together, and Victoria gestures for me to sit. The table is already prepped with plates, silverware, napkins, and a pair of ladles. I end up sitting between Ever and Asher, with the mothers sitting on the opposite side of the long, sleek table.

I scan the table for some salt. Sure enough, there are silver salt and pepper shakers right in front of Asher. I nudge him in the shoulder, whispering, "Can you pass the salt?"

His eyes waver to the salt and back to me. He forks a morsel into his mouth and swallows, a mischievous glint in his cobalt eyes when he whispers back, "No."

I narrow my eyes at him. Rude.

"Fine then," I huff, under my breath. I reach over him, the side of my body brushing against his, and grab the salt.

"Wren, darling, just ask Asher, he'll pass it to you next time," Victoria gushes, noticing me. I smile politely at her and nod, while Asher stuffs his face with food in a clear attempt to hold back his laughter.

I ignore him. Soon, Ever's eyes start drooping, and I have to stop her tiny head from plummeting into her unfinished bowl of vanilla ice cream. It's so adorably funny, and I have to refrain from laughing.

"I'll carry her to her room," Asher offers. He picks her up with ease and slings her across his chest, her sleepy head resting on his shoulder. He's actually sweet when he isn't being utterly infuriating.

Rising from my seat, I utter a quick, "I'll go too."

I run after Asher's retreating back so that I don't get lost. I eventually catch up with him and start trekking up the elaborate staircase. He's aware of my presence; he's just awfully quiet.

"Why are you so quiet?" I ask, trying to keep up with him on the stairs and not fall, break my neck, and die.

He turns to face me, with light in his eyes. "You talk enough for both of us."

I frown at the irony of his statement. We reach the second level of the house and he wades into what has to be Ever's room. I can tell by the painted wooden letters on her door that spell out *Everly*.

I watch as Reed places her onto her single bed, treating her like fine china. My frown morphs into a smile as he tucks her in and places a discreet kiss on her forehead before joining me at the door.

"Cute," I say.

He rolls his eyes as we descend the staircase, but I don't miss the way his cheeks light up. When we're downstairs, he pulls his jacket from the coatrack and a navy-blue beanie from the pocket of said jacket.

"What are you doing?"

"When was the last time you did something fun?"

"Uh, I don't know?" I frown.

"Put on your coat," he orders.

"Why?"

"Just put it on, okay?" He motions to my gloves resting on the lower shelf of the coatrack. "And the gloves."

Rolling my eyes, I do as he says, giving him a strange look the entire time.

He grabs my hand. "Come with me."

# CHAPTER 20

## *Asher*

I drag Wren outside in the freezing cold, my hand still clenched around hers. Judging from the way she shivers slightly, she probably needs something like cocoa, or a warm shower, and what I'm about to do next makes me feel half-bad.

When she's not looking my way, I scoop up some snow and mold it into a ball. Then, just as she turns to face me, I send it flying, watching as the thick ball of snow breaks on her face.

She shrieks, her honey eyes wide and her mouth open in shock. "*You did not just—*"

I try my best not to burst into laughter. "I did."

Annoyance is practically radiating off of her when she bends to scoop a decent amount of snow into the palm of her hand. I blink innocently, fully aware that I started a war.

That's when she hurls it, and it breaks before I have time to register and dodge it. I'll give her credit, it lands right on target:

my face. My skin freezes as bits of snow collapse in fragments on the collar of my jacket. I can see why she yelped now—shit actually stings.

I dust it off, my face now damp. When I glance up at her, her eyes widen by a fraction and she knows it's her cue to run.

Pure exhilaration runs through my veins as I cut through the snow after her. She slows down, a flash of a smile lighting up her face, probably thinking I won't make up ground too fast because of my knee.

She can't be more wrong.

A few seconds later, I'm ambushing her with snowballs from the back, the ice slipping into the crevices of her coat and down her back. Wren squeals the entire time and I can't help but laugh.

Gritting her teeth, she turns on her heels, managing to grab some snow in the process. She tries to chuck it at me but I reach her fast enough to stop her, holding her arms behind her back and pressing her flush against me.

I can feel her pulse quicken as I lean in closer and surprisingly, she does the same. There's something blooming in my chest, a bright, effulgent heat I can't explain. Then—

"Think fast, Reed!" she yells.

In a flash, she loosens her hands from my hold and smashes snow onto the sides of my face. I frown—a delayed reaction—and she laughs. Her cheeks are flushed and her honey eyes are bright as she stares up at me.

There are still bits of snow on my cheeks I haven't cared to wipe away, so she reaches up and brushes them away with her gloved hand. My frown morphs into a half smile. I blink. "You look cold."

"Nice observation skills," she mutters, rolling her eyes.

I chuckle and take off my beanie. "Here."

I place it on her damp hair, and the soft wool brushes her forehead. She's about to say something, but I get her with a huge snowball to the midriff. Wren lets out a frustrated growl as she trips over herself, the snow cushioning her fall. Laughing, I hold out a hand. She passes me a look that could kill, but takes my hand so I can pull her back to her feet.

"It looks better on you," I add, motioning to my beanie.

She wrinkles her nose. "I highly doubt that."

"Let's go inside," I say. "I'll make you hot chocolate."

"I hate you," she mumbles, shoving me in the shoulder.

I grin. "Keep telling yourself that."

∽

Staring at the white and pale-pink marshmallows bobbing like balloons on the surface of the mug, I figure I make a decent cup of cocoa.

"How is it?" I ask, while taking a gulp from my mug.

"Actually, pretty good."

My gaze lingers on her damp clothes. "Do you want me to get you something to change into? You're probably freezing in those."

She lifts her eyes to mine, probably to refuse. I don't wait for her response and pull her to the guest room before she can utter a protest. Disappearing into my mom's room, I scrounge through her wardrobe. I doubt Mom will mind. I only find one small pair of jeans. Back in my room, I find a small Nirvana shirt. Soon, I walk back to Wren with a neat pile of clothing folded in my arms.

"It was pretty hard to find something small enough," I say, "but I think this'll do."

She takes the pile from my hands gingerly with a silent nod of gratitude.

"I'll wait outside." I pause for a moment, light filling my eyes. "Unless, of course, you want me to stay."

She rolls her eyes and gives me a spirited shove, and I escort myself out of the room with a guffaw. After waiting for well over a few minutes, I'm impatient. "How long are you—"

Just then she opens the door, cutting me off. She's wearing my shirt, and her cheeks are rosy from the cold. I'm taken by surprise, and I can't help the words that fall out of my mouth. "You're stunning."

She blinks. "Oh, um . . . thank you."

My lips lift as I grab our coats and guide her outside again, trying to take my mind off how good she looks in my shirt. We sit on a low-lying wall above the snow. The sky is a black abyss, and the only source of light glints from the ornamental lights attached to the wall. Our legs dangle off the edge, and the silence is soon sliced by my voice.

"Why'd you always try avoiding me?" I ask, cautious as I turn to face her. She frowns. "Back when I met you outside the library," I elaborate. "And even after I picked Ev up from your place."

She glances at me, surprise and a little guilt swimming in her eyes. "I didn't try to *avoid* you."

I give her a pointed look, and she can tell I'm not buying it, because her expression turns sheepish. "Okay," she says. "Maybe I did, a little."

"Why?"

She sighs. "Remember middle school?"

"No." I laugh. I don't want to come off as an asshole, but I don't remember half the shit I did as a stupid middle schooler.

"Yeah, well," she rambles, "I do. I remember you sitting next to Drew McKay when he bullied me in front of everyone. And . . . I remember you laughing."

My chest tightens. Clearly, I'd blocked off middle school because I'd done more screwed up shit than I'd like to admit, but hearing this? It's like a knife to the fucking chest. I don't even remember the day, but it makes me feel worse, because all along I've wondered how Wren had formed her opinion of me—why she used to look at me with caution.

"I'm sorry," I say. "I know I might sound like a cliche, but I really have changed. I'm not the same dumb kid anymore."

"It's okay." She shrugs. "I would've forgotten about it if you didn't bring it up, anyway."

"No," I say, "you wouldn't have. You don't need to try and make me feel better." A bitter smile finds my lips at the irony. "Drew was the one who gave me this injury, you know?"

Wren's eyes are wide. "Really?"

I nod. "It's a long story. But basically, he thinks I snitched on him, stole his place, and still has hard feelings because his sister had a thing for me and I turned her down."

Her gaze is delicate. "Which isn't true?"

"Not entirely," I say. "I didn't snitch on him, I just refused to break into school. I *did* break his sister's heart, but I didn't mean to. And as far as taking his place is concerned . . ."

I glance at Wren. Her expression is rapt, her honey eyes soft and inviting. She hasn't said a single bad word, hasn't judged me even once. I trust her. And so when I turn to her, something compels me to come clean.

"My dad left us when I was young," I start. "He was smart. A great businessman. But he'd say the meanest, most degrading shit ever. And I was always trapped in this pathetic chase for his approval that I couldn't see. Not even when his words cut. Not even when he raised a hand to me.

"I sat with Drew in third grade. I really didn't want to, but I did anyway. He did some pretty awful things. But if he didn't like me, no one would. I joined him, and whatever he did, I didn't stop him." I pause, taking a breath. "I couldn't. And I know that makes me as bad as him, if not worse.

"It never occurred to me how fucked up it all was. Not when Dad left. Not when Drew left. Because all along, I was still liked. But recently with the injury . . . everything sort of hit me." I look at her. "And I'm learning not to care so much.

"And I'm still learning that . . . " I take a breath, gazing at Wren as she considers me. "The ones who really care are the ones that stick by your side. And you . . ."

Her eyes flicker up to meet mine. "Me?"

I draw back. "Nothing. That's all of it. After knowing everything, are you still willing to be . . ." I pause. "Friends?"

She stays quiet as I anticipate her response, frowning when she doesn't reply immediately. My chest cracks open, and she watches as remorse clouds my features. I almost regret telling her everything when—

"Yeah," she says. My head snaps up.

"Why would you think that I wouldn't want to be friends with you anymore?"

I sigh, running a hand through my hair as I keep talking. "Because I might hurt you. I might do something to hurt you while trying to impress other people or get them to like me. I've done that so many times I've lost count. You don't deserve that. No one does."

She shifts a little. "You're being too harsh on yourself. You've changed."

"But what if I haven't?" I ask.

"You *have*. I know you have. Because the Asher you're describing . . . it isn't the Asher I know. The you I know . . ." Her soft, hesitant gaze flickers my way. "He's highly confusing. And he frustrates the living daylights out of me. But he's also the one I trust. The one I—"

"*Asher!*"

The sound of my mother calling my name startles us both, and a faint flush creeps up Wren's neck as she stands abruptly, averting her gaze. I sigh for a moment, then rise to my feet. My mom calls for me again, and then we're walking back in, but my mind keeps replaying one thought.

*She trusts me too.*

# CHAPTER 21

## Wren

I'm sitting in the spare room, the one that used to belong to my sister, that's now a storage space with my old books on the shelves and my abandoned art easel. And I'm just staring—just marveling over and over again at the expensive paint placed on one of the many scattered boxes of my old belongings.

*I won't give up on something that makes me that happy that easily.* I mull over Asher's words. *If there's a possibility that I can still do it? I'd make sure to do everything to make that possibility a reality.*

Maybe I'm internally mourning because I can't afford to pick up a paintbrush. Maybe it's more the fact that I really, really want to. Maybe Reed's words have been replaying in my mind so often they've begun to make me sick.

I know that this could make or break me. That the simple

act of holding a paintbrush—layering paint, feeling it on my fingers—has the potential to cause so much harm. To me. To the progress I've made so far.

I could relapse, my PTSD flaring if the images I painted magnified the nightmares. But then again, maybe nothing would happen and I could go back to doing the thing I loved most without fearing that it was a trigger. High risk, high reward. I take a deep breath and make the decision.

I'm going to paint.

Which is precisely why I, the girl who never voluntarily wakes up earlier than seven in the morning, am positioned on the stool in front of my art easel at 5:52 a.m., paintbrush in hand.

Twirling the brush ever so slightly between my fingers, I stare out the window. The sky is the palest shade of pink, soft against the shadows of the trees. The sun hasn't come up yet, but I still feel an unaccustomed warmth within. I can't describe it, but as soon as I dip the brush into the color on the palette, I know exactly what I'm going to paint.

I fall in love with the creamy texture of acrylic paint, the give and take between the brush and stretched canvas. Pigment on top of pigment, varying shades colliding with each other to form shapes. There's something honest and authentic about the art of painting. It feels organic and true. Earthy. Visceral, almost.

The feeling is foreign yet so natural. Pushing pigment around on a stretched canvas makes me feel alive.

I've been feeling better recently. The past two years have torn me to pieces, until all that was left of me was shredded fragments of raw, discarded paper.

The accident.

Not being able to say good-bye to either of them.

But I'm healing. Slowly. Piece by piece. Stroke by stroke. I can paint. I can do it.

I can save myself.

And just like that, paint fills the canvas in vibrant shades. Time rushes by, visible as my hands and fingers get worn out and gradually smudged with contrasting shades of color. As time passes, the coats of paint start to dry in refined layers on the canvas.

The quietness and tranquility of the room shelter me, and I drop the paintbrush, telling myself that it's never going to be perfect.

Then I resort to staring, losing myself in the focal point of my artwork. I chose to paint something that I could never criticize, something I could never hate. Taking a deep, contented breath, I leave my canvas to dry further and stride downstairs to appease my growling stomach. I'd been painting for four hours straight but my veins are still pulsating with bubbly liquid.

"Someone's up earlier than I expected." My mother's voice fills the air, and I'm pretty sure there's a distinct twinkle to her eye when she speaks. "I heard you tinkering around at six in the morning from down here. Are you all right?"

"Thanks for mocking my sleep schedule, Mom," I murmur dryly, pouring out my Froot Loops.

Amusement douses her features. "What made you think I was mocking you and your diurnal mannerisms? I'd never do such a thing."

"Diurnal?" I scoff. "And you say *I'm* a science geek."

"But you are. Remember how happy you were when you got an A on that one—"

Just then the doorbell rings, serving as a pause to our light conversation. Mom turns swiftly in the direction of the door, uttering a quick, "I'll get it."

I hear faint chattering from the door, and a voice that's marginally familiar. The owner walks in no less than a few minutes later, my mom trailing not far behind him.

I've seen Asher almost every day of winter break. Since Mia's still away in Vermont, and Brody and Zach are spending their ten-day breaks away as well, the two of us have resorted to spending the bulk of our free time with each other, and with Ever. I don't even know if that's a good or bad thing—maybe a bit of both.

Seeing that I finished all my college applications, I have much more free time. Writing essay upon essay was one of the most challenging things I've had to do, but now that I'm done, I just have to play the waiting game.

Reed winks discreetly, and his gaze coasts down my pastel pink pajamas in a way that it definitely shouldn't with my mom two steps away. I roll my eyes in response, my mouth too full of Froot Loops to supply him with a sarcastic comment.

He walks over, swipes the bowl of cereal from my hands in a swift motion, and proceeds to *eat* from it right in front of me.

I gasp audibly, while he just pulls one of his casual smirks. My mother stands to my side, still sipping her apparently piping hot coffee, an amused smile playing along her lips.

"You're not going to do anything about this?" I say to her, casting a momentary glance at the devil incarnate before redirecting to my mother.

"I'm okay with anything that doesn't physically, emotionally, or mentally harm you, honey. And as far as I can tell, the boy isn't ticking any of those boxes," she says. Then she gives Asher a wary glance. "Yet."

"Your argument is flawed on so many levels, Mom," I say, but just she smiles, still amused, and walks away.

"You're going to have to sterilize that spoon!" I holler at her retreating figure. "Or maybe just incinerate it to stop anyone from catching hepatitis or something!" The last thing I hear is her muffled laugh in the distance.

"I'm right here, you know," Asher says then, somewhat offended. "By the way, your mom loves me."

"Just like the hundreds of other girls at our school," I mutter inaudibly under my breath, and I have to hold myself back from rolling my eyes for like the tenth time since he walked in or they might fall out or something. "I heard you two talking at the door. What did she say?"

He grins. "She told me to be careful around her daughter and that if I'm planning on hurting you any time soon, I should probably rethink my decision."

My eyes widen. "What did you say?"

"I don't really plan ahead most of the time, ma'am."

I huff a stunned laugh, shaking my head in disbelief. His attention turns back to my cereal, which he *stole* from me. "I'm so used to eating healthy things like oats and fruit for the hockey season. This stuff's pretty good."

I narrow my eyes in response. "You *love* annoying me, no?"

"Sure," he replies, winking suggestively. "But I'd like to do more than just annoy you."

That's when I splutter and start choking on air—because that's how attractive I am, naturally. I make a mental note to train myself to stay calm in situations like these. He laughs openly at my reaction, obviously gaining something from it.

I clear my throat. "Why are you here?"

"I needed to ask you something." He pulls out a rectangular piece of paper, the page creasing beneath his fingers. There's

185

vibrant pictures of a lake and a forest on the page, and I squint, trying to read the fine print. He notices, then recites the words on it. "'Waterfront Lake.'"

"What about it?"

"Come with me," he says with a slow grin. "It's always been the guys and me, a sort of silent tradition we follow by driving down south for spring break. But it'll be the last time we do it before we leave for college. I want you to come with us."

I blink slowly as his words sink in. It seems like such a special place to him. And he wants me to come with? "I . . . don't know."

The smile on his face falters and he slowly withdraws the hand that holds the crumpled paper. I chew on the inside of my cheek, feeling a bit guilty. "But I'm willing to give it a chance."

For a moment, there's just silence as he looks at me with a ghost smile, as if he's trying to figure something out. As if he's trying to figure *me* out.

Then he snaps out of it and nudges me in the shoulder. "So how long do I wait before I get a painting of my hot self? You know, all Victorian, *Mona Lisa* style?" he jokes, pointing at the paint smudges on my arms.

I smile at the fact that he noticed. "Actually . . ." I drawl.

He eyes the look on my face, and his expression breaks into disbelief. "*No way*. You actually painted a picture of me?"

I laugh then, largely fueled by the look on his face. "No." I scoff, still amused. "I *did* paint something, but that something isn't you, although it has some relation to you."

"When did you get the time to paint anyway?"

"This morning," I pipe, tying my hair up using a stranded blue ribbon from the countertop.

"Right," he says, eyes narrow like he doesn't entirely believe me.

"You don't believe me?" I lift a brow, contemplating whether I should let him see my fresh canvas. I wonder what his reaction will be, and whether he'll like it. But I guess I'll never know if I don't give it a shot. Eventually, my mind gets the better of me as I grab his arm and tug him to the stairs. "C'mon. I'll show you."

We end up at the entrance of the room, and when I realize that my hand is still encircling Asher's wrist, I quickly retract, creating a little more distance between us to lessen the chances of internal disaster. It doesn't seem like he notices, though.

Stepping toward my easel, I extend my hand over the thin sheet covering the canvas. Slowly, I lift the sheet, revealing the color underneath. I turn to see some sort of reaction from Asher, but instead, I find him just standing there, completely silent, and I begin to doubt my decision to show him. Just as I'm about to throw a comment about it not being perfect, he speaks.

"Holy shit!" he exclaims, his blue eyes bright. "You painted my sister."

"Yeah," I confirm, releasing a breath I never knew I was holding. "I painted Ever."

"It's . . ." He edges closer to me and the canvas, his eyes not wavering from the painting. "It's *amazing*."

An awkward smile spreads on my lips as my gaze sweeps over my art again. Sure, I'd spent a whole lot of time on it. But it really isn't as perfect as he's making it to be. I still love it, though, because I can't help the warm feeling that spreads in my chest every time I glance at it.

You can make out the specks of hazel in Ever's large eyes, the pink tinge in her cheeks. I'd especially paid a lot of attention to her hair, the locks intertwining around her adorable face.

"You going to make this a career one day?" Asher asks, his

serious gaze still fixated on the piece while he looks like he's trying his best to refrain from touching the now-dry layers of acrylic paint.

"I don't think so," I reply honestly. "I can't really imagine making art for money."

"Understandable," he replies. His eyes shift to me, connecting with my own. I've never been a fan of eye contact, but I hold his stare for a while. I bite my bottom lip, averting my gaze in an attempt to break the awkward moment.

"Don't do that," he says.

I lift my head to face him, with my brows scrunched. "What?"

"That," he says, pointing to my lips. "Biting your lip. It's distracting."

Rolling my eyes, I move away from him to place a cover over the canvas to prevent it from getting dusty and damaged. But really, all I'm trying to do is prevent him from getting an edge over me again. I am *not* going to get all flustered over this idiot.

"You know what I noticed?" Asher calls, randomly.

"What?"

"You don't blush."

I'm a bit impressed that he noticed, but I don't show it. "Yeah. It's because my cutaneous blood is deeper, because basically, my capillaries don't widen."

He smirks. "Since you seem to have a scientific explanation for most things, why don't we try out a little experiment?"

I narrow my eyes. "What do you mean?"

He says nothing then, merely taking a tiny step closer to me. I stare at him, as if doing so will make him stop edging toward me. It obviously doesn't work, though, because he continues his little venture forward from the other side of the room.

"Does this make you blush?" he says, at a sizable distance from me.

I frown, refusing to comply with his stupid *experiment*. "No."

Instead of backing away, he walks even closer to me. I feel my palms getting increasingly clammy, and I squirm under his concentrated gaze.

"How about now?" he says, now at an arm's length from me.

"Nope," I manage, feeling the edge of the desk against my palms behind me as I lean against it.

He takes a huge stride this time so that I have no other choice but to make eye contact. I can feel him inhaling, his chest not far from mine. He leans in closer, sending my stomach into a catastrophic turmoil.

"Does this make you blush?" he whispers, sending shivers down my spine.

But before he can advance, and before I can think against it, I'm yelling, "Mom!"

And just like that, he rips away from me faster than a wildfire spreads, a look of panic taking over his pretty face. When he realizes he's just been duped, the look he gives me is predatory.

All I do is laugh, though. My laughter is literally uncontrollable, and I have to lift a hand to cover my mouth. Because for the first time in forever, I've outsmarted Asher Reed at his own game.

My mom appears at the door, concern written on her face. "Yes?"

I clamp down on my jaw. Clearly, I didn't think this through. "Nothing," I lie. "I . . . uh, tripped but I'm fine now."

She gives me a wary nod, her gaze sliding over to Asher. "Make sure this door stays open."

I nod, chewing back my smile. "It'll be open."

She nods slowly, lingering in the hallway for a while before her footsteps head downstairs. When I turn back to face Reed, I grin. "Oh. My. God," I wheeze. "Your face, the look . . . priceless."

He smiles to himself as his cool, calm demeanor returns. "You know, you really shouldn't have done that," he says, his voice eerily composed.

"Why?" I chuckle. "Because you're going to make me blush?" I snuffle unattractively, breaking into another round of laughter.

"No," he says, grinning evilly, pulling something out. "Because I found this seventh-grade diary and I'm thinking it'll be quite interesting to read it. Hmm . . . where should I start?"

"What the heck?!" My eyes widen and I focus on the pink diary in his hand. I lunge for my diary, but more importantly, my seventh-grade self's dignity. "Give me that!"

It's futile. Each time I reach to claim the book, Asher dodges smoothly with his stupid athletic ability, or elevates my diary higher than it's possible for me to reach.

Then, he does exactly what I dreaded.

He opens it.

"'*Dear diary!*'" he says in a high-pitched girly voice, which makes me want to strangle the life out of him. "'Today in math I sat next to Luke. He's actually really cute, with those big, nerdy glasses and supercool pens. I don't know, though, boys are weird.'"

I cover my eyes and groan. "*Stop!*"

He doesn't listen. Just continues in that annoying high-pitched voice that I do *not* freaking sound like. "'Dear diary, today was most definitely the worst day of my entire life. It was really embarrassing, and everyone laughed at me. I just feel like burying myself in a human-sized hole. It all started when I got up from my seat . . .'"

My eyes widen as I realize what comes next and before I can stop myself, I pounce on him, struggling for my diary. He just smirks and pulls it out of my reach once again, the jerk.

I shuffle over him, still struggling for that stupid diary I regret writing when I trip—which serves me right for lying to my mom earlier, I guess. He stumbles, which means I stumble on top of him too.

If only it's as graceful as it sounds, which unfortunately for me, it really, really isn't.

My eyes widen when I register our position, which isn't proper in any way.

I'm currently straddling him, and he's spread flat on the floor, his hair spread across his forehead. He stares at me, his deep-blue eye scouring every pore on my face. My heart beats in self-consumed fury, scorching hot, skin tingling from the contact. I can feel his abdominal muscles shift under my hands.

I might just be overreacting, but imagine this: the first few seconds of a roller coaster, as the cart is climbing up the lift hill. You're leaning back as your heart is pumping in your ears, and you're building up the force to scream, and you're wondering if you can't turn around now, if you can't press the Stop button and go back, or if time could just freeze, and you could at least stay in this spot for a little while longer.

That's how being with Asher feels. That's how it *always* feels, but right now, the feeling is magnified about a thousand times.

Asher's eyes are bright as he stares up at me. "Gee, Martin, if you wanted me that bad, you could've just asked."

"Shut up," I stutter, frozen to the spot as heat surges to the surface of my skin.

"Wren?"

"W-what?" I falter, and my voice is followed by a silence occupied only by the sound of my erratically beating heart.

"I might not be able to get you to blush." He smirks. "But if you need anyone to get your heart racing, you can call me anytime."

᠊ᢧ᠊

After Reed leaves, and I get over the near heart attack he induced, I venture downstairs to ask Mom about the Waterfront. I can't believe I'm even considering it, and I'd be lying if I said a part of me isn't hoping she won't agree. Peering into the kitchen, I find no trace of her.

"Who are you looking for?"

I yelp, fumbling on the last stair and trip over my feet. Luckily, I catch myself before I fall. Mom stands in front of me, an amused smile on her face.

I throw my hands in the air. "I could've died!"

She lifts a brow. "I think you're being a little dramatic."

It's silent for a while. Mostly because I'm conjuring ways to ask my mother if I can go. It would just be so much more convenient if I didn't have to go, because then I wouldn't have to *ask*.

"Wren?"

Right. I'd been silent for a whole minute now. I snap out of it, going straight for the kill. "Asher asked me if I wanted to go to the Waterfront with him and some friends for spring break."

My mom's expression is pensive.

A small frown sits on my face. "You don't like him?"

"No, no. I do. He's a nice boy. I just want to make sure you're comfortable. And . . . I noticed you haven't been wearing that hoodie you have an obsession with as often."

"I don't have an obsession," I counter.

There's disbelief in her features. "You wore that thing for a month straight. At one point I had to practically rip it off of you while you were sleeping so that I could wash it."

"That's because it was cold."

She clucks her tongue. "It was the peak of summer." And then she switches the topic so fast I get whiplash. "Do *you* like him?"

"Who?" I blurt dumbly.

She gives me a blank look.

"Oh . . ." I swallow, and because I know my mom can read me like a book, I feign nonchalance. "Besides stealing my cereal, and a few annoying comments, he isn't that bad."

My mom sighs. "What are the friends' names?"

"Brody and Zach."

And that wary glance returns. "They're both boys?"

I lift my hand to the nape of my neck. "Well, yeah. I guess."

Hesitation marks her features. "I'll speak to Victoria about it."

I twist my arms around my mother's body, hugging her. "Thanks, Mom."

She just shakes her head, but I can feel her smile. "I just never believed I'd see the day that my teenage daughter would actually ask me to leave the house."

～

Time rushes by uneventfully, and I hear nothing from the colleges I applied to. It's a day before I leave for the Waterfront, and I'm sitting at my desk by the window. Studying. The trees have begun to bloom again, but only barely, and the last of the snow has melted.

My eyes skim over the pages flooding my desk as a buzz shakes the scattered papers. I let out a sigh. I hate when I have to move through the mess to find my lost phone. The light shining from my screen catches my attention. Scooping up my phone, I find a text from Mia.

MIA: *Can you pack a hair dryer for me? Mine may have just exploded*

Behind me, my suitcase is very open and very empty. I got it out yesterday, and I was supposed to pack. Unfortunately, good ol' procrastination paid a visit, and I'm still unpacked. But it's only eight at night, and I tell myself I have more than enough time to gather all my clothes.

Unlike Mia, I pack light. She's convinced that you need to pack for every possible situation. Which is literally impossible. When she went to her gran's place for the spring break last year, she took a unicorn floatie. I was fine with that until she told me that there wasn't even a pool.

Rolling out of my chair and onto my bed, I pick up a book from the side. Turning the room lights off and putting my lamp on, I make myself comfortable. I move the pillows around before opening to the page I'm on. After reading for a few hours, the dim lights in my room lull me to sleep.

～

"Wren."

I pull my pillow over my head, trying to block out the noise.

"Wren, honey! Wake up!"

Groaning when my sheets are ripped off me, I flip over, my hair covering my face. Slowly, I sit up. I bring the back of my hand to my eyes, rubbing them. A glance at the clock near me tells me it's eight.

"Ugh, Mom, it's so early," I groan, yanking my sheets from her grasp. "I'm going back to sleep."

"Wren!" She yanks the sheets back. "Mia's here."

I spring back up. "What?"

"You're going to that Waterfront place today, aren't you?"

Waterfront.

Oh fudge. *Waterfront.*

I shoot out of the bed and push my mom out of the room. "Tell her I'll take a while."

I take the quickest shower in the history of showers, and when I run back to my room, Mia's there, but she isn't doing much to help. She's sitting at the edge of my bed eating potato chips.

"Mia! Quit eating and help me pack."

She stares at me. "How many times have I reminded you not to leave things to the last minute?"

"Several," I admit. "Now help me!"

"Ugh." She sets down the packet of chips. "Fine."

She starts picking at the clothes I hastily threw into my suitcase before my shower. "Have you packed your toothbrush?"

"Yep."

"Underwear?"

"Yep."

"The hair dryer?"

"Yep."

"Swimsuit?"

"Ye—" I pause. "What?"

"Swimsuit. I'm pretty sure you're going to need one of those."

"What? Why?"

She stares at me. "Uh, because it's a swimming site?"

"Really? I don't think I'm going to swim."

"C'mon, Wren! It's spring break, live it up a bit! It'll be fun. Trust me on this one, okay?"

"Okay, fine." I groan. "But it's your job to find me a swimsuit in there. I haven't used one of those for months."

"Wait a second, didn't I buy you one?" she asks, after thinking about it for a moment.

I frown. "No."

"Yes! Yes, I did!"

The frown remains on my face as I watch her rummage through my drawer fiercely. I'm still wondering what she's talking about.

"Here it is." She's holding a black one-piece. "I found it, look!"

Then, my mom hollers from downstairs. "Wren, Mia!"

My eyes widen and so do Mia's. I didn't expect them to be *this* early. Mia bids me a temporary farewell, leaving me to zip my bag up myself.

The traitor.

I can't help but feel like I've forgotten to pack something, and it picks at my brain before I force myself to stop thinking about it. I've stuffed everything into a small bag, which means that I have to go to great lengths to actually zip it up.

Sighing, I sit on my bag to squash it closed. My fingers find the zip and I struggle to get it to move, the contents of the bag overflowing. *Ugh*, why don't I just use a bigger bag?

I let out an animalistic groan, one that *does not* sound good at all. Of course, Asher finds this a perfect time to enter my room. He raises a brow. "You all right there, birdie?"

"I'm fine," I huff.

Finally, the zipper moves. I haul myself off the bag, and it bulges again because of the absence of my weight. Asher gives me a smile before lifting my luggage easily. He makes his way out of my room, calling out behind him, "You can stop checking me out now."

I suck in a guilty breath, cringing as I follow him out of the room silently. I follow Reed downstairs, greeted by the sight of my mother, whose gaze settles on him.

"Victoria is one call away, mister," Mom warns him.

Asher smiles. "I'll keep that in mind."

"What about the rooms?"

"Mia and Wren will share one cabin while the boys and I'll share another one."

"All right." Mom gives him a grim smile in return before she looks at me. "Take care of my baby, will you?" My mother glances at Asher. "She can be quite clumsy at times."

Asher grins. "Will do."

What the heck? "I'm right here," I scoff.

She gives me a slight push toward the door, and I move along with it. "Have fun, honey."

As I stride outside, I immediately notice the red car parked at the curb. Zach's leaning against it as he speaks to Mia, and Brody's packing something into the back of the vehicle.

Asher joins him while I stare at the car. It's a Rolls Royce, and it's a shiny red—the type you see in movies. It's vintage and so pretty I could stare at it forever. The roof of the car is absent; the seats are a neutral beige shade.

"Someone likes the car." Zach smirks when he notices me staring. "Don't drool."

I hold back a smile. "Not my fault it's prettier than you."

Mia snorts, and Zach places a hand over his heart. "You girls wound me, you really do."

Brody closes the trunk. "I'm driving."

To this, Zach scoffs. "Sorry, but who's the owner of this baby again?"

Brody glares at his friend. "Your mom."

"Can you just start the car?" Asher mutters.

"Mia's shotgun," Zach says, his eyes landing on me. "Sorry, Wren, but you're stuck in the back with those two."

I frown at him, not sure whether to take that in a good or a bad way. Mia takes it the latter, shoving him in the gut.

"Ow!" He slides into his seat with a frown. "You've got to stop reading *Fifty Shades*, babe."

"I don't read that!" Mia yells. She frowns as she slides into her seat, crossing her hands over her chest. Zach sneaks a kiss on her cheek, and she rolls her eyes with a small smile.

I hold back a smile of my own as I open the door then take the seat next to Brody so that he's sandwiched by Asher and me. Finally, Zach starts the car, and with a slight purr of the engine, we're in motion.

The road before us is a tarmac ribbon, a velvety black winding shape. A white line running down the center is eaten ferociously by our car. I plug in my earphones and play Troye Sivan's *Blue Neighbourhood* on shuffle.

༄

I jolt back to reality when we hit a bump. Peeling my eyes open, I register the smell of bubble gum. Suddenly, I'm given the sight of Asher staring down at me. He's smiling—so gentle and soft that

I want to smile back. Until I realize my hands are circled around his arm, half of my body leaning against his. I can feel the warmth emanating from him.

Wait, where's Brody?

I unravel myself from Asher, and a frown appears on his face. I notice Brody then, sitting where Asher had been.

"Why did you two swap seats?" I ask.

Brody turns at the sound of my voice, glancing at Reed. They stare at each other, each silently motioning for the other to explain.

Zach breaks the silence. "Asher wanted to sit—"

Reed swats him on the head. "I won a bet."

I give him a confused look, glancing at Zach, who's sporting an amused grin, as if he knows Asher has left out some important details. He drums his fingers along to a song, though, not revealing a thing. Maybe it's a stupid bro code thing. I let it go, exhaling.

Asher's thigh brushing against my own sends tingles through my body. My heart is still beating a little faster than normal, but he doesn't seem to know or acknowledge it. He's too preoccupied with his phone.

The sky's shifted into a velvet blue by the time we close in on a sign that reads *Waterfront Lake Resort,* and all three boys let out a feral cheer that makes me jump.

I notice the lake just touching the edge of the forest as the car stops amid a collection of cabins. We get out, and I stretch. My hair tumbles down my shoulders, my ribbon suspiciously missing. Asher gives me a mischievous glance.

"I'm going to go fetch some kindling," he says. "Want to come?"

I shrug. "Sure."

We wander into the forest, and I bend to pick up a big chunk of wood.

"Hey," I say, "there aren't any wolves in this forest, right?"

Asher winks. "I'm the only wolf around, Little Red."

I roll my eyes, but that's when I realize something.

I forgot to pack my hoodie.

I haven't been wearing it as much lately, but I still feel insecure without it. I swallow down the anxiety and try not to think about it. I'll be able to manage without it. Hopefully.

When we get back to the campsite, the car is unloaded, and Mia, Zach, and Brody are sitting along the raised area around the nonexistent fire.

"It's about time," Brody quips.

Asher unloads the wood, forming a girdle. He sets it alight with a lighter. Brody turns his attention to the developing fire, blowing slowly into the red coal. Within minutes, the coals glow orange, and Asher reaches to his pile of wood for some kindling.

"I brought graham crackers and marshmallows, bitchachos!" Zach yells, lifting up a bag of pink and white marshmallows. "Time to roast these babies!"

Grinning, I grab one as everyone else does, and join them around the campfire. Asher takes his last, taking a seat next to me. We make eye contact for a few seconds before I tear my gaze away, poking my marshmallow into my stick and extending it into the fire.

When my dad and Emma were still around, we'd go camping at least once a year. Making marshmallow s'mores brings with it a feeling of nostalgia, but I swallow it down.

I miss my hoodie.

I want it here with me, now.

Absentmindedly, I touch my marshmallow, not even considering the fact that it's really, really hot.

"Ow!" I hiss, retracting my fingers. Asher's eyes flick to me, and when he notices, he shakes his head and grabs my hand, inspecting it. He blows a little on my finger, but by then there's no pain at all.

I remember the time something similar happened—when I tripped and hurt my hand and Asher took it into his own and brushed off all the stones. Just like before, pure concern fills his eyes. It makes me smile a little, and I can't hide it.

"It'll be fine," he says.

He doesn't even notice me smiling.

# CHAPTER 22

## Asher

I'm lured awake by the scent of something cooking. Edging out of bed, I check the time on my phone. It reads 12:30 p.m., and I groan when I find it hasn't charged fully overnight. Maybe I didn't push the charger in enough last night. Perfect.

Taking a glance around, I notice the two empty beds next to me. I open the door of my cabin and step out, finding Brody placing pieces of wood in a pile. Chandler's sleeping on a camping chair. When he wakes up, he's definitely going to complain about his back.

I stride over to him and flick his forehead. His eyebrows furrow as a string of expletives leave his mouth, clearly not happy to be woken up so early. Stifling a laugh, I walk over to Brody. He's making burgers, I quickly find out, which was what woke me up.

Brody lifts his gaze to me. "Get the buns from the box in the car?"

Nodding, I tuck a hand in my sweats and stroll to the car parked out front.

"Yo, wait," Brody shouts, pulling the keys from his khaki shorts and chucking them over to me. "Here's the keys."

Eventually, I reach the car. Upon opening the trunk, I see I'll have to forage through countless brown boxes. What the hell? Where did Zach and Brody think we were going? Fucking France? I should've known they'd do something like this, though. They always overpack.

Brody didn't even tell me anything specific to help me find the buns. Hell, now I have to go through all of the boxes. I start with the first one, pulling out batteries. Christ knows when we'll need them. I throw them back in.

Finally, I spot a plastic bag with several buns in it. Whipping it out, I slam the trunk closed and lock the car. Once I hear a loud beep and the clicking of the locks, I head back over to Brody, who's still cooking.

"Your buns." I fling the packet his way before taking a seat next to a snoring Zach.

Brody looks at me with his eyebrow raised. "What did the buns do to you?"

"Are you kidding me? It's a fuckin' maze back there."

He snorts. "What? We organized everything."

I huff. "*Oh* yeah. So tell me why the buns were packed with a case of beer, a Monopoly box, and bars of soap?"

Brody laughs, and Zach finally stirs awake at the sound. He rubs at his eyes, stretching in his camp chair. Just when I'm about to comment on how dangerous that is, the chair tips and Chandler falls straight to the ground.

Whining about how his body hurts, he gets up on his feet.

Brody laughs and I just shake my head. Zach groans. "If I wasn't up then, I'm up now."

"Why were you sleeping out here?" I ask, my eyes hopping between the two.

Brody opens his mouth to say something, but Zach's quicker. "This little asshole throws my sheets off of me at five in the morning because he *can't sleep* and *doesn't want to sit outside alone*."

I snicker. "Is baby B scared of the dark?"

"Piss off," Brody murmurs. "I'm too used to waking up early for practice."

It's silent for a while, until I notice the two are in some sort of eye signal battle.

"What's going on?" I ask. Zach violently pushes Brody with his shoulder. Knight responds with a glare. I raise a brow. "So?"

"We were wondering how your knee's doing," Brody says. "You know, after the surgery and all."

I raise a brow. "That's it?"

Zach interrupts before I can say anything else. "Well, yeah. Last time we asked you almost bit our heads off, dude."

Bringing a hand to the nape of my neck, I try to explain myself. "I admit I didn't take the news too well . . ."

"So, is it good?" Brody asks.

I nod. "I can go up the stairs normally without walking like I have a stick up my ass. So yeah, I'd say it's doing pretty well." I pause. "But I haven't told Coach anything yet."

Their eyes widen.

"You should tell him as soon as we get back," Zach says.

"Yeah." I nod. "Yeah. I will."

A few minutes later, Mia joins us, offering to help out. We're still busy making burgers when the sound of crunching leaves from the direction of the girls' cabin catches my attention. I turn my head toward the sound. Wren lifts her eyes until they meet mine, and my chest constricts.

"Hey," she says, peeking over at the pan on the grill. "What are you guys making?"

"Breakfast burgers." Brody grins. "Made by yours truly."

Zach scoffs. "Shut it, dickface. I made most of it."

"Sure, you did," Brody and I say.

"Aw, it's okay, Zachy," Mia says. "We all know you're a terrible cook."

Zach's features soften in a way that's almost shy. Almost. After a while, Brody serves a burger to Wren on a white plate, bowing a little. "Milady."

She chuckles, receiving the plate with equal grace and a little curtsy. "Thank you, good sir."

I'm annoyed. It's irrational, but I can't help it. As if he can sense it, Brody's gaze flicks to me. I ignore him, looking away. I don't miss the grin that creeps onto his face.

After we're done eating, Mia promptly drags Wren to their cabin, while Wren groans. "What *now*?"

The guys and I head to ours after cleaning up. I change into a pair of black swimming trunks and carry a spare T-shirt I can change into later for hiking. Knight whispers something to Chandler, whose eyes find mine immediately and widen in reaction to Brody's comment. They stand next to me, staring at me with weird smiles on their faces. There's an awkward silence.

"What?" I finally crack, turning my head to face them.

"When are you going to admit that you're in love with Wren?" Brody asks.

I frown. "I don't know what you're talking about, man."

Zach makes a disgruntled sound at the back of his throat, and Knight just looks at me, tilting his head. "So, you don't mind if I go ask her out?"

My jaw clenches, because no fucking way I'm letting *that* happen. "Fine, I like her. Happy?"

Zach shrugs. "Not so hard to admit, was it?"

"No." I narrow my eyes. "But I swear to God, if you two say anything, you'll end up joining the club of people in a cast this year. Got it?"

Brody grins. "Got it, lover boy."

Leaves crunch and I follow the sound to the figures walking over. Wren's wearing a thin cardigan over her bathing suit, and she looks . . . perfect. So much so that I don't even notice Mia standing next to her, phone and sunscreen in hand. Wren, on the other hand, is holding a book.

I know she likes reading but seriously? A book to the lake? The crazy is strong with this one.

When they near us, Brody and Zach are too busy with their own little banter to even notice them. Mia breaks up their conversation by muttering, "Shall we leave?"

Immediately, that draws their attention to the girls. Wren's eyes meet mine, before her gaze drops. She sucks in a breath.

"You can stop staring now," Mia murmurs dryly.

Brody laughs and Zach just smirks. I roll my eyes at the two of them, edging closer to Wren as we start walking down to the lake. "You look good."

"W-what?" she stutters.

I laugh, angering her further. "Ah, birdie. You're so incredibly cute."

Finally, we reach the shore, and I walk over to the guys, who are already in the water. The lake's a serene, flat body of water. From the tall pines around the edge there's no sound, no movement of branches. Even the birds are quiet. This place has been magical for as long as I can remember.

Wren settles on the bordering bank, and I watch from the water as she reads, getting lost in the bone-colored paper. I give her around ten minutes, watching as Zach teaches Mia how to use the rope swing. But Wren makes no attempt to even *look* in the direction of the water.

Before I can decide against it, I'm walking out of the lake, water sluicing off me. She doesn't notice me until I lift her up from the ground, and her book flies from her hands.

"*Ah!*" she shrieks. "*My book!*"

I laugh, and wade into the lake.

"Let *go* of me!"

"Your choice," I mutter, dropping her into the water.

Before she figures out what's going on, she opens her mouth to scream, but it's futile, because it only means she's inhaling water. I dive in after her. She resurfaces, a coughing spectacle, spitting out water and rubbing furiously at her eyes. To be fair, the water *is* pretty cold, and it probably comes as a shock to her body. I stifle a chuckle as her hair sticks to her face.

"Are you *insane*?" she yells, staring up at me, the light catching in the honey of her eyes. Her shirt got lost somewhere in the process, leaving her in just the one-piece.

I lean closer to her, moving through the water, leaving a trail of goose bumps on her skin. I grin. "Only for you."

She takes this as an opportunity to swing her elbow back and bring it forward again in the water, splashing half of my body. I'm already lunging for her, but she disappears underwater.

My arm encloses her underwater, and she tries to wrench it away, but I pull her to me, closer and closer and closer until we can't breathe any longer and we're forced to resurface.

And when I do, she's staring into my eyes, her face covered by rivulets of water. We're close now, so close I can feel her chest on mine—feel her small hands on my chest. I send a hand through her wet hair, pushing it away from her face. I lean in then, closer and closer and closer until I can almost taste her lips.

And then she pulls away, smiling as if to say "Payback," before she wades back to the shore.

I flash my eyes at her back, about to pass a comment when—

"Brody! Get off your fat ass and help me get stuff for the hike," Zach yells, distracting us. He makes his way to us with a towel in his right hand. He's already pulled on a shirt over his swimming trunks.

"Says the one with the biggest ass," Brody mutters as he changes.

Zach scoffs. "Oh, come on, you know you want me."

"Yeah. I want you—to get a life," Brody responds, with a pointed look.

"Whoa, whoa," Wren says, covering herself with her towel. When our gazes meet, she looks away. "Wait. We're going on a hike?"

They both turn to face her.

"Yes." Zach stares at me as if it's the most obvious thing in the world. "We are."

Mia appears then, with a towel of her own and half dressed already. "Wren, why do you look like you're going to puke any second?"

"Because we're going hiking, apparently? Which means long distances and *energy*. You know I'm sports deficient."

"Quit being a drama queen." Mia laughs. "It'll be fine."

THE HOODIE GIRL

I sneak up to Wren and ruffle her wet hair. "Yeah, what she said. You're too lazy for your own good."

"Excuse you." She swats my hand away and narrows her eyes. "I'll have you know I'm actually extremely busy training for a Netflix marathon."

Mia snorts and chucks clothes at Wren.

The boys and I gather all the stuff and shove it into bags. After cleaning up and throwing on some sneakers, we're ready to go. Wren glances around at all of us, realizing everyone's carrying more stuff than her, so she picks up a packed bag, slinging it across her shoulder in an attempt to seem busy.

I detach the bag from her shoulders and sling it across mine. "That's mine."

She rolls her eyes and huffs, walking behind Zach, who's already started off. The plan is to hike until a certain point, then set up the food for lunch. On the way, Brody chucks Wren a water bottle, and she looks surprised when she catches it.

"Nice catch," he says.

Knight turns to face me. "You good to hike?"

"Yeah." My knee's been doing pretty good lately, and maybe it's just in my head, but it might even be stronger than my uninjured one after all the concentrated therapy it's been getting. According to Dr. Greene, it's mostly healed now—I just need to be cautious and make sure that I don't screw it up.

Brody slows his pace to stay behind me. There are no roads or buildings, nothing except for a dirt path leading through the wild to the top of the mountain. Only one dirt path. The woods seclude us from the rest of the world.

There's a calm flow of the streams and a never-ending supply of fresh air cools my skin.

"It's when you get to the larger rocks that you know you're getting close to the top," Brody explains to Wren. "It gets more fun."

I think she wants to disagree with him on that one, because she looks like she wants to collapse and never wake up again. She leans down and rubs at her calves.

"See?" Mia cocks her head. "It's not that bad."

"Look at this." Wren points to herself. "Look at me. I'm *dying*. I'm slowly deteriorating, and you say *it's not that bad*?"

Mia shrugs. "You're just hungry."

I glance at Wren, who looks as if she's about to argue with her, but then closes her mouth, realizing it's true. I chuckle under my breath, watching as she pouts and trudges along. Cute.

I'm about to chip in a word of encouragement, turning my head to her when I hear her yelp. Her sneaker's slipping on a large rock. I reach out on impulse, but before I can reach her, Brody's arm shoots around her back, keeping her slanted but upright still.

There's a slight smile on his lips but it fades as he becomes aware of the fact that I'm staring at them. Brody must sense something in the way I glare at him, because he lets go of her and—

She falls.

Holy *shit*. I can't help but laugh.

"Brody!" she yells. "Why the heck did you let go?"

She pushes herself up, and Brody chooses to help her up by taking one of her hands. There's an embarrassed look on his face, but he's also trying very hard not to laugh. Wren clenches her jaw, huffing. "I hate both of you."

Brody and I look at each other before erupting into laughter again. Wren turns her back to us (and we're *still* laughing) to catch up with Zach and Mia.

Turns out that when she catches up with the other two, Wren realizes she made it to the top, judging from the surprised look on her face. I see Zach and Mia staring over the edge of the peak, and all that can be heard is my feet trudging across the sparse grass as I near them.

The view from the top is breathtaking, but I find myself stealing glances at Wren the whole time. She soaks up the view with longing in her eyes. Like she wants to paint it. All of it.

When her gaze meets mine, I don't look away.

∾

After lunch, we hike back down and head to our cabins. We agree to meet up in the main room to watch a movie after showering. The girls disappear and we assume they've gone off to do some girly shit. After a shower, I join the guys.

"What the fuck were you doing in there?" Zach mutters. Then he shakes his head. "Actually, never mind. I don't want to know."

There's some weird ass sexual scene on the screen, and they're both pretty invested in it. Stretching over, I pick up the remote and switch to an action movie, their groans and whines echoing throughout the room.

"Asshole," Zach mutters under his breath.

Ignoring them, I take out a blue pen and scribble across the page. I scratch out a few words and start again.

"That a diary, weed?"

Just as I'm about to deny it being a diary, Wren and Mia walk in.

Wren's gaze drops to the small book tucked between my fingers, and my knuckles whiten as my grip on it tightens. I try to tuck it under a stash of pillows, clearly trying to hide it from her. I'm an idiot. Her voice perks up as she points at my hands. "What's that?"

My eyes widen. "Nothing."

"It can't be nothing." She lunges forward. "Let me see!" My reflexes are quick, though, and she ends up weirdly stretched out on top of me, still out of reach of the little brown book.

"Well, if you guys are going to be all over each other," Zach drawls, "at least take it to the bedroom to spare our eyes."

"Shut up, Zach!" at least three people say. Zach disappears somewhere with a smile, and when Wren looks back at me, the book is gone. I wink at her.

"Come back here, birdie." I motion to my lap. "Since you like being close to me all the time."

Wren glares at me and sits as far away from me as possible— which, coincidentally, is next to Brody. I clamp down on my jaw, my attention splitting when Zach reenters the area with a chocolate bar, singing "Don't Cha" by The Pussycat Dolls at the top of his voice.

Mia looks unbothered by him, her eyes trained on the TV screen. I think she's accustomed to it by now. Zach squishes himself between Brody and Wren—and I'll admit, I could kiss him for it—and she moves over to the edge of the couch.

Zach grins. "Hey, Wren, do you know what Asher's nickname was in middle school?"

My head whips up and I narrow my eyes at him. "I swear, Chandler, one more word and I'll—"

"No, no." Wren smiles, leaning in. "Go on."

"Ash-wipe," Zach says, and after that he laughs so hard it

drowns out everyone else. And to think I was willing to kiss this asshole just a few seconds ago.

"You rat," I mutter. "Unfollow me on Twitter."

"I can't do that."

"Why not?"

Zach bursts into laughter. "Because I'm not following you in the first place."

# CHAPTER 23

## Wren

It's a while before I'm able to come to terms with the almost kiss at the lake. Hell, I can't even maintain eye contact with Asher without freaking out internally. So naturally, it's a while before I can bring myself to tell Mia about it.

I'm lying on my bed; Mia is on the other one, flipping from one side to the other on her mattress. She's silent for a while, and I think she's asleep. Sitting up a little, I see the moonlight splashed across her face. She's still awake.

"Mia," I whisper, but I'm not sure why.

"Yes?" she whispers back.

"Asher almost kissed me," I blurt. "And I think . . . I think I like him."

"Oh?"

I'm not sure what I was expecting, but it definitely wasn't *that*. It's the first time I've admitted it out loud, and honestly, it shocks me more than it does Mia. But I know her, and she definitely should be overreacting right about . . . now. In the dark, I lift a brow.

"You're not going to like this," she says, detecting my suspicion. "But I kinda already knew."

My eyes go wide. "What?"

And in the dim light, I can make out her nonchalant shrug. "Oh yeah."

"What the heck?" I groan, covering my face to hide my mortification. "I can't believe it was so obvious."

"*What the heck,*'" she mocks, reaching behind to grab her pillow, and when she swings it my way, I'm too slow to dodge it. I'm still yelping when she says, "Why are you only telling me now?!"

"I was trying to process it all!" I yell.

"Never mind that." Mia waves a hand, a fervent look in her eyes. "What did you say?"

I look at her blankly. "Nothing."

"What?"

"I said nothing."

I don't get to finish because Mia literally kicks me off my own bed.

"*Hey!* What was that for?"

"I'm trying to knock some sense into you." She shakes her head. "I mean, what were you thinking? I can't believe you sometimes."

"I wasn't thinking *anything.* That's the point." I lift myself off the floor, sitting as far away from Mia as possible as I rub my side. "I blanked." I sigh. "I'll figure it out soon."

"You better," Mia shoots. "It's like . . . it's like my ship has no captain right now."

I laugh. "What is that even supposed to mean?"

"It means that it's going to sink very, very soon if you don't get your ass into gear and tell that boy you like him."

Mia sings an off-key version of "White Flag" by Dido as she collapses back into her mattress. There's a strange sense of relief in my chest after admitting my feelings to her. In a way, I admitted them to myself, as well.

The pain of today's exercise will kick in tomorrow morning, and for now I'm beat. I just lie on my bed and stare at the ceiling.

For one whole hour.

Fudge.

I can feel the bags forming under my eyes, which isn't healthy at all. It's times like this when I'm reminded of just how terrible my packing skills are.

Rubbing vigorously at my eyes with my fists, I walk to the bed next to me where a sleeping Mia lies. My hand hovers over her shoulder as I contemplate waking her up. I halt when I remember that Mia takes her sleep seriously. She'd probably chop off a limb or two if I woke her up.

Sighing, I open the door to our cabin. The glow from the campfire coals is a terrible excuse for light. Trudging over the unbalanced and slightly damp ground, I make my way to the campfire.

A shadowed figure hunched by the fire catches my attention. I slow, trying to make out who it is, until I step on a twig. At the noise, the figure turns, facing me.

"Birdie?"

Reed has a confused look on his face and his hair is all over the place.

My eyes widen. "Oh, um . . . I couldn't sleep, and I didn't want to disturb Mia so I came . . . out here. Wait. Why am I here? Oh my gosh, I'm sorry. I should just—"

"Wren." He laughs. "Stay."

Alarms should be ringing at this moment, but they aren't. I notice a camping chair in the dim light, and I edge toward it. I'm about to fully collapse on it when Asher protests.

"I wouldn't do that if I were you." He lifts the bottle-green camping chair and places it neatly beside him. "Zach fell off that chair this morning. Sit on this one instead."

After a moment's hesitation, I walk over and fall into the seat. Taking a blanket from Asher's grasp, I make a cocoon for myself, appreciative of the warmth.

We sit in silence for a while, gazing at the stars in the sky. The wind blows lightly, rustling the leaves. Asher puts some wood on the fire so it crackles and burns, throwing an orange hue onto his face as he looks up, deep in thought.

"Why are you out here?" he asks, finally.

"Couldn't sleep," I remind him. Snuggling against my chair, I turn my head to him, watching as he stares intently at the constellations. "I left my hoodie at home and . . . it just doesn't feel right."

Reed swivels to face me. "What's the deal with it, anyway?"

"My hoodie?"

He rolls his eyes. "No, birdie, my jeans." He glances at me, and my blank stare must persuade him to clarify. "Yes, your hoodie. What's up with you wearing it all the time?"

I shrug, "I like it."

He shakes his head. There's a soft pause before he says, "You have other hoodies, right?"

"Yeah," I say, not seeing his point.

"Then why *that* one?"

The question brings up a flurry of memories. Me, returning home after the accident. Mom, too devastated to comfort me.

I remember feeling cold. Unbearably cold. I somehow made it upstairs. Opened my drawer and pulled out the first thing I could reach.

My hoodie.

And when I cried myself to sleep that night, the hoodie was the only thing that brought me comfort, the only thing that tied me to reality—that sheltered me from it too. But I can't find it in me to explain it all to Asher, so I just give him a smile and hope he understands. "I *really* like it."

He holds my gaze for a moment, then pulls away, shaking his head with a small upward tug of his lips.

I know he's about to question it further, and in an attempt to stave it off, I turn my attention to the fire instead. It crackles as it burns, the bright hues of burning orange and red giving way to yellow and white near the center, where the heat is the greatest. "It's beautiful."

Again, it's a while before he responds, like he knows I'm avoiding his questions.

"Yeah," Asher finally breathes, but when I turn to face him, he isn't staring at the fire.

He's staring at me.

Then, he's edging dangerously close to me, close enough that I can feel his warm breath on my cheeks. His gaze lowers to my lips, giving me a second to pull away.

I don't.

And in an instant, and before I can fully anticipate it, his lips are on mine.

It knocks the wind right out of my lungs.

My eyes widen and I'm held firmly by his strong hands, bringing me closer to him. Excitement bursts inside me like a fervid flame, each tendril curling around my soul in intricate patterns and grasping on tightly. His lips are soft—so soft—and they become my oxygen.

I don't do anything, and I guess that's the problem.

I don't do anything.

A cloud of rejection hovers in the air and settles around us as he shuffles away from me. There's an unreadable expression in his eyes when he opens his mouth to speak.

"Sorry." His voice is strained. "I shouldn't ha—"

Impulse guides me as I lean over and kiss him.

He's taken by surprise—a rare occurrence—but soon catches on. He smiles against my lips, and the ghost of his smile lingers. Why does his smile against my skin feel so good?

Slowly, unknowingly, I move my lips along his, soft and sweet. He gently swipes his tongue along my lower lip, parting them. He tastes of sugar and something familiar, a combination that entices me more than anything.

His hands are wrapped around my waist, mine locked around his neck, pulling him down to me. My skin is on fire—nothing compared to the one before us. Every single pore set alight by his touch, the feeling foreign and exhilarating. The irregular beat of my heart seems to switch my mind on. Asher Reed is kissing me.

And I'm kissing him back.

# CHAPTER 24

## Asher

I finally build up the courage to tell Coach about my updates. It hadn't slipped my mind. I just didn't want to see the disappointment in his eyes. Raking a hand through my hair, I let out a breath. I don't want to do this, but I don't want to keep avoiding him either.

My hand hovers over Coach's office door as I hesitate. *Fuck it.* I knock haphazardly.

A deep voice speaks. "Come in."

Coach is someone I've always looked up to. He's been my role model for years, even when I didn't know him personally. Hell, he's been more of a father to me than my actual dad. Coach is one of the best players I've ever seen, and one of the Leafs' greatest forwards.

Elliot Brown. The name on everyone's lips around thirteen years ago. The youngest player to ever play in the NHL. That was him. One night, someone from the Bruins injured him. It was messy. Articles and rumors had been plastered all over the news.

Coach vanished for a while, and everything had died down by the time people discovered that he was here, coaching at Eastview. His name on the ice disappeared, and it was like he never existed.

If anyone understands me right now, it should be him. The thought should comfort me but it doesn't. Not completely. I don't want to be the person who reminds him of the bad parts of his life.

But I'm already here, and it's too late to back out now.

Stepping in, I train my gaze on the floor, finding it more interesting than the person sitting in front of me. My eyes finally flicker up. Coach sits upright, his gaze scrutinizing. I can't get a read on him.

"Reed," he huffs, gesturing for me to sit down. "How are you doing, son?

Slowly, I slide into the chair in front of him. Clearing my throat, I say, "I'm good. I just want to get back on the ice. I miss it, and," I pause to catch my breath, "I hope everything is fine with the team . . ." I trail off.

He nods. "Do you need anything?"

"I actually got my medical results a while back . . ." I falter as he leans in and crosses his arms. "I won't be able to play hockey for the rest of the year. I'm on a physical rehabilitation program. They say I might be able to get back on the ice by next year."

It's out. Staring at the trophies lining the rear wall, I find myself gazing at my team's picture at the bottom. I scan the wall for my face, finally finding myself next to Coach, a grin on my face.

Eventually, I look back at Coach, who has a blank expression on his face. Finally, he says, "I'm sorry, son."

I rattle off the same old reply. "It's fine."

He clears his voice, and I furrow my brows. He's normally not like this. Coach always speaks his mind, never really hesitating to say anything.

"I also have to talk to you about something." He looks up at me, playing with the pen in his hand. "I understand that this isn't something you expected to happen. The team and I weren't prepared for it either. I hope you know that your injury affected the team."

I nod in understanding.

"Last week, during practice, one of the boys said that we should name a new captain to replace you." He pauses to look at my reaction, but I keep my expression nonchalant.

"I would like to keep you as captain, but it's not possible when you don't come to practice. The team doesn't want to say anything to you in case they upset you. You're an amazing player, Reed. Brilliant. One of the best I've ever seen. I hope that after your recovery you still continue to play hockey if you can. Eastview has been lucky to have a player like you on the team for four years."

Muttering a small thank you, I stand and turn around, ready to leave the room. It's suffocating me. Holding the handle of the door, I twist it, pull the door open, then step outside. One breath at a time.

I should've seen it coming. I mean, what did I think? The guy who screwed up his knee and can't play anymore can still have his position as captain? It isn't possible. I should've realized.

Sitting in the car next to my mom, I know she can sense that I'm not in a good mood. She's worried; the stress lines on her forehead prove that. I contemplate telling her but decide against it. I keep my mouth shut until we reach home. Getting out of the car, I swing my backpack over my shoulder.

Walking inside, I start talking as she puts down her bag. "Coach told me that I'm being replaced as captain."

Her expression falters. "I'm so sorry, honey."

"It's cool, Mom," I murmur, resigned.

My mom has always tried to do everything she can to prevent Ev and me from getting hurt, but sometimes it's inevitable. I get it. Pain is something my mother experienced. She doesn't want me to go through that, but as much as I appreciate it, she can't protect us from everything.

She sighs. "I'm sorry I couldn't keep my promise, Ash. I really did want you to get back to playing."

"It's okay, really," I say with my head low. "It's not your fault."

I walk to my room and close the door behind me. Chucking my bag in the corner, I flop onto my bed and pull out my phone. Swiping through my gallery, I look through all my hockey pictures. Several chaotic selfies scatter across the screen. I remember all the times my teammates stole my phone and flooded my camera roll with the weirdest shit.

There's a photo of us laughing, me looking at Zach, who's looking down his pants. I chuckle, knowing how one of us shoved the puck into his pants and it got stuck there. I wish I was back there—I'd tell myself to enjoy it, because it would end soon.

Chucking my phone aside, I veer downstairs, and for the first time in forever, I slide into my car. *My baby.* I missed this. I send a quick text to Wren then pull out of the garage, one hand on the steering wheel. Did we kiss? Yes. Was it the best kiss I've ever had? Also yes. Do I plan to do something about it? Hell, yeah.

On the way, I notice something on the side of the road. I narrow my eyes, and can't help the grin that finds my lips. No way.

Rolling up her driveway, I don't even have to think twice.

Taking the keys out of the ignition and stepping out, I shove them in my back pocket. Wren opens the door. Her hair is pulled into a messy bun held in place with a black ribbon, and she's wearing her red hoodie with a pair of black sweatpants. When she finds it's me, an embarrassed look takes over her face.

"What are you all smiley for?" she asks, raising an eyebrow.

I shrug, but she notices my faint blush. "Nothing."

"Okay, so if it was nothing important, then I'm just going to—"

"Wait!"

Wren pauses, staring at me. "What?"

"Let's go." My hand encircles her wrist as I drag her out the door and to my car. "We have to hurry or they're gonna leave."

"Calm down!"

"Hurry!"

She raises a brow but concedes nonetheless, probably wondering what's gotten me so riled up as she slips into the passenger seat. We eventually pull in at the grassy area on the side of the road that I spotted earlier. The grass is chopped low, and it's a deep shade of green. It's just trees and a couple of bushes and a random bench.

"Well, you have a lovely choice in surprises," she mutters dryly.

"*Shh.*" I shut my door softly and stride over to her. "You'll scare them away."

"Scare who away?"

"Them." My voice is light as I motion to a giant tree. Her eyes follow my line of sight until she finally sees it. The bulbous roots of the tree morph into thick bark, branches, and then finally, foliage. But if you look carefully, just a little more, you notice them.

Birds.

Hundreds of them. They're all tiny and brown and camouflaged within the greater scheme of things. If you're quiet enough you can hear them too—their chirps are small and soft.

But then Wren realizes something. I know this because she looks at me with wide eyes.

They aren't just any little birds.

They're wrens.

I can feel her excitement bubbling, and she smiles so hard her cheeks must hurt. "*Wrens?*"

"*Shh.*" I hush her with a silent laugh. I notice a few of the birds jumping at the interruption, moving away from the tree.

Wren nods, and we near the tree as slowly and quietly as possible. Despite the efforts we take to not disturb the birds, most of them sense our motion and flutter away. I smile a little, eyeing a tiny bird with brown plumage and beady little eyes. Up close, it seems more delicate; more natural.

"It's so cute," she murmurs.

My eyes meet hers. "I know."

I breathe, my eyes flitting to her lips. She sits on the bench next to me and I snap out of my momentary daze. "But you were already on the way to my place?"

I freeze for a millisecond. Damn, she's smart. "Well, yeah."

"So, the whole bird sighting thing was unexpected?" Her brows knit. "What were you really coming over for then?"

Shrugging, I say, "I wanted to bring you here anyway. And you're right, the birds were just . . . really convenient." I pause. "We haven't, you know, talked about that kiss yet," I say. She freezes. "And I thought we could do that here."

"What are we?" Wren asks quietly.

I grin. "Well, I don't know about you but I'm one good-looking piece of—"

"You know what I mean." She rolls her eyes. "What are we? What am I to you?"

"You're my birdie," I say. "And we can be anything we want to be."

And before I can think against it, I say, "Despite knowing nothing lasts forever, and we'll inevitably turn to dust, Wren Martin, will you be my girlfriend?"

My heart is beating fast, and my throat is dry, and my mind is on fire. It seems like an eternity passes before she finally speaks.

"Yes," she breathes. "Yes, I'll be your girlfriend."

I blink.

"You drive me insane, you know," I say. "I figured you out sooner than I'd like to. I mean, birds are ultrasensitive, you know. Make one wrong move and they're gone. Do one wrong thing and they slip away from you before you can touch them."

Wren furrows her brow. "You—"

"It's just every time I'd been holding myself back, the more I was attracted to you. It was like every second I didn't spend with you was wasted, and," I ramble, "all I want to do is kiss you again."

"Then do it," she mumbles.

I pause for a moment, studying her, eyes calculating. Did she just say that? Maybe I heard incorrectly.

"What?" I ask, wondering if my mind is playing tricks on me.

*Say it again.*

"Kiss me."

She doesn't need to ask twice. I lean forward and kiss her, and everything else fades in comparison. It's different; fiery and red and fervent, yet comforting in ways words could never be. My hand rests below the shell of her ear, my thumb caresses her cheek as our breaths mingle.

Wren runs her fingers through the soft hair at my neck, tugging me closer until there's no space left between us and I can feel the beating of her heart against my chest. I forget about everything—the bitterness and rejection of being replaced, the betrayal of my teammates.

Because kissing this girl comes as naturally to me as breathing, and I wonder where she's been my entire life.

# CHAPTER 25

## Wren

I'm not one for surprises.

So, when I walk into my room on Saturday afternoon and see something I don't expect to see, I nearly freak out.

Lying on my bed, neatly, is a new set of clothes and a note. There's a pleated floral skirt and a black top with elbow-length sleeves. Slightly adjacent, there's also a pair of nude Oxfords. Trying to contain my surprise, I pick up the note. In neat, blue writing it reads:

Date at 2.

PS: I hid all your hair ties.

PPS: And ribbons.

PPPS: I hid your wallet too.

PPPPS: Nice underwear drawer.

~ A.

Each line of the note leaves me with conflicting feelings. In the end, I decide to ignore the parts about the underwear and missing wallet and hair ties and realize I'm actually going out. On a *date*.

I don't want to seem pessimistic, but one hour is a dangerously small amount of time to complete the necessary. Without further thought, I rush into the bathroom for a shower, squealing the entire time.

When I return, I stare at the clothes, becoming increasingly suspicious. Surely Asher doesn't know *that* much about women's clothing. I have a sneaky suspicion that Mia had a hand in this. Only she would be able to concoct an outfit that somehow fulfills both of our preferences.

She's always telling me to wear skirts more. I really don't like wearing them, though, because to do so I'd either have to shave or risk everyone being given a view of the Amazon forest.

I decide to ask Mia about it later, slip into the clothes and leave my hair loose over my shoulders. I mean, I don't really have a choice since Reed kidnapped all of my hair ties and ribbons. Seeing as I don't have much time to do anything fancy with my hair, I just run a brush through the knots, leaving the strands in a relatively straight condition.

I actually try using eyeliner, and it doesn't come out half bad. It's similar to using a really fine paintbrush. I draw the line at mascara and lip balm, not wanting to wreak further havoc. A look at my wall clock tells me that it's 1:56 p.m., and I make my way downstairs with my phone in my hand.

"Wren, honey." My mother's voice stops me. "All decked up for your date I see."

I turn to stare at her bright, amused face, wondering how she knows exactly where I'm going and why. "You're in on this too?"

"Of course." She smiles. "Have fun."

I shake my head to myself as I walk past her. Opening my door, I find Asher standing there with his hands in his pockets.

I take in the sight of him, his hair disheveled, and his dark shirt absorbing light. He smiles when he sees me, and I punch him in the shoulder.

"You looked through my underwear drawer?" I ask, incredulous.

He ignores my question and catches me completely off guard. "I have a really pretty girlfriend."

"Oh . . . um, thanks, I guess."

He chuckles. "Who said I was talking about you?"

I raise a brow. "You have multiple girlfriends?"

"Take a joke for once, birdie." He takes my hand. "Besides, I don't need anyone else but you. C'mon," he says, tugging on my arm. We're on foot for this one until we get to the bus. I thought I'd switch things up a bit."

As we near the stop, it seems that our timing is perfect, because people cluster around as the bus pulls in. Asher stays behind me, allowing me to get on before him.

We find seats at the front, and when I sit down, Asher's hand is in mine again. I'm not complaining, and it's hard to fight the smile that tugs on my lips I try to control my heartbeat, and the sound of the bus restarting masks it. Asher is silent, although I feel his eyes on me for a brief moment.

There's a carnival in my stomach, and I get incredibly flustered. I can't figure out whether I like it or not, but conclude that I do. I love it, in fact. Being close to him always comes with this inexplicable high, one that only wears off when he isn't in sight.

After fifteen minutes, the bus comes to a halt, and everyone files out of it. The sun settles on our skin, and when Asher sneaks his hand into mine again, it seems natural. We walk past countless street vendors, with no real purpose, but it's strangely comforting.

A bunch of colorful balloons catches my eye. I don't realize that I'm just staring at the balloons until Asher slips one in my hand.

I stare at him in surprise. "When did you buy this?"

"While you were staring at them for fifty seconds flat."

Smiling, I stare at my little floating balloon. He chose a blue one, and it blends in with the cloudless sky.

Asher reclaims my hand in his, and he tugs me back onto the footpath. I can feel everything in our intertwined hands, and to feel everything and pretend to feel nothing is more difficult than it might seem.

We come to a standstill in front of a wall covered in paint. Street art. It's an overly large picture of a black car being hoisted into the air by millions of brilliantly colored balloons. The colors fill my eyes, and I reach out, running a hand over the cool surface of the wall.

"Wow," Asher breathes.

"Yeah." I've been around town but never come across this before. Maybe it's new. "Reminds me of the movie *Up*."

"Obviously everything has to relate back to a Disney movie for you," Asher mocks with a lazy smile.

I snort. "It's Pixar."

He shakes his head, then asks, "You hungry?"

"Always."

We eventually end up at a street vendor. He smiles at us. "What would you two like to have?" he asks, his accent slipping into his words.

"Uh," I start, pausing to decide. "I'll have the chicken tramezzini."

"And you, sir?" he asks.

"I'll just have whatever she has."

"That'll be fifteen," the man says handing me the food as Asher takes out his wallet.

"Thanks!" I say, while Asher pulls me along.

"My pleasure." The vendor's smile is huge as we walk away.

I roll my eyes as I bite into my tramezzini. "You hid my wallet too."

He beams. "Yep."

"You're really weird, you know."

"I've been told."

"But I like it."

"I know," he says.

"Are you sure you're ready for this?"

"What?" He raises a brow.

I motion to myself. "This."

"I was born ready."

"I cry a lot."

"I have tissues."

"Like, a *lot*."

"I'll buy more."

"I'm really awkward, and you're not going to understand what I'm saying at times."

"Trust me," he muses, "you're going to wish you didn't understand the things that'll come out of my mouth."

I manage to not choke on anything this time.

"Hey." He pulls me in for a hug. "I walked into this knowing the consequences. Do you wanna know the truth? I like you. A lot. You make me happy. You make me laugh. You're smart. You're a little crazy, strange at times, but your smile alone can make my day."

I lean closer into his chest, liking his words and scent far too much.

"You're just a work in progress."

"Oh my God." I laugh, separating myself from him. "You totally got that off Tumblr."

"Nope." He grins. "I got it off Pinterest."

I laugh at his dorkiness, then reach out to brush away the hair falling across his eyes. He leans in closer.

"You have something on your lips." He runs a thumb across them, supposedly brushing away a crumb of bread.

It's enough to send shivers under my skin. "Subtle."

His lips lift. "Sometimes you gotta be obvious."

Fast and slow at the same time, his lips are on mine.

The world around us fades away. My skin burns under his cold touch as he bites gently on my bottom lip, tracing my cheek with his fingers. It's funny how a single kiss can make you feel immortal.

～

When I return home, my pulse is still racing, and I'm on a sero-tonin high. I'm about to open my door when my phone buzzes. I slide open my lock screen, and my heart drops when I see the email notification. It's from the Yale admissions office. I could wait to open it on my laptop but I need to know. Now.

With my heart in my mouth, I open the email before I can psych myself out.

*Dear Miss Martin,*

*Thank you for your application to the Yale Fund Scholarship. We have had a large number of exceptional applicants, and regret to inform you that you have not been selected for the award.*

# CHAPTER 26

## Asher

Pushing the doors of the arena open, I make my way to the lockers. I know that I'm no longer the captain, or even on the team, really, but I figure it doesn't hurt to sit in on practice. I've had my fair share of wallowing in self-pity and I've had enough of it.

Fine, I missed the scouts. Fine, I missed my senior year of hockey. And yeah, it might suck, but it's not the end of the world. I realize that now.

But everything freezes when I get outside the locker room and catch the tail end of a conversation that's enough to drive me over the edge.

"Reed still with that prude?"

And what's worse is a few chuckles resonate in the room. Before I can help it, I'm slamming the door open, pinning the culprit immediately. "You know, Harv, you should watch your fucking mouth."

They stare at me, shocked. I've been keeping quiet for weeks, convincing myself that these guys are my friends. The sad reality? They aren't. They never were.

"Wren has been a real friend to me for a while now. You guys . . ." I pause. "Almost all of you guys were with me for four years and this is what I get? Saving all of your asses from Coach, staying late to help you practice, pushing you so that you don't fall behind. So that you stay on the team. All that for *this*?"

The door opens and Brody and Zach enter the room, hovering behind me, but I continue my rant. "I've tried to come to every single practice after you complained that I didn't. I'm here even after you replaced me as captain. Just to hear you talk shit about me in the lockers? Fuck that. I'm done. I'm *done* trying to please all of you."

I turn my back and reach for the door before spinning around. "Oh, and Harvey? You aren't funny, man. You're just a dick."

Coach's eyes follow me as I leave the arena. I'm not in the mood to explain exactly why he could hear me cursing in the change rooms.

Eventually, I find myself in my car, and I rest my head on the top of my steering wheel as I sigh.

Maybe I should do something I was supposed to have done years ago. Right when all this shit started. I jam the keys in the ignition and crank the engine before pulling out of the parking lot. Driving down the familiar road, I park in the driveway of the grey house I once used to frequent almost every day in middle school.

I climb out of my car and pace to the door. My hand hovers over the wood. Brushing aside all hesitation, I bring it down, knocking one time. Two. Three. Someone opens the door. Drew.

His eyes are wide. Confused. "Why the hell are *you* here?"

Pushing past him, I climb the stairs, walking to the door on the right. I knock again.

Finally, Gemma's voice sounds from inside the room. "Come in."

I push the door open to find her sitting on her bed, reading. Gemma glances up at me and freezes.

"Hey," I say.

She clears her throat, sitting up on her bed with wide eyes. "Uh, hi?"

I sigh, taking a breath before I dive straight in. "I know this is weird, seeing as you haven't seen me since you transferred out of Eastview." I chance eye contact with her but her stare is blank, so I press on. "I just wanted to say that I'm sorry. I didn't have to do that to you. I knew you liked me, and I strung you along and then broke up with you. I'm sorry."

She sits and looks at me. And then, after a while, she speaks. "I, uh . . . have no idea what I'm meant to say right now, Reed. I mean, I . . . uh, I hated you for a long time, honestly. But I got over it, eventually."

"Great," I say. "I, uh . . . I just needed to do this."

*I needed to not be like my dad. Like his cruelty, and everything he stood for.*

"Well, that's all I wanted to say. See you around, Gem." I make a beeline for downstairs, heading to the front door, right past Drew. Shaking my head, I'm about to leave when Drew's voice stops me.

"Asher."

Narrowing my eyes, I turn.

There's something so close to human emotion on his face, a

shimmer of the boy who, despite everything, possessed some shred of kindness.

His gaze lingers on my knee before it coasts back up to me. He swallows. "I'm . . . I'm sorry, man," he says. "For everything."

And since the bareback apology is more than I bargained for, I nod firmly and walk out of his house. And I don't look back.

∽

After my impulsive visit to Drew's place, I come home feeling lighter. It was stupid, and impulsive, but it was also long overdue. As I walk up to my room, I notice the spare-room door is open. Strolling into it, I'm greeted by the view of all my hockey equipment sprawled across the floor. I think I may have broken a thing or two.

Feeling the need to clean up the mess I made, I find some big plastic bags and boxes and take them up to the room. Dropping them on the floor, I start sorting my things out.

I don't immediately notice the figure standing by the door, but then I hear a sound. Mom. She gives me a smile and walks in, looking at the mess surrounding me.

"I dumped everything here a while ago," I murmur.

She jumps over the collection of padding. "Do you need help?"

I look around, wondering how the hell everything fit in my room. "Sure." I pause. "If you're not busy."

I start picking up my old jerseys and throwing them in boxes. Finding my one from this year, I gaze at it. It's not worn out like the others, so I pick it up and chuck it down the hallway, deciding to keep it. I'll pick it up later. My eyes flick back to my mother. She's crouched, picking up my glove with two fingers, her other hand covering her nose.

"When's the last time you washed this thing?" She flings it at me in disgust as I burst out laughing.

"Before hockey season started."

Throwing it in another box, I start with the pile of pucks lying in the corner. I place them in a netted bag and put them away. I glance at Mom, who's silently gazing at all my accolades. Pictures, trophies, medals, and certificates sit in a huge pile. She shakes her head.

"You know, you were such a bright little boy," she starts.

"I'm still pretty bright. Sometimes," I say, "when I walk into rooms, people have to look away."

Mom rolls her eyes. She picks up a picture of me sitting in the arena when I was in seventh grade. "When you first started you couldn't stand on the ice for a split second."

"I wasn't *that* bad."

She gives me a look of disbelief then continues. "But the determination I would see on your tiny face was amazing. A little five-year-old always flopping onto the ice for the first few months, but you still got up and tried again and again and again." She pauses and scans the expression on my face. "You can get whatever you want if you put your mind to it, you know."

She sets the frame on the neat pile in the box and walks out of the room. "I'm going to catch up on some work. Don't forget to eat something."

After some serious cleaning, I have two packets of old gear and jerseys, two boxes of other padding and helmets, four more boxes full of awards, and lastly, some old sticks held in a black bag.

I decide to chuck the things that I can't use anymore and move the others back to my room. After a lot of running between two rooms and organizing everything, I'm finally done.

My room's no longer the empty room where I ripped out every memory of hockey. It looks full, my hockey stuff back in its place. It feels a little like home.

Hockey was my life. Everything I did revolved around it. All the friends I made were from the sport. The parties, the image people had of me, the teachers who saw my sport achievements rather than who I was, the girls . . . everything was from hockey. Nothing I did made people like *me*; they only liked a certain facet of me. The hockey facet.

This time things will be different.

᷍

I haven't checked my phone in a while, so I'm surprised to find a shit ton of messages from Wren.

The first seven are ones she'd sent and then deleted. The others are practically essays. One repeated phrase catches my attention. *I'm sorry.*

I frown. What is she sorry about? I can't remember her doing anything wrong. Racking my brain, I start reading. Scrolling to the top, my eyes glaze over the words, and each cuts a clean, precise hole in me. Right through my chest. I don't understand. What happened? Did I do something wrong? I thought everything was good. I thought we were good. Amazing, actually.

The ache in my chest gets deeper and deeper with each word. I pace around my room, my phone tightly gripped in my hand.

There's got to be some reasonable explanation for this. I let the breath I was holding out before my eyes flick back to my phone. I pull it up and read the rest. For a moment, my heart stops. It's like someone's holding it tightly in their fist, and my chest is caving in on itself.

*What the hell?*

My mind is racing, running over every small scenario it can recall. I wonder where I could've gone wrong. What I could've done better. Maybe I was overbearing. Maybe she just . . . needs a little time. And space.

Sitting on the edge of my bed, I can't help but stare at my phone again. Over and over, her words replay in my mind.

*I don't think I can do this anymore.*

# CHAPTER 27

## Wren

Sometimes, life goes the way we want it to go. When I really think about it, life *has* tried its best to undo the wrongs it has subjected me to. I got a lot of second chances. I got Asher. And Ever. And all the other little pieces that try their best to fill the cavities in my existence. But life did not fail to remind me of the flaws in my narrative.

My eyes flit to the acceptance paper in my mother's hands. I didn't want to tell her myself, so I printed out the letter and left it on the kitchen counter where I was sure she'd see it.

"You got into Yale?" she asks, her eyes full of shock.

"Yeah."

"But you didn't get the scholarship?"

"Nope."

Her gaze turns soft. "It's okay, baby," she says. "Have you gotten a response from any of the other scholarships?"

"No. But I'm pretty confident that I'll get at least one."

There's a tentative silence before my mom chooses to fill it.

"Wren?" she says, slowly. Carefully. "I'm going to ask you a question. And I want you to answer honestly."

I nod warily. "Okay."

"Why Yale?"

Even though I knew it was coming, the question still takes me by surprise, and I'm mortified when my eyes begin to tear up, the pent-up emotion from when I saw that email bubbling over. I look up at my mother. I know she suspects what my answer is going to be, but she wants to hear it from me. So I give it to her. "Dad went to Yale."

The air turns stale. I spread out over the couch, blinking away the time. And the tears. It's the first time I've said it out loud. But now that I've said it, I realize how true it is. I've always felt that going to Yale would be something special. Something meaningful.

A way to keep the thread between my dad and me intact. One of the last bits of hope I had to keep those fading memories. And knowing that it was one of the best colleges was the glazed cherry on the top.

"Honey." My mom's eyes are filled with an unknown emotion. "You don't have to do things you think he would've wanted you to do. Because he would've wanted you to be *happy*. He would've wanted to see you make your own choices. Always. So, this time I want to ask you another question, and if you say yes, I will do everything in my power to help you. But you have to be honest, baby. To me and yourself." There's a beat before she speaks again. "Do you want to go to Yale?"

I pause. It's never been put this way before. I've never had to stop and think about college the way I do right now. And when I force my mind to wrap around the concept, to truly think about it this time, the answer is crystal clear.

"No," I say. "I want to study medicine. And I'll take whatever college offers me a scholarship."

Mom is quiet for a while. "Are you sure?"

I nod, and finally, for the first time in a while, I *am* sure. "Yes."

But this revelation doesn't change the fact that I lost the scholarship. It was something I'd been working hard for the entire year, for my *entire* high school career, and I can't help but wonder where it all went wrong. And as much as it makes my chest painfully constrict, I have to admit it: I'd been fooling around with Asher.

But then again, I'd truly tried my best. I studied. Hard. Asher had never been a distraction. We only just started dating, and yet here I am, blaming him for the parts of my life that hissed and snarled. Blaming him as soon as things went wrong.

It's unfair.

He deserves better. And then I realize how *not ready* for this relationship I really am. I'm messy. Unhinged. All over the place.

And suddenly I'm panicking, and all the reasons we shouldn't be together, all the reasons we'd never work, come soaring in: I'm too boring. We're too different. And maybe the starkest realization: we're short lived.

We have completely opposite lives. We run in different circles. How long until those differences finally catch up with us?

We'll never be forever.

We're not going to the same college, and this is just some stupid high school thing.

I'm crying now, choking back sobs, and before I can stop myself, I'm typing out a message. As I ruin one of the best things that's ever happened to me, my vision is so blurry I can't even read what I've typed, but I'm forced to blindly trust my autocorrect.

I click Send.

～

I don't go to school for the next three days. I can't get out of bed. Can't sleep. Can't eat. Mom's worried, but she can't force me to do anything other than eat a few bites, but nothing tastes like anything. When I'm not studying, I read, but I can't make it past a page without reading the same sentence over and over. I can't find it in me to focus.

I leave my phone on silent, because Asher has been calling incessantly. A few days ago, he'd stolen my phone and made his face my wallpaper. For some reason, I haven't changed the lock screen, so every time my phone lights up with his face, my chest twists painfully.

Every single time I find myself smiling at the sight of his face, and every single time my eyes tear up when I realize that I tore it all up. I ruined everything. So, when my phone lights up with his face once again, I don't think much of it. And when my mom calls me downstairs, I don't think much of it either.

Except I should've.

Because Reed is standing on my porch. It's raining outside— *pouring*—and he's drenched. And he's *standing on my porch*. He's right here, in front of me, now, and I want to cry. Then his eyes meet mine, and they blaze.

Staring at him, guilt clogs up my throat. My eyes tear up before I can control anything, but I stay quiet, waiting for him to say something.

"We need to talk," he chokes out. And I notice the dark shadows under his eyes. Mine probably look the same, if not worse.

For a second, I freeze in the hallway. My mind's a mess. I look terrible. I should tell him to go. Tell him that I meant what I said. That I'm not worth it. That I'll never be worth it. But it would all be one big, festering lie. So wordlessly, I nod once. Twice. Then I step aside and let him walk in.

"I've been calling," he says.

"I . . ." I trail off as he frowns and edges closer to me. His hand reaches for the side of my face as he tips my chin up with his thumb, peering down at me. I try to picture what he sees. It's not pretty. It's dark circles and puffy eyes and desperation.

"What exactly," he says, steely calm, "is going on, Martin?"

"I—"

"Where were you?" He rips his hand away from my face like it pains him. Then, frustrated, he runs his hand through his hair again, messing it up further. "Jesus Christ. I've been calling and texting. For *three days*. No reply. And you haven't been coming to school. I've been trying to give you space, and then I thought *Fuck it*. And now I'm here. What else was I supposed to do?" His voice breaks. "Tell me, Wren, what else was I supposed to do?"

"You were supposed to forget about it," I say quietly. "About me."

For a second he just stares at me, incredulity painted all over his face. He looks like he wants to burst, but he takes a deep breath, and that steely calm from before returns.

*When I was sixteen my dad died in a car crash,* I want to tell him. *My sister was in the car when it happened. She died too.* I want to tell him that what happened that night changed me so much that I don't know who I am anymore.

But I stay quiet. I say nothing.

"Forget you?" He lets out a dry laugh. "*Forget* you? Do you really think it's *that* easy?"

"I didn't get the scholarship."

His face falls, and my chest aches when his anger is replaced by genuine surprise. "I'm sorry," he says. "I'm really sorry, birdie. But I still don't understand how—"

"There's no chance of us getting into the same university," I say, dumbly. "Zero."

He furrows his brows, clear-cut confusion dousing his features. "I don't understand how that's a problem. I thought you knew that this would happen." His voice turns wary. "Are you saying that you're going to find someone new in college?"

The thought of being with anyone other than him makes my stomach churn. And he must notice, because he smiles bitterly.

"Exactly," he says. "I trust you. You trust me. And I literally don't care how far we are from each other—if there's trust then everything will work out."

"You're not being realistic," I say. My voice is empty. Tired.

"Fine," he says gruffly. "You want realism? It's going to be difficult. It's going to be real fucking difficult. But that doesn't mean I'm going to let you go. I just . . . I can't. I know I'm being selfish. I'm sorry, Wren, but I can't let you go."

There's a soft silence that exists between us then. It's comforting knowing that we don't really have to talk to understand each other. I stare at his profile, the smooth angle of his jaw and the stray strands of hair falling across his forehead.

I bite down on my jaw. "You have to."

"No, I don't."

"Yes," I say. "You do."

"*Why—*"

"Because I'm scared!" I yell. "I've lost almost everything that means something to me, and I'm *terrified* of losing you too."

Everything freezes. The world goes silent for a moment, and so does Asher. His gaze is a shadow as something dawns on him. "There's more, isn't there?"

My throat constricts. "No."

But he's too intuitive to not know, and too stubborn to let it go. His deep-blue eyes flare. "You're not telling me something."

I glance at him. "You don't want to know."

"What makes you think that?"

"It's . . ." I swallow. "It's a lot."

He sighs. "You should know, Wren Martin, that 'a lot' does nothing to deter me. 'A lot' is what drew me to you in the first place. There will never be a day when you're not 'a lot'. And there'll never be a day where I'll judge you for it. So, whatever you're going to tell me, say it. I promise I won't run. I'll never run."

I breathe slower, fighting tears. Fighting every instinct telling me to run. But he's right here, and even if I run, trip, fall—he'll be here. With a net to brace my fall. So I take the leap.

"When I was sixteen," I say slowly, "my dad and younger sister died in a car accident."

He freezes.

"My dad died on scene. My sister didn't survive ICU. I don't know why, but I got out with minor burns. Sometimes . . ." I smile softly, wiping my face with the back of my hand. "Sometimes I wish I died with them that day too."

His features cloud with a mixture of emotion—not pity, thankfully—and he wraps his arms around me fiercely, his soft jacket absorbing my tears.

"No." His jaw sets in a hard line. "No. You have so much to live for."

Asher remains quiet for a while, his jaw set in a hard line. Then, without warning, he presses his lips to my temple—a soft, tender touch. "Thank you for telling me. It means everything to me but changes nothing between us. You deserve all the happiness in the world, Wren, and it's about time you realized that."

"I don't think we can do this, Asher," I say. "I'm too . . ."

He frowns. "Too what?"

"Messed up," I say. "Self-destructive. I ruined us before we started. And I wasn't kidding when I said I cry a lot. You shouldn't have to tolerate that. You shouldn't have to tolerate *me*."

"*Tolerate*—" He runs a frustrated hand through his hair. "What do I have to do to prove to you that I'm serious about you, Martin?"

I swallow. "Give me some time."

ᔕ

A week later, I still don't go to school. Asher keeps his promise to give me time. And one morning, I wake up and it's like the fog has cleared. I know what I have to do.

I haven't been to the cemetery for months—I couldn't bring myself to go. The last time I visited was on the anniversary at the beginning of the year. Then, I couldn't bring myself to even enter. For the past two years, I've never properly visited them.

I take out my phone and my finger hovers over a single name on the screen. Mia's busy today. She has a family gathering to attend. So, before I can stop myself, I hit Call. The ring resounds in my ear.

"Hello." I speak into the receiver. "Asher?"

His reply comes fast and surprised. "Birdie, hey. What can I do for you?"

I can tell that my call's woken him up. He still manages to sound good even on the phone, drowsy yet crisp—a feat I thought to be practically impossible. I manage to sound like a frog in voice recordings.

"I need two flower bouquets." I sigh, wondering if it's going to be too much for him. "And a lift to Churchstone Cemetery."

But he doesn't say a word, and an hour later I utter a small thank you as I take the flowers from his hands and slide into the front seat of his car. He bought pure white daisies. I resist the urge to smile. Asher Reed is a mystery. I'll lose my mind trying to understand him.

As I hold the flowers between my fingertips, the thin wrapping grazes my scuffed palms. The drive is filled with comfortable silence, with me sneaking glances his way to stare at the V-neck shirt he has on.

I tear my eyes away from him as the car comes to a halt in front of a street leading up to the cemetery grounds. He looks around the somber place and then looks at me, his gaze concerned, lips set in a tight line.

"If you want, you can leave," I say as I unbuckle my seat belt. "I really don't mind."

He opens his door. "I'm not leaving."

I'm surprised—I mean, a cemetery isn't the coolest place to be on a Saturday morning, especially for someone like him, who must have a million other places to be except here, with me.

"Your choice," I mutter. "I was under the impression that meeting someone's buried family would be slightly awkward, but all right."

Asher looks at me, unsure how to reply. But he doesn't stop walking for a second. I hold back a smile. He isn't going to change his mind.

As we move past the tall black gate, a feeling of nostalgia overwhelms me. I exhale in the cool air. We walk through the rows of tombstones with moss-covered engravings, and white marble mausoleums. Dad would've hated this place. How can it be so full and yet so empty at the same time?

My throat constricts as I see them—the two stones standing side by side. It has been so long since I last came, but this image is one I can never forget. It's quiet, and I can hear Asher's footsteps behind me.

I stand in front of the graves, in front of the tombstones of my family, skimming the inscriptions. My breaths are slow as I'm no longer able to hold in the tears. I kneel, slowly depositing the flowers next to each white memorial.

I reach out to touch my sister's tombstone, but it's cold and hard and inanimate—everything she wasn't. Whatever I came here for isn't here. This graveyard is full—of stone, moss, and yew trees—but it's empty. There's nobody here but me and my sadness.

Everything falls into place in my mind.

Asher pulls a piece of paper from his pocket. "I found this for you." He offers it to me. "Maybe it's a little better than me trying to say something—I'm bad at this sort of stuff."

I take it from him cautiously and peel open the paper, which reveals his signature in blue ink.

"Do Not Stand at My Grave and Weep" by Mary Elizabeth Frye.

After I read the poem, I stare at Asher, who averts his gaze; very unlike him. I edge closer to him and wrap my arms around his neck, his chest flush against my own. He smells of sweet summers and soap, and his warmness encases me like a tiny haven.

Eyes full of tears, I say, "Thank you."

"They'd want you to be happy," he says.

I spend a lot of time wondering what we are, and what we are not, then.

We're human. Skin and bones and beating hearts. Flawed and painstakingly average.

We aren't forever. Or permanent.

We'll rust and burn and fade away, with the faith and hope that our souls will be what we could not: infinite.

But our mortality is what makes our lives all the more remarkable.

"I am," I say, as I bury my face in his shirt. "Now."

# CHAPTER 28

## Asher

I knock on Wren's door at nine in the morning. She's already left for school, so this is the only time I can get to see her mom. I can't deny it—I'm nervous.

"Coming!"

I wait anxiously at the front door before it opens. As she glances up, confusion marks Wren's mom's face.

I clear my throat. "Morning."

"Morning, Asher." Still confused, she pauses. "Wren's not here. She's at school, which started an hour ago," she says slowly, probably insinuating that said school is where I should be too.

"Yeah, I know, Mrs. Martin. I was wondering . . ."

She raises a brow. "Wondering?"

"If I can have the keys to the house."

Wren's mom shoots me a perplexed look. "The what now?"

I scratch the back of my neck. "The keys to the house."

She nods slowly, digesting the information. The coffee cup in her hand stops steaming as she stirs it. "Can I know what for?"

"I want to ask Wren out for prom, if that's fine with you."

An amused smile lights up her face slowly. She takes a moment to stare me down before she goes back into the house and returns a few minutes later. The jingling of keys in her hand makes me grin. She chucks them at me. "No funny business when you're in here, okay?"

I nod. "Yes, ma'am."

∾

When she reaches home, Wren trudges inside, her footsteps heavy on the hardwood floors. I'm taking a lucky guess and I'm going to say she's tired. She walks near the stairs before doubling back. Blinks once. Rubs her eyes, wondering if I'm sitting at the kitchen island on a bar stool, eating Froot Loops.

"What are you doing here?!"

*Oh, you know, casually running up and down, trying to sort this arrangement of about hundreds of colorful balloons I shoved inside your room.*

They're different colors—red, blue, pink, yellow, purple. I think I almost drowned in them at one point. I couldn't see the furniture, and eventually a whole lot of them floated out the door. I had to run out and shove them back in again. It was undoubtedly one of the hardest things I've done in my life. No joke.

I also made a huge poster with the help of a couple of the guys from the team—seeing as pretty much anyone can draw better than me. On one side, there's a picture of a house floating up while strung to countless colorful balloons. On the other, the big, bold lettered words:

WILL YOU FLY *UP* TO PROM WITH ME?

It took me weeks of searching online and combing through Pinterest, but I eventually found something Wren would like. I'm pulled from my thoughts when she starts talking.

"It's four in the afternoon and you're in my house eating my favorite cereal?"

I nod. "Precisely."

"How did you even—?" Wren pauses, and I know it's the exact moment she decides to let it go. I really didn't want to know what she was going to say anyway. Probably chastise me for bunking school just to sit in her house all day. She pours some of the cereal and milk into her own bowl, and takes a seat across from me before scarfing it down.

"Why'd you ditch today?" she asks.

"I had some stuff to do."

Technically, not a lie. Wren keeps her eyes on me for a few seconds longer but I maintain eye contact with her, eventually winning when she blinks, deciding not to pursue it. I smile.

"Hey—that stuff I said about not letting you go?" I say. "I meant it. I know this might seem pretty stupid. I mean, this is high school and we're not supposed to be this serious, but I'm willing to try. For us."

I stare at her eyes. They seem warmer now.

"I'm willing to try too." She smiles, holding up the cereal box. "For Froot Loops."

I bite back a grin. "For Froot Loops."

I pick up the milk carton, and we make a pact with the two.

I chew on the inside of my cheek, growing impatient. She's not going upstairs . . . and she kind of needs to go upstairs for this to work. I figure this shit's gonna need some activation energy.

"Hey, do you have your math textbook?" I say, trying not to be suspicious.

"Yeah," she says. "It's in my room."

"I need to borrow it."

"Sure."

"Right now."

"Oh, uh, okay . . ." She frowns as she finishes her cereal and leaves her bowl in the sink, her eyes meeting mine. "I'll be back."

I nod, and she finally heads upstairs. I hear her open the door. Then there's silence. What if she actually doesn't like it? Shit, what if she's allergic to balloons? Can someone be allergic to balloons? What if she got stuck in there and can't breathe because there's so many fucking balloons?

I'm halfway to the stairs when I hear quick footsteps, rapidly approaching. Wren stands at the top, looking down at me.

Then she races down, catapulting on top of me like some sort of marsupial. I don't crumble under her, standing strong as she wraps her arms around my neck. Her heart beats so hard I can feel it against my chest.

A huge smile that must hurt her cheeks appears on her face as she pulls away to meet my gaze. It's like something else is running through her veins. Something more than blood.

"*Yes, yes, yes.*"

I smile, holding her tighter.

"'*UP*', Reed, really?"

I shrug. "You like Disney."

"Pixar," she corrects. "There's, like, a million balloons up there."

"Five hundred and thirty-nine."

"What an awkward number."

"Well yeah, it was meant to be five fifty," I say, "but I popped a few."

∽

Two days before prom, I text Wren. Zach and Brody wanted to go shopping for things we'd need. So here I am, at Helen's. The saleslady has her hands full trying to tell the boys not to touch anything. Pulling out my phone, I pop the question.

ME: *What color is your dress?*

WREN: *You can guess. It'll tell me how well you know me*

WREN: *Have fun shopping!*

Okay, so that helps. I rack my brain trying to find a color Wren would wear. The first thing that shoots through my mind is two completely opposite colors. A bright red and a pale, pastel blue.

Wren's hoodie makes me want to believe that she'd wear a red dress. But the blue balloon she stared at on our date? The blue wall in her room? It's definitely blue. If it isn't, I'll just buy a ton of colors and hope one is right.

Heading to the counter, I pull out the tie I picked. Picking up my card, I swipe it, then head out of the store. Soon, Chandler and Knight come out, holding shopping bags of their own.

∽

The day of prom, my mother refuses to let me go without taking pictures of me. She takes hundreds. Thousands, maybe. Mom was meant to come with me to Wren's house for more pictures, but she told me she had to go somewhere with Ever.

I take one more glance at myself in the rearview mirror, making sure my hair's neat.

Knocking on the door, I find Wren's mom. "Evening, Mrs. Martin."

"Come in, Asher." She gestures for me to enter. Slowly walking in, my nerves increase tenfold.

"Honey, Asher's here!" she shouts up the stairs.

Looking up, I get an obscured view of Wren as she walks slowly and steadily down the staircase. Her brown hair's in a low bun, curled, twisted, and pinned with a few stray strands hanging along the sides of her face, framing it lightly.

My eyes flicker to her dress. Soft blue. Hell, yeah. I got it right. Her eyes widen in surprise as she notices my tie. The iridescent beads on her dress glisten when light hits them, glowing a different color with each different angle. It's stunning. *She's* stunning.

"You got the right color?" she murmurs.

At the sound of her voice, I turn my gaze to her face. My eyes sparkle as I look at her shamelessly. I clear my throat.

"Well, yeah, apparently," I say. "And if not, I have the entire fuckin' color spectrum of ties in a box that I brought with."

She gives me an incredulous stare. "*What?* You're crazy."

I wink. "Only for you."

"But then why did you choose to wear the blue one?" she asks me, composing herself quickly.

"It looked sexy and brought out the color in my eyes," I offer dryly.

Her mother's voice bursts the little bubble that's forming around us. She's returned from her hunt for a camera, apparently. Suddenly, we are attacked by flashes. "Okay, smile for the camera!"

"Are you just going to stand there?" Disbelief is evident in her voice. "Give me some *oomf!*"

I turn to Wren. Before she knows it, I place a small kiss on her cheek and the camera flashes once more.

"Cute!" her mother says. She's got to have taken over a hundred pictures by now.

"Okay, Mom, we're going to go now," Wren says.

"Wait, just one more!"

"Seriously, Mom." Wren laughs. "We have to go."

She sighs. "Okay, okay. Have fun." She offers me a cautionary glance. "Take care of my daughter."

When we reach the car, I shuffle over and open Wren's door for her.

"Wow, Reed, you're opening a door for me?" she jokes.

I walk over to my side of the car and slip in. "You're worth it."

While driving, I can't keep my eyes off her.

She laughs. "What?"

"What?"

"Why are you staring at me like that?"

I grin. "Like what?"

"Like . . . *that.*"

"I have no idea what you're talking about, birdie."

I get out first and refuse to let her open her own door, and she lets me be chivalrous. People turn to flash their eyes at us, but they're quick and fleeting. I wrap my arm around my girl's lower back, and she sinks farther into me. She smells of citrus and strawberries.

Since it's the archetype masquerade ball theme, everyone's wearing masks. Mine is black. Wren's is silver. It has a butterfly perched on one edge, bathed in silvery glitter. Her honey eyes are bright.

A girl with curled dark hair rushes toward us. Mia. She's wearing a light-pink gown made of soft, satiny fabric, long and loose. A semicircular, high collar made of silk-like material frames her face. Her mask, like her dress, is salmon pink.

Not far behind her, I recognize someone who's definitely Zach.

"Wren!" Mia gushes. "You look beautiful."

"Says you," Wren counters.

"What is this school trying to promote?" Zach mutters, fidgeting with his mask, "These masks are so kinky."

I roll my eyes. "Where's Brody?"

Just then, a couple enters. I recognize the girl from her flaming red hair. Not to mention the long, nude-colored dress, which looks like it cost a fortune and a half.

Faye.

But the guy at her side. . . ? Tall, sleek suit, chocolate-brown hair. . .

"Is that Brody?" Mia asks.

Why, yes. Yes it is.

He walks over to us with a small, nervous smile. Surprisingly, Faye follows.

Zach whistles. "Holy shit. You said you weren't bringing a date!"

Faye holds back a smile, walking over to the buffet table. Wren swaps an amused glance with Brody, before leaving for the buffet, too, and something tells me that she knew about Brody and Faye. Which is fucking hilarious, because I didn't have the slightest clue.

Zach and I are halfway through chewing Brody off for not saying a word about his secret date when Wren returns to the table with a single serving of chocolate mousse.

"Hey." I motion to the left corner of her lips. "You have something over here."

She mirrors me, her finger moving to the right corner of her lips to wipe away the remnants of chocolate.

"Is it gone?" she asks me. I shake my head.

"No." I take out a handkerchief and bring it to her face gently. "Here."

"Ladies and gentlemen," the MC's voice booms on a microphone. "The moment you've all been waiting for—it's time to announce our prom king and queen!"

"Prom king is . . ." The MC pauses to read off the open envelope. "Brody Knight!"

Brody stands with a small, almost hidden smile then walks to the stage slowly. Zach and I engage in a weird celebratory handshake that just looks very aggressive to anyone witnessing it.

"And prom queen goes to . . ."

The crowd falls silent, eager to hear the next result, although most of them know the answer already.

"Faye Archer! Congratulations! Please make your way up to the stage for your crowns and the honor of starting the dance."

The crowns are placed on Faye's and Brody's heads, and they join hands before making their way back down the ramp to start the dance. The first few seconds are filled with the school watching the two masked people swaying in the middle of the floor. Quickly, others join.

Wren is caught by surprise when I take her hand in mine and pull her into the sea of people who have already assembled on the dance floor.

While she's still trying to figure out the steps, I softly push her back, draw her close, and turn her around along to the music.

She's too surprised to say a word. Under the mask her gentle honey eyes are looking straight into mine.

"Do you think . . ."—Wren tilts her head—"they would've voted for you if you weren't with me?"

"No," I say. "And if that's true then I don't want their votes anyway."

Wren smiles primly. "If you say so. You—"

I don't let her finish, leaning down and placing my lips on hers. They're soft. Gentle. Angelic. She's slow to react, but when she does, it's a kiss that makes the world around us fade to black. Everything is dim in comparison. We're in technicolor. Bright. Brilliant. Beautiful. And I know, without a doubt, that I've fallen for the girl in my arms.

# CHAPTER 29

## Wren

The laptop screen in front of me is blank. I'm about to go insane. Graduation is coming up soon, and I still haven't gotten to writing my valedictorian speech. Yes, valedictorian.

I got two scholarships. One from Cairne and one from a state college. They may not be Yale, but that's okay. I'm still more than happy and appreciative that I won't have to figure out a way to outlay the insane amount of cash needed for college.

I emailed countless people at Yale a week ago regarding my application. It got under my skin as to why I wasn't accepted into the scholarship program. When I finally got a response, I read the email about a thousand times.

*Thank you for reaching out to us regarding your queries about the Yale Scholarship Fund. I have gone over your portfolio and others who have been accepted into the program.*

*It is no doubt that you are a young lady with above average intelligence. The only factor that sets you aside from the other recipients are the extra activities that they have participated in. On your application you have put down service. Other applicants have participated in sports, play instruments, and are part of debate teams.*

*We regret not having such a bright student at our institution. I hope that answers your questions.*

And I finally understood. It was me. I was holding myself back the whole time. Not joining more clubs and societies because I was too afraid to climb out of my shell. Not speaking up during class. I didn't realize how damaging and self-destructive my habits were becoming. I wasn't *allowing* myself to be happy. To be open, bold, confident, and . . . free.

Asher, who's sprawled on his bed, isn't making writing my speech any easier. He's being overly chatty. I've been at his place for almost two hours, and I chose to completely ignore him around forty-five minutes ago.

"I know I said I like your company and asked you over and everything," he says, "but you've got to at least acknowledge my presence."

He's met by a broad silence as I continue to stare at my computer screen, hoping the words will appear from nowhere. There are moments like these when I really wish my head had a USB port. How easy would life be if things could go from your head to paper in a few seconds?

"Birdie.

"Wren.

"Wreeeen." He sounds like a sheep.

"Hello.

"Talk to me.

"Give me something to work with here.

"Why so hostile?"

Once again, he's met by silence. But my God, is there ever a boy more persistent than Asher Reed.

"Come on.

"Wren.

"Birdie.

"*Babe.*"

That's it. I'm going to stab someone.

"*Reed.* Can't you see I'm trying to write? For the love of all things holy!"

He laughs, flat out. It's so loud it fills every crevice of the room and bounces off my face. He knows exactly how to get on my last nerve.

"There's nothing on the page."

I narrow my eyes at him. "Thanks. It makes me feel like a complete failure."

He laughs again. "The valedictorian of Eastview High calling herself a failure."

"Stop it," I mutter, grabbing a pencil and hurling it at him. He jumps, narrowly escaping.

"Damn, birdie. If you're trying to blind me with a pencil you've got to at least get your aim right."

I feel my left eye twitch.

"I think there's something in your eye." He points at my face. "Come here."

I'm about to respond when he tugs me off my chair onto the bed. It knocks the wind right out of me. I'm attacked by an onslaught of emotion, first surprise, then annoyance, and then I'm flustered.

Asher's blue eyes are in my direct line of sight, and I can see every pixel of the faint freckles dotting his nose. He has to be bad for my health. I push him off me a little.

"There's nothing in my eye, you irrit."

"What the hell is an irrit?" His attractive face warps into confusion.

I laugh, despite myself. I guess he does get me out of my mood, in a way. "An irritating person."

The door creaks, followed by, "Wen!"

"Ever!" I yell back. "How are you, my little ray of sunshine?"

"I'm starting school." She lifts both her hands in clear excitement. "And guess what? Mason's coming to the same school as me!"

"Mason?"

"*Mason?*" Asher repeats with a frown.

"Oh yeah." I snap a finger in mental recognition. "I remember Mason."

Ever nods.

"Wait, hold up, I still don't know who the fu—" Asher pauses when I glare at him, then nods in Ever's direction. "—dge Mason is?"

"I want him to marry me," Ever says.

"*What?*" Asher and I howl.

"Do you know what that means, Ev?" Asher asks calmly, but I can see how hard he's trying to keep from bursting.

"'Course I do! Even you and Wennie are married."

"*What?*"

Ever rolls her eyes. Her brother looks like he's about to implode at any moment. "Mom said that people got married when they like each other *a lot*. Like you and Ash."

"But—"

I turn to Asher for help, but he just looks amused. He doesn't look like he wants to correct Ever either. I narrow my eyes at him. Guess I'm on my own.

"We're not married," I say. "And getting married is a lot more than just rings and two people liking each other, all right?"

She nods slowly, but I don't really think she understands. Then she shrugs with a small pout. "Mason doesn't like me, anyway."

Asher sighs and rolls up his sleeves. "I could always *make* him like you."

I gasp. "You will do no such thing."

"Why not?"

I eye him. "One, he's a little boy, you monster! Two, Ever's way too young, and three, it's supposed to happen naturally."

"Nacho rally?" Ever asks, under her breath, her face warping into confusion.

"Naturally, you say?" Asher repeats, an evil smirk taking over his face.

I frown, but it doesn't deter him. If anything, he edges closer to me. Although I know he loves me, there are still minuscule parts of me filled with doubt. The parts of me that try to convince me I'm not enough. They are also the parts of me constantly telling me there's nothing special about myself—that I'm boring.

Don't we all have those parts?

Reed proves those parts of me wrong. He's the same charming boy I know. Despite everything that is changing around me, Asher Reed remains constant, and I couldn't be more grateful. He snakes his arms around my waist, pulling me against him.

"You know what else comes naturally to me?" he teases.

"What?"

He brings his lips down to mine. "This."

"*Mom!* Ash is trying to eat Wen's face again!" Ever yells.

I pull away from Asher immediately. He starts laughing, showing no remorse. Jeez, the boy made me forget that poor Ever was in the same room as us. We probably just scarred her five-year-old eyes.

"Is he now?" Victoria responds, appearing at the doorway. "Would you like some ketchup with that, Ash?"

"Mustard will be fine, Mom," Asher responds, with an equal amount of snark.

"This boy," Victoria mutters under her breath, but I catch the smile on her lips. She picks up a slightly lost Ever. "Try being a good influence for once?"

I might be mistaken, but I think she winks at me? Asher must've learned from somewhere, I guess.

"I'm always a good influence," Asher says. "And maybe you should give Ever a proper definition of marriage."

"*Marriage?*" Victoria looks appalled. "Asher Reed! Your sister is five years old. Have some decency."

Asher frowns adorably, and I laugh. Ever seems to know when to keep quiet, because she looks extremely content playing victim in the arms of her mother. I almost forget she's the same Ever who promised to continue the raging war on her brother.

"Ever," Victoria calls over her back. Ever offers me a little wave over her mom's shoulder, and I offer a little wave back.

Asher shakes his head, a small smile peeking. He pauses. His eyes latch onto something behind me—my hoodie—and he sobers up.

He pulls me off the bed. "C'mon."

"Where?" I whine. "I'm busy writing my speech."

"You obviously need a break."

"But—"

"Don't ask questions." He stands. "Grab your hoodie. It's coming with us."

I frown, reaching an arm out to take my hoodie off the bedside table. He reclaims my hand in his and tugs me downstairs lightly. It's around five, and the sun has begun to set already. It casts a dim shadow on us as we make our way to his car.

～

"No *way*, you wanted to kill me this entire time?" I muse.

Asher doesn't respond, but I notice the small flash of amusement in his eyes. Without a word, he walks on. He obviously expects me to follow him, so I do.

We finally reach an area deep in the woods that's cleared out, possibly a hot spot for picnics or camping. Trust him to know a place like this. A pile of blackened ash lies in the middle, presumably the remnants of a dead fire.

"You planning to burn me alive then?" I ask him, pointing at the ash.

He gives me a blank stare.

"Okay, fine." I'm curious. I can't help it. Suspense is something I'm not designed to handle. "What are you planning to do, then?"

"People become attached to certain objects to satisfy specific emotional needs," he says, slowly. "Often the threat of loss of the object triggers anxiety because it threatens the loss of some status or security."

I raise a brow. "What?"

He points at the hoodie nestle in my arms. "You have an emotional attachment to that hoodie."

"An emotional attachment to my . . . what are you trying to say?"

"Think about it," he persists. "When have you worn your hoodie?"

I meet him with a perplexed gaze. "When I'm cold?"

He frowns, giving me a look that says I should cooperate. "You've got to think a little deeper than that for me, birdie."

I frown. "Asher, what exactly are—?"

"When you feel socially inept, when you feel your anxiety building up. I'm telling you that you don't need your hoodie. I'm not saying getting rid of your hoodie will get rid of all negative feelings, but it does mean you can't hide behind it anymore. It's human to feel sad or angry or nervous. *It's human to feel.*"

"I still don't see the relevance."

"Burn it."

I stare at him, open mouthed. "What?"

"You heard what I said."

"No, I didn't."

"*Yes*, you did."

"*No*, I didn't."

He stares at me. "There's a difference between hearing and listening."

A deep silence follows, before I slice it apart with a sharp knife. "Don't make me do it, Asher. I can't."

"Wren. You *can* do it. For yourself."

"No." I shake my head. "You don't understand. That hoodie is more than just a hoodie. When I have it in my hands, I feel . . . I feel safe. Protected. I can't destroy that feeling."

"You don't *need* a hoodie to feel safe," he persists. "You can't just put on a hoodie and expect it to solve all your problems. You need to face them. Stop running away from them. They're eventually going to catch up with you. Confrontation is key."

I stare at him, unable to counter that.

"*Burn it.*"

"Are you positively insane?" I exclaim. "What makes you think I'm going to burn a piece of my clothing just because you're asking me to? It actually does keep me warm, you know." I glare at him with angry eyes that then turn placating. "It's my favorite hoodie."

"I'll buy you another."

"I don't want another."

"Fine." He sighs. "You can have one of mine. Whichever you want."

I think about it. Most of his clothing will smell like him, and it *would* be nice to carry one of his hoodies with me to college. I huff. "Fine."

Reluctantly, I set my hoodie down on the pile of ashes. Asher hands me his lighter, which I flick on and hold against the material. It catches quickly, and I move away with a hole in my heart. The flames grow higher, licking the red material. It gradually turns a deep, rust color.

There's something wet on my cheeks. When I lift a hand to my face, I realize I'm tearing up.

"I love you, Wren Martin," Asher says.

My throat dries. Everything comes to a standstill. The rustling of the leaves, the flames of the fire, my heart. I stare at him, wide eyed, wondering if I heard right. With the fire dancing in the pools of his eyes, he looks more alive than ever.

"It's hard not to fall in love with you. In fact, falling in love with you is inevitable. It's hard not to fall in love with your laugh, or even your smile. It's hard not to fall in love with the spark in your eyes when you're happy.

"It's even harder to ignore the little things about you, like how you play with your necklace when you're nervous, or how you frown when you concentrate, or how your hair falls into your face when you don't tie it up. Sometimes I feel like looking at you forever. Being with you forever.

"And I know I can't promise you the forever you're searching for, but I *can* promise you now. I can promise you I'll do whatever the hell I can to make sure that smile never falters when I'm with you.

"When you're sad, I'm sad. When you're happy, I'm happy. And if this isn't love, then I'm not sure what it is. All I know is I love you, Wren Martin. And it's taken me an awfully long time to admit it, but I am in love with you."

# CHAPTER 30

## Asher

"What did she say?" Brody asks me.

"Nothing."

They give me incredulous looks. "You just professed your love for her and she said nothing?"

"Precisely," I state.

Zach opens his mouth. "Why aren't you more bothered about this, man?"

I stop writing in my little brown book, swiveling on my chair to face them as they sit on my bed. I point the pen at him. "Because it's Wren. I can't force anything on her, and I don't want to. She needs time. And she can have it."

"Hm. Guess that makes sense," Brody says, shrugging.

I turn my attention back to what I'm writing. I scribble across the page. I don't notice the two guys creeping up on me until the hardwood floor near me creaks. I spin as Zach and Brody run back to the bed, jumping on it.

"What?" Brody asks.

I raise my eyebrow. "What are you two doing?"

"Nothing. We're just sitting on the bed. Looking at your back. You know?" Zach rambles.

Shaking my head, I get back to what I'm doing, not paying attention to the two behind me. They don't bother me for a while, so I presume they're entertaining themselves.

Suddenly a hand shoots out and steals the book from my grasp.

"Whoa man, is this a *lurve* poem?" Zach prods. "All *Romeo and Juliet* style?"

"Fuck off!" I yell, running at him. "Give it back, Chandler, or I swear to God I will—"

I take him down, knocking the wind out of him. I reach for the book, pull it back, and dump it in a nearby bag, which happens to be my hockey bag.

Zach smirks at me while I flip him the bird.

"Wanna go play *Call of Duty*?" Brody asks me.

"No."

"C'mon."

"No."

A few minutes later, I'm wishing I never agreed to play with them.

"Jesus, Zach, you can't just shoot everything!" I yell, tugging at my hair.

"Yes, I can." He doesn't even look at me, his eyes fixed on the screen in front of us. "And I will."

Brody and I swap glances, then pick up our consoles and join him. My character ducks, swerving between boxes and hiding. I aim at the person in front of me. Taking a shot at him, I run off again.

"Who shot me?" Brody asks.

"Don't know," I lie, shrugging.

He huffs and turns back to the screen. The game soon ends, and when we see who wins, I nearly throw the entire console set.

"Hells, yeah!" Zach shouts.

∽

In the midst of shoving the books aside in my locker, I don't notice that someone's behind me.

"Reed?" a male voice booms.

Turning, I come face to face with someone I haven't seen in a while. "Coach?"

"My office, please."

I nod curtly and follow him to his office, an eerily quiet place. Coach takes a seat as I look around. I gaze at the team photo taken for this year. I'm not in it.

"You don't have any idea as to why you're here, Reed?" Coach asks, his eyes calculating.

"Is it because Zach and I made the shower floors slippery?" I say slowly. I watch as he raises an eyebrow. I furrow my brows, quickly realizing it wasn't about that. I already start losing track of the freshly started conversation.

"I've been doing some research on the medical results you gave me earlier. It took a while, but I've got a plan." He chucks a folder in front of me. I pick it up and flip gingerly through the pages. "You can still play, boy."

He huffs out a breath. "As you can see, I contacted Grover. Unfortunately, as you know, they said they won't be able to accept you this year. However, they did say that if you attend another school and apply to them the following year, you'll definitely get in."

It takes some time for it to sink in. I blink, then blink again, and suddenly I'm smiling a numb smile.

"I'm pretty sure you know what this entails. You'll have to work harder, Reed. I know you won't disappoint."

I blink. "Yes, thank you, Coach."

"You don't need to thank me, Asher. You've done a lot to get to where you are now and it'd be a damn shame to lose a player like you. Get back in the game. Don't let this chance go because you're scared. Don't be like me, Reed," he says. He meets my gaze. "Be better."

Throat tight, I nod. "I'll try."

❦

I haul myself out of the car, and walk toward Wren's house. She opens the door and I wink at her.

"What did Coach say?" she asks as I ruffle her hair. She doesn't even bother fixing it.

"I still have a chance of getting into Grover." I can't help but smile. "Not for next year, though. But the following year, yeah. Coach gave me this folder with all the details," I say, waving it in her face.

I see her face change as she mirrors my smile. She pauses for over a second, as if thinking something through, and then her features cloud over.

"What?" I ask, worried. "What's wrong?"

She looks at me blankly, before taking a seat on the porch steps. Still confused, I take a seat next to her.

"I love you," she murmurs, after a while.

My eyes widen. "What?"

There's a beat before she replies. "I'm not repeating it."

"Wren." My fingers trace her jaw. I snake my arms behind her back and under her thighs, shifting her to my lap so she's vertically across me. It feels strangely comforting, so she stays quiet, leaning into my shoulder lazily.

I drop my face to her level, unnaturally happy.

"What exactly . . ." she starts, her voice trailing off, "are you doing?"

I tilt my head, and our lips touch for the briefest moment before I lace my fingers in her hair, making it fast and fervent.

My brain wants to pull away, tells me to stop, but my body has a mind of its own. I brush the tip of my tongue against her lips, coerce her into opening her mouth. When she retracts, the warmth retracts with her.

Wren looks flustered, while I just run my hand through my hair, now at a breathable distance from her.

It's weirdly comforting, being able to hear her heartbeat and feel her close to me. She's alive and breathing and with me, and that makes it enough.

I thought that I needed to define my life by a finite set of things. But I couldn't have been more wrong. There's no such thing as carving out facets and sticking to them for years. Because the moment this girl walked into my life, there was a facet already there, polished and shining, waiting for her to claim it.

Everything you need is all in you, and you can create and

destroy and carve out your life exactly the way you want it to be. Free of other people's opinions. And my mom was right. You *can* get anything if you put your mind to it.

I got Wren, after all.

# EPILOGUE

## Wren

### Three Years Later

I push through the crowd, hoping to spot a soul I can identify. Mom, Mia, Victoria, and Ever are all hidden somewhere here, and I squint up in the stands filled with people waving their hands and homemade signs. It's Grover against Varietas today.

The cheers coming from the crowd make it hard for me to hear. Finally, I catch sight of Mia, and I cut through the sheets of human bodies until she can see me too. She shoots me one of her million-dollar smiles before pulling me toward her until I'm standing beside her and we are able to get a reasonably good view of the rink.

Mia's leaving for Vermont in two days. She studies there and only came back to watch the game and spend the weekend with me. Her family's forcing her to spend time with, well, *more* family before she heads back to college, not to be seen again until Thanksgiving.

Zach took a year's break, and now he's studying business. He's not in the same college as Asher and Brody, but all three guys still meet up and wreak just as much havoc as they did during high school.

After faint chatter with Mia, she signals for me to shush as the players are introduced to the rink.

Suddenly, our players emerge, and there's a deafening roar and applause from the stands. Asher's staring up at the crowd around him, lips lifted. Varietas also emerges, dressed in tree-green as opposed to our dark blue. I don't recognize anyone from their side, though.

Asher swerves in a circular motion, his eyes searching for something specific until his gaze lands on me. Realizing that he's found what he's looking for, he raises his hand, touching two fingers to his lips, and stretches his arm out.

He's pointing in my direction.

His eyes are fixed on no one else but me. I feel something rise in my stomach, and spiral down again. Countless people turn to look where he's pointing. Somehow their wandering eyes stray through me, as if I'm invisible.

Becoming conscious of the fact that no one knows what's going on, or more specifically, who Asher's act was meant for, I fire the biggest smile I can at him, hoping he can see it from such a distance.

Surprisingly, he does, and a grin of his own takes over his awfully attractive face. Mia catches on pretty soon, and she jerks my arm, squealing intensely.

"That was the cutest thing ever!" she cries. I ignore her, a smile still plastered on my lips.

"The game's starting in five!" I hush her, oh-so-obviously trying to divert attention from my little scene. Leave it to her to make things more awkward. She narrows her eyes but concedes nonetheless, turning her attention back to the game.

The puck is in Asher's hands. It's passed with a flick of the wrist from person to person until the real hits start. It took me a while to figure out how this game works, and I still don't know much. But I try my best to learn.

I remember when I used the term *crease* in front of him and his team. Reed immediately pulled me closer to him, practically squashing me. He gave me a megawatt smile, and ruffled my hair, saying *That's my girl.*

It's been three years since senior year. I'm not going to say it isn't hard, because it's been one of the hardest challenges I've ever faced. Pre-med is a really time-consuming field of study, and hockey takes up a ton of Asher's time, but we make it work.

He makes sure to visit me whenever he has time. I'm sure the cost of his flights have made a dent in his bank account, but he reminds me time and time again that it's worth it.

Asher phones me every day, always making sure that I'm okay. One time, I came down with a flu and ridiculous fever, and he immediately flew over, kicking up a fuss and knocking on my dorm-room door, bags of medicine and food in his hands.

We also made a pact, that whenever I went to his place for the holidays, he'd help me learn how to drive. I would get in his car, and he'd sit in the passenger seat, instructing me.

I *actually* learned how to drive. Yeah, can you believe it? It only took about three more failed tests, and about fifty buckets of tears, but I did it. I'm going to be honest, though, I don't take failure as well as SpongeBob.

Loud cheers interrupt my thoughts. I glance at the boys on the ice, trying to find Asher. It isn't hard. The white *89* on his back is the biggest indicator. There's also something in the way he plays. I don't know how to describe it, but it's different.

By the third period, my boyfriend's team is winning by two points. Mia disappears for a while, resurfacing with a bag of popcorn, fries, a corn dog, and a hot dog.

Too soon, the fries and hot dog are in my hands, and my face is stuffed with popcorn. Mia rolls her eyes as if to say "Typical," but grins playfully anyway, enjoying her corn dog.

I watch as the puck flies in Varietas' possession. Asher is on the ice with the rest of his line. The other team manages to cut through our line, but the puck is out of sight as our defensive players try to recover it. They play it back to our center and it heads straight to Asher.

He collects it, moving right towards the boards. A player skates toward him, but Reed swerves to the side, popping the puck in the air and bringing it back down to the ice. He reaches the crease and hits the puck with so much force that it bounces up and flips into the goal. Reed skates behind the net, slowing down.

I stand with the rest of the crowd wearing green, cheering as his team rushes to Asher.

"Holy shit," Mia yells. "He's good."

I grin, nodding. My eyes are laser focused on the boy in front of me. I lift my gaze to the timer on the wall.

There's five minutes left.

This time, when the puck's dropped, Varietas take possession. They maneuver through our line, weaving in and out of the players. Nearing our net, the player takes a wrist shot at the goal. I'm at the edge of my seat, fidgeting with Asher's jersey, which I'm wearing.

Our goalie kneels to the left, and I watch as the puck bounces off his padding. I let out a sigh of relief.

Our players immediately get the puck, pushing it from player to player. I look around, searching for it. Suddenly, it appears with Asher.

His skates cut into the ice with laser-like precision as he speeds toward the opposition. He holds the puck with him, as Rangers fly at him like moths to a flame. They're desperate. If we score this goal we win.

I stand up again. Reed still holds on to the puck.

"Pass it, Reed," the coach screams from the side.

The tension in the arena is so thick you could cut it with a knife. The players seated on the bench stand up and yell at Asher, who keeps the puck with him and moves down the ice.

I glance back at the timer. There's fifteen seconds left. Anxiety creeps over me as my knuckles turn white from holding on to my jersey tightly.

*Come on, Reed. What are you doing?*

A Varietas player dives in, moving to check Asher. He looks up for a minute, and then clears the puck to the opposite side of the rink, right to one of his teammates, who swings his arms, releasing a quick shot into the net. The whistle blows. Game over.

The score is 3–2. We won. The crowd goes wild. Someone throws their popcorn in the air, and it sprays everywhere. I smile as Mia holds my hand, moving us through the insanely loud crowds to the players' bench, where the team comes off the ice. Victoria takes Ever, moving out of the stands to the exit.

"I'll be at the front." She waves back at me. "See you later."

I nod at her, before walking out with Mia.

"I have to leave now," she says, sadness marking her face.

I get it. Flights are difficult to schedule, and besides, it means everything that she flew over to spend the weekend with me. I wrap my arms around her, hugging her tightly. "Text me when you reach home, okay?"

She nods. "I will."

Waving to her, I watch as she disappears into the crowd. My head turns back to the rink.

Reed skates off the ice with ease. He recovered quickly from his injury, and as soon as his doctor gave him the sign, he was back on the ice and staying late in the gym. He's still wary of surroundings when he plays, making sure he can see the whole rink before he does anything.

He's talking to a teammate about something as I stand at the side, watching him. His face lights up as he explains. I lean against the wall, tilting my head. He lifts his head, almost as if he knows I'm staring at him, and greets me with a kiss, wrapping his hands around my waist and pulling me closer.

"You played great," I say, popping on my tiptoes to poke his dimple.

He shoots me a smile, and as he's about to reply, his coach calls, "*Reed.*"

He ruffles my hair. "I'm gonna head back to shower. I'll meet you at the front?"

I nod as he pecks me on the forehead before heading off. I walk to the entrance of the rink, staring at the large amount of popcorn that's scattered across the floor.

"Yo, Reed's girl," someone yells. "Wren!"

Turning around, I face one of Asher's teammates. He holds a

black duffel bag in his hand and a water bottle as he walks toward me.

"Reed forgot his bag by the stands," he explains.

"Why don't you give it to him? I'm not allowed to go to the locker room. He'll need the clothes to change."

He shakes his head. "Nah, he has a separate bag for that."

"Oh." I give him a small smile. "Okay. Thanks."

He nods and drops the things in my hand before walking away.

Deciding that it would be better if the water bottle was in the bag, I try to open the duffel while walking. That's the first mistake. The second is not looking where I'm going, because I literally walk straight into a trash can.

I sigh as everything falls out. Perfect.

Huffing, I squat and pick up my boyfriend's spare hockey clothes and equipment and place them back in the bag. My hand hovers over a little brown book. I swear it looks familiar. I tilt my head; where have I seen it before?

I rack my brain trying to find an answer. Frowning to myself, I stare at the small brown book with doubt. My hand itches to open it. Curiosity wins.

Slowly, I open it to the first page, finding a red ribbon bunched up. I pick it up, remembering that I used to wear it almost every day in high school. Then one day, it disappeared. I should've guessed.

The page is filled with fine, deep blue scribbles and scratching. The rest of the pages are the same. I start reading,

"The Hoodie Girl" — A. R.
She was more beautiful than anything he'd ever seen;
Her hair the shade of coffee beans

*A hoodie sheltered her in a sheet of red*
*That slowly seeped and gently bled*
*And when she laughed*
*She crept her way into his heart.*
*Broken pieces, tied together,*
*A sea of stars that were forever*
*A mystery meant to be solved*
*And in a flash, his world evolved*
*A fearless bird soaring through a bright blue sky*
*Yet still as sweet as strawberry pie*
*Secrets bottled, stolen glances*
*Cloud-filled skies and second chances*
*And as time swept past in a quick blur*
*The lost boy fell in love with her.*

He wrote a poem about me? I didn't think I could fall any deeper for him, but it seems as though the cavern is never ending. My heart beats loudly in my ears, as I walk out into the open, feeling the breeze hit my skin.

The little brown book is clutched between my fingers and as I shove it back in his bag, I catch sight of Asher out front, showered and holding his other bags, waiting with his mom and Ever, who's seven now. I can't believe how fast time has rushed by. She still helps me out when I need to prank her brother, and she's gotten a lot better at it.

Reed grabs the bag from me when he notices I have it, and as he walks away, he mouths, "I love you."

"Wren." I recognize Victoria's voice. I turn to face her, and she smiles at me before continuing. "Thank you. This is the happiest they've been."

I catch sight of Ever running after an unwilling Asher, who, even though he won't admit it, is running at a slower pace on purpose. He's a boy filled to the brim with fierce love and soft affection, but most people move too fast to notice.

"In that case, I should be thanking you. Because it's the happiest I've been too."

"I guess we're even then," she says.

"I guess we are."

I'm glad that Asher hasn't promised me forever. I'm glad he hasn't made a promise he knows he can't keep. Because even if forever does exist, I don't want it anymore. I just want here and now, with all the people I love.

I've burned my hoodie and embraced my past, but in a way, I'll always be the hoodie girl. Thanks to a little brown book and neat blue handwriting, that is. Who knew it took so little to immortalize someone? To make them live forever?

Maybe this is what love feels like.

"I love you too," I whisper, staring at the blue-eyed boy.

# Acknowledgments

To my sister, thank you for the long, long nights spent reviewing countless drafts of this story. You are my number one cheerleader, my powerhouse, and my best friend.

To my mom and family, thank you for always supporting and encouraging me. To my aunt, thank you for your valuable insight. To my dad, I wish you could have been around to hold my book.

To my high school friends, thank you for introducing me to Wattpad. It was through this app that my thirteen-year-old self would realize her biggest passion and dream. To everyone at Wattpad—editors, illustrators, marketing and promotional teams—thank you for coming together to make the dream possible.

To Nurbanu, Jay, Brinda, Christa, and Abi, thank you for your help in reviewing *The Hoodie Girl* during its final stages of editing.

To Monica Pacheco, my talent manager, and Nina Lopes in

her stead, thank you for being there for me every step of the way. A big thank you to all the editors involved: Whitney French, Fiona Simpson, Deanna McFadden, and Rebecca Mills. Your tireless work to transform this story from a rough draft to its best possible form is greatly appreciated.

Lastly, to my readers. You laughed and cried with these characters. You grew up with these characters, and with me. You motivated me to complete Wren and Asher's story, and there are not enough words to describe how incredibly grateful I am for all of you. Stay gold.

# About the Author

Yuen Wright lives in Cape Town, South Africa. She began writing online at thirteen, and her debut novel *The Hoodie Girl* has since amassed over eighty million reads and won a 2016 Collector's Edition Watty Award. When she's not writing, Yuen can be found fangirling over Taylor Swift or studying toward her degree at the University of Cape Town.

# Some love stories begin in all the wrong ways.

**The Bad Boy and the Tomboy** by Nicole Nwosu

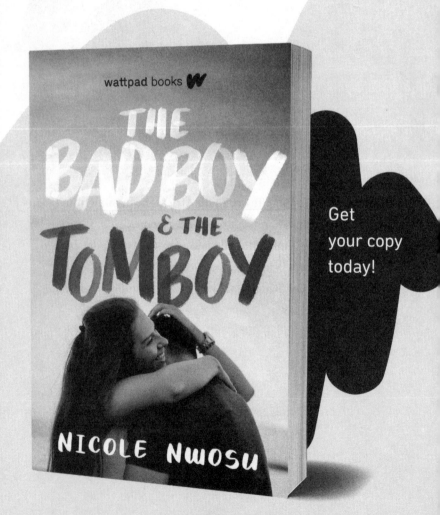

Get your copy today!

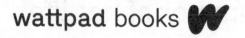